"You never should have put me up on that pedestal, honey. I was bound to fall off one day. I'm no hero. I'm just a man."

"You'll never be just a man to me, Ryan," Kirsty insisted stubbornly. "And I don't believe you're a womanizer. You're just saying that to put me off you for some reason."

How right she was. And how wrong. "I'm not that noble," he muttered. "Trust me when I say rarely a week goes by without my having a woman. But they have a very short shelf life with me, honey. Very short."

She gaped up at him with wide green eyes and deliciously parted lips. He stared down at them and thought the wickedest of thoughts, his flesh swiftly following his mind into the fires of hell. What on earth had he been thinking of, taking her into his arms like this? He should have known he wouldn't be able to resist her.

"I did warn you, honey," he growled as his mouth began to descend toward hers. "You really should have believed me."

Dear Reader,

When I first wrote the SECRETS AND SINS series, I never envisaged revisiting the Whitmore family. I thought all my heroines had finally found happiness with the right heroes and their stories had been told. But when my editor suggested I write a spin-off book eight years on, I got to thinking that perhaps there was more to be said, especially where Gemma and Nathan's relationship was concerned. I started wondering—would their marriage have survived the test of time?

Along with that intriguing question came another. What about Kirsty, Nathan's rebellious and spirited daughter by his first wife, Lenore? How did life turn out for her? What had happened to her during the past eight years? Being born into a wealthy family is not always a recipe for happiness....

The idea of Kirsty having been kidnapped at some point struck, as all good ideas usually do, in the dead of night. And in the dead of night came other ideas. Of danger and desire. And a hero unlike any hero I've ever created before.

Ryan doesn't think of himself as a hero. He's far too hard and cynical in his dealings with women for that role. But in Kirsty's eyes, he's always been her hero. When she was seventeen he rescued her from kidnappers, and she fell madly in love with him. The trouble was, he was married at the time. Now, five years later, he turns up in her life again, no longer married. Kirsty thinks fate has been kind! What she doesn't know is that one of her kidnappers has received early parole and Ryan has been hired by Nathan to protect her while Nathan takes Gemma on a second honeymoon, hoping to save his floundering marriage.

Kirsty thinks all her dreams are finally coming true, when in reality, a nightmare even worse than her kidnapping is about to begin.

This book could be categorized as romantic suspense. But I would describe it more as a suspenseful and rather erotic romance. Just my cup of tea! I hope you enjoy Ryan and Kirsty's story, plus the final chapter of Nathan and Gemma's long and tempestuous relationship.

Miranda Lee

Hearts of Fire
MIRANDA LEE

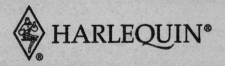

TORONTO • NEW YORK • LONDON
AMSTERDAM • PARIS • SYDNEY • HAMBURG
STOCKHOLM • ATHENS • TOKYO • MILAN • MADRID
PRAGUE • WARSAW • BUDAPEST • AUCKLAND

ISBN 0-373-83507-8

HEARTS OF FIRE

First North American Publication 2002

Copyright © 2001 by Miranda Lee

This edition published by arrangement with Harlequin Books S.A.

Visit us at www.eHarlequin.com

Printed in U.S.A.

Nathan Whitmore
Adopted son of Byron Whitmore, Nathan is a talented playwright. But after a desperately troubled childhood and a divorce, Nathan is utterly ruthless and emotionally controlled. Will he ever be the loving, caring husband of whom Gemma has dreamed?

Gemma Smith-Whitmore
On her father's death, Gemma discovered a magnificent black opal worth a small fortune, and an old photograph that casts doubt on her real identity. In search of the truth and a new life, she goes to Sydney, where she is seduced by and then married to Nathan Whitmore.

Kirsty Whitmore
The divorce of Nathan and his first wife, Lenore, sent their teenage daughter Kirsty off the rails. But now she is older and wiser. Having inherited her parents' love of the theater, Kirsty is committed to pursuing a career as an actress. Then Ryan arrives on the scene, and proves to be more than a little distracting....

Ryan Harris
Recently divorced, irresistible bodyguard Ryan has spent his newfound freedom indulging in a series of no-strings affairs. Ryan refuses to allow his emotions to interfere with his liaisons with women. But then Kirsty walks into his life—and *everything* changes!

HEARTS OF FIRE is the sequel to Miranda Lee's bestselling six-book series, set in the glamorous, cutthroat world of Australian opal dealing.

Secrets and Sins

PROLOGUE

THE funeral the previous day had been bad enough, but the thought of clearing out her mother's things was even worse.

She didn't know where to start, yet there was only this one room. One miserable room. In a miserable boarding-house. The kind of dilapidated dump which flanked the dingier streets of Kings Cross, catering for the down-and-outs of Sydney.

Not much to show for a life of seventy years.

She squared her shoulders and just started, dumping all her mother's clothes from the rickety wooden closet straight into a garbage bag, destined for the charity bin.

The contents of the ancient chest of drawers in the corner could not be disposed of quite so easily—except for the tattered underwear which went straight into a second garbage bag, this one destined for a dumpster. The other three drawers were full of assorted things. No doubt tasteless and worthless, just like their owner.

But they would have to be gone through, she supposed with a wearily resigned sigh.

The first two drawers contained fashion ''accessories', for want of a better word. Scarves and belts and jewellery. All cheap and nasty, but usable.

She tipped them in with the clothes.

The next drawer held various purses and handbags. Not expensive bags in themselves, though there was one quite pretty beaded evening purse which she almost kept.

But she didn't want any mementos of her mother. She wanted to forget the woman named Lorna Manson had ever existed. She'd even legally changed her surname so that there was no obvious connection.

The beaded purse joined the other things in the charity-destined garbage bag.

The last drawer presented a bit of a problem. It contained photos.

Sitting down on the bed, she went through them methodically and ruthlessly, keeping all the ones where she was alone and only a couple of herself with her mother. Nice shots when she'd been a baby. She made a second pile of the rest, including the ones of her mother with men-friends.

There were heaps of those, often provocative, with the men naked to the waist and their hands all over her mother, who was in various degrees of undress. The younger her mother was, the more risqué the photograph.

She shook her head at the endless parade of flesh. And the endless parade of men. When it crossed her mind that one of them could very well be her father, she started looking at the men's faces more closely.

None showed any resemblance to her own looks, however. None was even blond, which her father must have been, given she was so fair and her mother had been so dark.

Stupid, really, to even look. But it was difficult not

be curious over the man who'd made her so different from her pathetic mother. Most likely her father had been one of her mother's casual tricks, not an actual boyfriend. Up till Lorna had totally lost her looks, around fifty, she'd worked as a prostitute whenever she needed money. Getting pregnant had been a mistake. A *big* mistake. Or so her mother had often said, especially when she'd been drunk. Which had been pretty well all the time over the last few years.

It had been inevitable that the demon drink would eventually kill Lorna Manson. And it had. Though not exactly as her daughter had anticipated. Death had come courtesy of a driver who hadn't seen a very drunk Lorna lurch out onto William Street till it was too late.

Not a nice way to go. But better than dying of cirrhosis of the liver.

The last of the photographs sorted, she dropped the larger pile in the garbage bag with the underwear, and slipped the smaller pile into her own quite expensive leather handbag.

There was nothing in the last drawer now except a magazine, one of those women's publications which used to contain recipes and household tips but now peddled glossy photographs and sleazy gossip about the rich and famous. She picked it up, and was about to throw it away when her eye was caught by an article on Nathan Whitmore, the man who'd written the play she was rehearsing at the moment.

Had her mother bought the magazine because of her daughter's connection? Probably. Lorna had not been given to wasting money on a magazine when those dollars could have been better spent on gin.

Perhaps her mother *had* loved her, in her own warped way. Although she'd been disgruntled about her daughter pursuing a career on the stage. Perhaps because her mother had fancied herself an actress in her younger days. A highly unsuccessful one.

Sitting down on the side of the bed, she flipped over the pages till she found the article, which had more pictures than words. She was looking at one of the photographs of Nathan Whitmore and his young wife, and thinking what a stunning-looking couple they were, when there was a tap-tap on the door.

"It's Joan. Can I come in, dear?"

It was the old biddy from the room next door.

"The door's not locked," she called back while she rapidly scanned the article for mention of the play.

But there wasn't a word about *Sisters in Love*. The article was nothing but gossip about the wealthy playwright's marriage being in trouble. Apparently, Nathan Whitmore's wife hadn't accompanied him to New York recently, where he'd been presented with a Tony Award for his most famous play *The Woman in Black*, which was still breaking box office records on Broadway.

"They do print a lot of rubbish in these magazines, don't they?" she said to Joan, who'd come in and was standing next to her. "Take this article, for instance. Not a scrap of fact. Just speculation. I'll bet Nathan Whitmore's marriage is still going hot and strong. Just look at that wife of his. Talk about beautiful. Of course, she *is* a lot younger than him. But so what? He's still drop-dead gorgeous, even at his age. And with more money than you can climb over."

"Have you ever met him?" Joan asked.

"No. He's not having anything to do with the production I'm in. He rarely directs plays any more. Or even movies, for that matter. I read somewhere he doesn't like being away from his wife and family for long. Sounded like he's the perfect husband and father to me. Nothing at all like this article is implying—as though he's some kind of Bluebeard, not to be trusted by any woman or wife. For heaven's sake, he's only been married once before. That's hardly a crime these days. I've never heard anything about his sleeping around. And, believe me, if he *was* a womaniser, the theatre grapevine would know about it."

"You sound like you admire the man."

"I do. He's a brilliant writer. A creative genius, really. Who knows? Maybe I *will* meet him one day."

"I think that maybe you should..."

"Maybe I *should*? What do you mean by that?"

"Oh, dear. I've said it now, haven't I?"

"Said what? Joan, do stop dithering and just say whatever it is you are trying to say."

"This is going to come as a shock to you..."

"*What*, for pity's sake?"

"Nathan Whitmore..."

"Yes? What about Nathan Whitmore?"

"He...he's your father."

"My *father*!"

"Yes." Joan nodded her grey-haired head.

"But that's impossible!"

"No. It's the truth all right. Lorna told me one night when she was in her cups—and she always told the truth when she was drunk. She made me promise the next morning never to tell you, and I've kept that promise. But she's in her grave now, and I'm telling you because you have a right to know.''

"That's not what I meant by impossible. *Think* about it, Joan. I'm twenty-seven years old. Nathan Whitmore's only forty-three. It says so in this article.'' She jabbed at the page, her heart pounding madly in her chest. "My mother was forty-three when I was born. Are you saying Nathan Whitmore fathered me when he was *sixteen*?''

"I know it sounds unlikely, dear. Trust me when I say I was shocked when I heard, too. But it's still true.''

"But my mother had lovers by the bucketload. Why would she go after a mere boy? It doesn't make sense.''

Joan shrugged. "I gather Nathan Whitmore at sixteen wasn't anything like any ordinary boy of sixteen. He was fully grown and utterly gorgeous.''

"That's no excuse. My mother would have been old enough to be *his* mother, for pity's sake!''

"Lorna knows she did wrong. Why do you think she never told you? She was deeply ashamed.''

"But…but…how on earth did she get to meet him in the first place? Everyone knows he was adopted by that millionaire philanthropist when he was just a child. They would hardly have moved in the same worlds.''

"He was sixteen when he was adopted by Byron Whitmore—shortly after his affair with your mother. Lorna told me she first met Nathan when he was around twelve. His mother was one of those teenage runaways who came to the Cross in the late fifties and carried on haunting it throughout the sixties and seventies, living on a steady diet of sex, drugs and rock and roll. Nathan was this girl's illegitimate love-child. She died of a heroin overdose just after his sixteenth birthday. When he had nowhere else to live, Lorna took the boy in. She swore to me that her initial intentions were the best, that she just wanted to mother the boy, but she said she became sexually obsessed by him after he confessed to her that he was a virgin.''

Joan laughed a not very nice laugh. "Lorna said she'd never had a virgin before. She confessed she drugged him one night and did it to him whilst he was incapable of stopping her.''

"Oh, my God…'' Her mother hadn't just been a lush and a slut, she'd been a pervert!

"Lorna said he didn't mind after the first time,'' Joan prattled on. "She said he soon became sex-mad. Wanted it morning, noon and night. For a woman like Lorna, that was pretty irresistible.''

"Don't tell me any more. *Please.*'

Joan looked a bit shame-faced for taking such salacious glee in the tale. "Sorry. I didn't think.''

"Did…did he know he got Mum pregnant?''

"No. Lorna didn't realise she was having a baby till well after Byron Whitmore swept in and carried your father away to a better life. He never knew about you.''

"This is all so…so unbelievable!''

"I know, dear. I know. Sorry for blurting it out like that. Still, I'm pretty sure it's true. And there are tests which can prove such things these days. Maybe it's time you told Mr Whitmore about your existence. He might be able to help you with your career. He is your father, after all. Regardless of the circumstances of your conception, nothing will change that."

No, she conceded. Nothing would change that.

Yet if she went to him and told him he would hardly welcome her into his life with open arms. The last person he'd want to know—or love—would be the illegitimate offspring of some woman who'd virtually raped him when he'd been a mere boy.

Lorna's assertion to Joan that he'd been more than willing to be her lover after the first time sounded like one of Lorna's sexual fantasies. He probably hadn't known what he was doing half the time, especially if drugs had been involved. The person who'd wanted sex morning, noon and night would have been her nympho of a mother, not that poor abused boy.

Thank God Byron Whitmore had come on the scene. Though not soon enough, it seemed.

Groaning, she let her gaze drop once more to the largest photograph of Nathan Whitmore—to the picture of the man, not the boy.

"My father," she murmured in a mixture of shock and awe. She traced the features of his handsome face with her fingertips, seeing the genetic similarities for the first time. The thick blond hair. The widow's peak in the middle of his forehead. The deeply set grey eyes. The full bottom lip.

She still found it hard to believe, but the evidence was there before her eyes.

Nathan Whitmore *was* her father.

The idea was overwhelming once it sank in. My God, he was one of the most famous playwrights in the world, a very influential man in the theatre.

"You are going to tell him, aren't you, dear?"

The prospect of confronting Nathan Whitmore, claiming to be his daughter, was far more terrifying than auditioning for a part in one of his plays.

She was used to being rejected as an actress. Acting was not a career for the faint-hearted. But to risk being rejected as a daughter, being looked at with disgust or being called a liar and a blackmailer.

No. She couldn't do that to herself.

"Nathan Whitmore already has three legitimate children," she told Joan. "Two sons from his second marriage. And an older daughter by his first marriage."

Addressing that last fact out loud brought a mixture of negative emotions. Jealousy. Bitterness. Resentment.

How different her life would have been if she'd been Nathan Whitmore's legitimate daughter. With him as her doting father it wouldn't have taken her this many years to get off the ground with her acting career. He could have helped her, paid for proper lessons, maybe even written plays for her.

It was all so unfair. But then life was unfair. If nothing else, being Lorna Manson's bastard had taught her that.

"So what are you going to do?" Joan asked.

"I don't know yet. Something. Oh, yes...I'll do something," she said bitterly.

That was another thing being Lorna Manson's bastard had taught her. The only way girls like herself got anywhere in life was by being tough and determined—and, on occasion, ruthless.

CHAPTER ONE

RYAN showered for some time, reluctant to return to the hotel bedroom. He had a feeling the woman he'd just made love to—far too well—wouldn't want to call it quits.

When he finally emerged from the bathroom, with one of the hotel's thick white towels slung low around his hips, Leanne was sitting up against the headboard, smoking. She was naked to the waist, her long tousled blonde hair not long enough to cover her bare breasts with their still erect nipples.

"I want to see you again," she said between puffs.

Ryan threw her an uncompromising look as he crossed the room to where he'd left his clothes draped over the desk chair. She was beautiful. *Very* beautiful. But this was the second time he'd met her in this hotel room and it was going to be the last.

"I told you before, Leanne," he said as he started pulling on his clothes. "It's against my personal rules to sleep with the same lady more than twice. That way, I avoid any emotional entanglements and the scenes which go with them when I say goodbye. And trust me, Leanne, I always say goodbye."

She laughed. "I assure you, Ryan, I won't become emotionally involved with you. You're not nearly rich enough. I just want you for the sex. You're the best

I've ever had. But you already know that, don't you?''

''Practice does make perfect,'' he said with a poker face.

Leanne laughed. ''You're an arrogant, ruthless bastard, Ryan Harris. Which is exactly what I like in a lover.''

''I'm flattered, Leanne, but the answer's still no.''

''What if I pay you a thousand dollars, plus expenses? Harold told me that's what you charged him recently for one day's bodyguarding.''

Ryan stopped dressing to frown at her. ''Harold still tells you his private business, even now you're divorced?''

It was a concept he couldn't understand. Ryan would never trust his own ex-wife with any knowledge about himself. Not that he was likely to. He hadn't clapped eyes on *her* for over two years. Which was still not long enough.

The smile which played across Leanne's full mouth reminded Ryan of what women like her were all about.

''Harold has a tendency to talk in bed,'' she said.

''He still *sleeps* with you?''

''Of course.'' She dragged deeply on her cigarette, then let it out very slowly. ''I'm a hard act to follow. Like you, lover. So what do you say? Same time, same place next week? I'll have the money with me. In cash.''

Ryan resumed his dressing. ''Sorry, sweetheart. My body's for hire for a lot of things, but sex isn't one of them.''

"And what a body," she purred, her eyes all over him. "What if I offered you two thousand?"

"You wouldn't. You're not that desperate. And I'm not that good."

"That's a matter of opinion. But what if I did?"

"My answer would still be no."

She made a snorting sound. "Every man has his price. Even you, Ryan darling."

Ryan was thinking that he'd already paid a far too hefty price for his boudoir skills when his mobile phone rang. He picked it up from the desktop, clicked the blue button and put the compact black instrument to his ear.

"Ryan Harris."

"Keith, here, Ryan. Sorry to interrupt your rather long lunch-hour," his boss said wryly. "But a job's come in for you. An emergency."

"What?"

"Nick Gregory is being released from jail tomorrow. He got parole."

"*What?* After only four years? But his sentence was for ten."

"Yeah, but you have to remember he was only young, and it was his older partner who masterminded the kidnapping. They say Gregory's fully rehabilitated."

"Who's they?" Ryan scoffed. "The do-gooders on the parole board? What in hell would they know? They're all white-collar fools who haven't a clue what makes a criminal tick. When you're inside, you'll say anything to get out."

Ryan knew that for a fact. He hadn't graced the cells of an adult prison, but he'd spent more time than he liked to think about in juvenile detention centres. Desperation for freedom was a forceful incentive to lie. And pretend. He'd like a dollar for every prisoner who claimed to have found Jesus in jail. No doubt their victims wouldn't be as easily convinced of their convenient conversions as the pathetic idiots on the parole board.

"The chairman of the parole board happens to be Byron Whitmore," his boss informed him.

Ryan's straight dark brows lifted at this news. Byron Whitmore was the "do-gooder" who'd helped *him* get his life on track when he'd needed it most. If there was one man on this earth Ryan thought highly of, it was Byron.

What he'd done for Ryan hadn't been a one-off, either. The wealthy Sydney businessman had apparently helped a lot of boys who'd found themselves in trouble through no fault of their own—poor, wretched kids to whom life had dealt a rotten hand. He'd even adopted one as his own son.

Ryan would not say a word against Byron Whitmore.

Still, what the hell was he doing, rubber-stamping the release of one of his granddaughter's kidnappers?

"Kirsty's father is going to go ape," Ryan muttered.

"It was Nathan Whitmore who just called. He wants to see you, pronto."

"I can well imagine."

During his trial Gregory had threatened that when he got out he was going do to Kirsty what he should have done when he'd had the chance.

Kirsty hadn't actually been assaulted during her

three-day captivity, but she'd been bound and blind-folded, and Gregory had terrified her with his filthy talk. The poor kid had had nightmares for months after her rescue. Ryan hated to think what this news would do to Nathan's daughter.

"Can you get over to Nathan's place straight away?" Keith asked.

"Can do. He still living in that mansion at St Ives?"

"Yep. Hop to it, Ryan. He sounded very stressed."

"I can be there in half an hour."

"Good. I'll call him back and let him know you're on your way."

Ryan clicked off the cellphone and was hooking it over his belt when he noticed Leanne was no longer in the bed. He stared at the shut bathroom door. The shower was running. He slipped his suit jacket on, grabbed his tie and walked in without knocking. She didn't seem to mind. Leanne was an exhibitionist of the first order. He supposed that went with the terri-tory of having a great body.

"I have to go," he said as he tied his grey-striped silk tie, bought to tone with his lightweight grey busi-ness suit. Ryan dressed well these days, if conserva-tively. His job required that he blend in to a corporate crowd, not stand out. "I paid for this room upfront, and the desk has my credit card number if you want Room Service. Feel free to order lunch."

She gave him a sexy smile through the steam.

"Thanks. And you feel free to call me again. Any time."

Ryan knew he wouldn't do that. Quite frankly, she wasn't nearly as good in bed as she thought she was.

CHAPTER TWO

NATHAN slammed down the phone then dragged in several steadying breaths. Nothing was to be achieved by losing it. He had to stay cool and rational. He had to see things as they really were, and not through the panicky eyes of a worried father.

Okay, so Nick Gregory was being let out of jail tomorrow. That was a *fait accompli*. He could do nothing about that. But was Gregory a real risk? Or not?

Byron had assured him he wasn't. And Byron was no fool.

But he wasn't the compulsive cynic Nathan was. And he'd never lived shoulder to shoulder with the scum of the earth. Creeps like Gregory could lie and connive without turning a hair. They could never be totally trusted. Never!

Rehabilitated? Nathan didn't believe in the word. Once a bad bastard, always a bad bastard.

He knew that for a fact.

Nathan smashed an angry fist down on his desk then stormed from the room, marching up the hallway to the foyer, where he pressed the button which automatically opened the high iron security gates. That done, he strode into the front living-room and headed for the bar he'd had built in after he'd bought Belleview from Byron several years ago.

A drink was called for. A stiff drink.

He grabbed a bottle of bourbon and poured a Lazarus-reviving dose into a glass. He didn't bother with ice. He didn't want anything to water down the effect of the alcohol. He had to calm his jangling nerves—and his fury—before Ryan arrived.

But, damn it all, this couldn't have come at a worse time. He was leaving on a cruise with Gemma tomorrow—a much-needed second honeymoon. The last thing he needed was to have something on his mind. All he wanted to do for the next nine days and eight nights was concentrate on the woman he loved.

His marriage had been on increasingly shaky ground since Richard's very difficult birth five years earlier—Gemma being furious with him for having had a vasectomy afterwards without consulting her.

He'd thought she'd get over it, that she'd come to see the common sense of his decision. But she hadn't. She'd become cooler and cooler towards him. She never approached him for sex any more, and when he did make love to her she rarely came, no matter what he did or how long he took. She didn't say no, except when she had her period. She just lay there in their bed and let him do what he wanted. But she never actively joined in as she once had. She never kissed him back, or touched him, or went down on him.

God, he missed that.

All her love and attention went into raising the boys. Nathan felt furiously jealous of his own sons at times.

The thought that she might have finally fallen out

of love with him horrified Nathan more than he could ever have imagined. Life without Gemma's love just wasn't worth living. She was the light to his darkness. The outer peace which stilled the inner emotional turmoil which had always plagued his life.

So he'd been delighted—and relieved—when she'd agreed to come on this cruise. Though maybe her saying yes had something to do with the fact that he'd asked her in front of her parents. Gemma didn't like to look bad in front of them. And a wife would look bad if she said no to her husband proposing a romantic second honeymoon cruising up the east coast of Australia to the Whitsundays and back. He'd have opted for a longer cruise of the South Pacific if he'd been confident she'd leave the boys for that long.

But he hadn't been, and had sensibly opted for the safer, shorter route.

Nathan was not above doing anything to get back into his wife's good books. Anything at all. He already had, hadn't he? And he aimed to do a lot more during the next week or so. But he didn't want to worry about the likes of Nick Gregory whilst he was doing it.

Hopefully, Byron was right about Gregory being a changed young man. Or at least smart enough to know that going anywhere near Kirsty was not in his best interests.

Life's lovely little experiences, however, had taught Nathan always to think the worst of people, then act accordingly. That way he didn't suffer too many nasty surprises.

He was on his second whisky and was standing, wide-legged, at the living-room front window, waiting for his insurance policy to arrive, when a black Porsche swung through the open gateway.

"Mmm," Nathan murmured as he watched the stylish car crunch its way round the red gravel drive and pull to a smooth halt at the base of the front steps. Ryan Harris was doing very well for himself these days. He'd heard he'd been made head of security at IAS.

Still, a promotion that was well deserved.

A good man in a crisis, was Ryan. Aside from his many and varied physical skills, he kept a cool head. He was also intelligent in a street-smart way which was often far more successful in life than academic cleverness.

A good-looking man too, Nathan appreciated anew as Ryan climbed out of the Porsche. No wonder Kirsty had developed a crush on him after her rescue. Nathan suspected that if Ryan hadn't been safely married at the time something might have happened between those two.

Kirsty, at seventeen, had been a very attractive package, with her lush nubile beauty and air of schoolgirl innocence. Ryan had only been young himself at the time. No more than twenty-three or four. He had to have been sorely tempted—especially with Kirsty batting big, adoring eyes up at him all the time.

Nathan suddenly remembered that Ryan wasn't married any more. Byron often chatted away to him about his second most successful protégé. Apparently Ryan had divorced that tarty-looking wife of his a year or two back, and was now living the life of a swinging bachelor in some snazzy unit overlooking

Bondi. He also had quite a reputation as a ladies' man.

Byron, naturally, was unimpressed with this latest development in Ryan's life, whereas Nathan understood exactly where Ryan was coming from. His sowing of his wild oats was a natural male reaction after marrying the wrong woman far too young. But, ultimately, marriage and family *was* the way to go, if you didn't want to surrender your soul totally to your dark side. All Ryan needed was to meet the right kind of girl.

As Nathan watched Ryan's long legs carry his powerful body up Belleview's wide stone steps two at a time, his ruthless mind began ticking away. Maybe he could kill two birds with one stone here. Protect Kirsty while he was away as well as present his stubborn daughter with the one man who might show her that her neurotically clung-to virginity was not the way to personal survival *or* happiness. Neither was play-acting her life away.

Women were meant for love and marriage, in Nathan's opinion. But first of all they had to be capable of love. And loving.

Kirsty had been in love with Ryan once. Maybe she still was. All *he* had to do was throw them together once more.

Ryan rang the front doorbell, sliding his hands into his trouser pockets and glancing around while he waited to be let in.

It was over five years since his last visit, but nothing had changed much. Belleview was still one of the most impressive homes he'd ever seen. Stately and

grand, the two-storeyed white stuccoed residence had
a wide white-columned portico, long symmetrically
placed windows and perfectly manicured grounds.
There was garaging for six cars on one side and a
solar-heated pool in the huge backyard.

Or there had been, last time he was here.

When he'd first started working at IAS Ryan had
been staggered by the wealth of some of their clients.
But over the years he'd grown used to their mansions,
and yachts, and cars. He had a fancy car himself now,
and a fancy beachside apartment. Which he owned
outright.

Success, he now believed, was better measured by
what you started out with. At seventeen, when Byron
had found him a job at IAS as the office boy, he'd
had nothing. No money. No skills. No confidence.
Not too many muscles either.

Twelve years and many night courses later, he was
now head of security, with a body that served him
well and a range of other skills useful to his profession. He was an expert marksman with both rifle and
revolver. He held black belts in kung fu and karate.
He could run ten miles without flagging and drive a
car like a getaway man. He could pick any lock and
had a sniffer dog's nose for electronic bugs.

Recently he'd taken a course in negotiation, anticipating a situation in the future where he might have
to talk himself out of danger. He'd also done an ad-
vanced first aid course after one of his clients had
dropped to the ground with a heart attack next to him
and someone else had had to do CPR, leaving Ryan
feeling stupid and inadequate.

Ryan hadn't relished the experience, and didn't aim

on enduring a repeat. His motto was an extension of the Boy Scouts' code. Be prepared. For *anything*!

Although he was now IAS's most sought-after personal bodyguard, Ryan only assigned himself to protect the richest and most famous of their clients these days. Mostly he oversaw operations, trained new operatives and delegated.

But there was no question of delegating when the client was Nathan Whitmore.

The door swung open and there stood the man in question.

Ryan knew everything the general public knew about Nathan Whitmore and considerably more, courtesy of the way the man had acted when his daughter had been kidnapped.

No police had been called. No one else told except Byron and Ryan's boss. Then, finally, Ryan. The demanded ransom of two million dollars had been discreetly organised and the drop carried out without a hitch. Using a disguise as a biker, Ryan had followed the older kidnapper back to where he and his younger partner had been hiding Kirsty, at a dilapidated farmhouse on the western outskirts of Sydney.

Fortunately the ramshackle building had been surrounded by overgrown trees and shrubs—good cover under which Ryan had been able to creep close, then easily assess the situation. Two men in the kitchen, counting the money on an old table. Female target still alive and alone, tied to a bed in a front bedroom.

Ryan had quietly entered the premises by a broken side window, disabling both men with a couple of strategic blows almost before they'd looked up from the loot. Then he'd gone to the bedroom, where he'd swiftly but gently informed a terrified Kirsty he was a friend and was there to rescue her. Despite being bound and blindfolded, and shaking like a leaf, she'd been physically unharmed.

Because of Nathan's bold plan and steely nerve, Nathan had got his daughter *and* his money back.

A most unusual man, in Ryan's opinion. A man to be respected, but perhaps a little feared.

"Ryan," Nathan said to him by way of greeting.

"Mr Whitmore," Ryan returned with a polite nod.

"Thanks for being so prompt. And do call me Nathan. Come in."

Ryan extracted his hands from his pockets and entered the cosily central-heated interior. Although the sun was shining outside, it was a typical June day in Sydney. Cool and crisp. The home's foyer, with its vaulted ceiling and marble floor, would have been chilly, had it not been heated.

"This way," Nathan said, shutting the door and striding off along the downstairs hallway.

Ryan followed him into a room he recalled very well. It was the study where they'd planned Kirsty's rescue. He and Byron and Keith and Nathan.

"Take a seat," Nathan offered, waving towards one of the two leather-studded armchairs which faced the large antique desk in front of the window.

Ryan thought antique furniture suited Nathan's looks. He was the sort of man who, if he'd been an actor, would have played the Scarlet Pimpernel perfectly. He was almost foppishly handsome, with that wavy blond hair and full mouth. Only his eyes gave away the man of steel underneath the surface elegance. Grey in colour and sharp with intelligence, their expression could change from charming to chilly in a split second. Ryan might respect Nathan, but he had no illusions about his character. He was not the gentleman his adopted father was. Not even remotely.

"Did Keith tell you what's happened?" Nathan asked as he sat down behind the desk.

"Yep. Gregory hits the streets of Sydney tomorrow morning."

"You understand my concern, then?"

"Absolutely. I can't believe they let him out this soon. But that's the Australian justice system for you."

"Byron says he's rehabilitated."

"Byron believes in rehabilitation," Ryan said drily, and Nathan laughed.

"I appreciate a man who thinks like I do."

Ryan felt that was going a bit far, but declined to say so. "What do you want me to do?" he asked.

"First I want you to put a tail on Gregory, from the moment he steps through the prison gates. I want to know what he does and where he goes, twenty-four hours a day."

"For how long?"

"For as long as it takes to reassure me he's no risk to Kirsty. Or the rest of my family."

"That could be a very expensive operation."

"Money's not a problem."

Ryan shrugged. "Fine. Consider it done."

"But I don't want Byron to know. He'd think I was being paranoid."

"Actually, I don't speak to Mr Whitmore all that often these days. But if I happen to, for any reason, then mum's the word. Does *my* boss know he's not

to say anything? I think he socialises with Mr
Whitmore occasionally.''

"Yes. Keith knows. There's one other thing.''

"What's that?''

"Unfortunately I'm leaving tomorrow on a nine-
day cruise off the coast of Queensland with my wife.
My two boys will be staying with their aunt Jade for
the duration. Gemma's over there now, settling them
in.''

"That doesn't sound unfortunate to me. It sounds
like a good idea—especially if you take Kirsty with
you. Get her out of town for a while. I'm sure if you
pull some strings you could get her a berth.''

"No point. She wouldn't come. Kirsty and I have
barely been on speaking terms since she left home a
few years back to pursue a career in acting. Trust me
when I say any suggestion of mine would be rejected
out of hand at any time, but especially now that she's
finally landed herself a good part in a play. One of
my own damned plays, would you believe it? Talk
about ironic. Anyway, the première was last weekend
and the critics gave it reasonable reviews. The initial
six-week run looks like being extended. Kirsty's not
going anywhere at this point in time, I can assure
you.''

"So Kirsty went into acting after she left school,''
Ryan remarked thoughtfully. "I have to confess I'm
surprised.''

"You and me both.''

"Reading between the lines, I gather you didn't
want her to become an actress?''

"Actor, Ryan,'' Nathan corrected drily. "Don't,
for pity's sake, use the word actress around the theatre

world or they'll have your guts for garters. But you're quite right. No, I didn't want Kirsty to follow in her mother's silly footsteps. You could have knocked me over with a feather when she told me.''

''When was that? After she finished school?''

''Not exactly. As you can imagine, it took Kirsty quite a while to recover from the kidnapping. She wouldn't even go outside the front door for ages, let alone go back to school. Anyway, when she did finally get it together, she came to me and said she didn't want to go back to school. She wanted me to pay for acting lessons instead.''

''She'd never said she wanted to act before this?''

''Not a word. I told her she'd be far wiser to finish her education, then find herself a real job in the real world. I couldn't have been more honest. I warned her of all the pitfalls of an acting career, especially on the stage. As far as I'm concerned, most of the men are gay, and all the women ambitious cats. The pay's pathetic as well. Unless you're one of the few lucky ones to make it on the big screen, that is. Even then you're not guaranteed a happy life. The movie world is a jungle, with far too many predators for a girl like Kirsty.''

''So what did she say to all that?''

''Refused to listen. Told me in no uncertain terms that I was a control freak, that I didn't always know what was best for everyone, even if I thought I did, and that she aimed to live her own life as she saw fit. She said acting was in her blood and she was going to become an actor whether I liked it or not.''

Ryan almost laughed. Fancy anyone, let alone a sweet young thing like Kirsty, having the balls to put it to her father like that. He'd have liked to be a fly on the wall at the time. Even repeating the incident was making Nathan go red in the face.

"When I informed my dear, darling daughter that I had no intention of financing what I considered a waste of time, she said she didn't need my twenty pieces of silver and that she would make it on her own. She even changed her surname and became a brunette so that no one in the theatre world would recognise her and give her parts just because she was my daughter."

"Wow. That's really telling you. But, you know, all that doesn't sound like the Kirsty I rescued at all."

"The Kirsty you rescued was not the real Kirsty," Nathan said ruefully. "She was a temporarily traumatised Kirsty. The real Kirsty is a real pain in the butt. She's always been a difficult child. *Always.* Well…perhaps that's not quite true. She was a delightful child till the divorce. It was after that the rot set in."

"How old was she when you split with your first wife?"

"Twelve or so when we first separated. Fourteen when I remarried."

"A touchy age."

"True. Look, don't think I don't appreciate the effect divorce has on kids. Everything parents do affects their kids."

And wasn't that the truth? Ryan thought bitterly.

"But Lenore and I were better off apart," Nathan went on. "We didn't love each other. If Kirsty was honest with herself, she'd agree. Gemma's been a wonderful stepmother to her. And Kirsty adores her two half-brothers. But ever since the divorce she's suffered from some kind of self-identity crisis—and a driving need to show me, especially, that she can make it on her own.''

''Most children with any guts want to do that, Nathan. Show their parents that they can make it on their own. I would think the daughter of a rich and famous man like yourself might have an even greater need than most. I wouldn't knock it, if I were you. You should be proud of her. She could have just sat around like some lazy rich bitch, sponging off her dad's money and spending her days shopping and having her hair done.''

''I *am* proud of her, damn it. Though I'm still not convinced that she has any great acting talent. I was at the play's opening night and, believe me, she didn't set the stage on fire. I suspect she was cast simply because she looks like the girl the director had already chosen for the older sister. Prior to this she's only been in bit parts. But that's not the issue at the moment. This situation with Gregory is. She still has nightmares about the kidnapping. Her mother told me. If Kirsty finds out that creep's on the loose, she might regress to the timid fear-filled creature she became after the kidnapping. You know what she was like.''

Ryan did. The girl had clung to him like a leech after he'd untied her that day. She hadn't wanted him to leave her, not even after he'd delivered her safely home. She'd sobbed and begged him to stay. Which he had. The whole of that first night. Sitting in an armchair in her bedroom. Then on and off during the weeks leading up to the trial. She'd kept asking for him, and he hadn't been able to refuse her.

It had been a strange experience. His wife had assumed the worst, her jealousy fuelled by Kirsty's looks. None of her nasty accusations had been true, but in hindsight there *had* been another element in the bond which had developed between them. Impossible not to have been, Kirsty was a beautiful young girl, sweet and adoring in her gratitude and attitude. What man wouldn't have been flattered, and attracted, even against his better judgement?

"I don't want Kirsty to know he's out," Nathan insisted, snapping Ryan out of his thoughts.

"Fine. Don't tell her. We'll simply put a watch on her as well. Where's she living, then? In a flat somewhere, I presume?"

"That's part of my problem. She does have a poky little bedsit close to town, but for the time Gemma and I are away she'll be living here. Alone."

"*Here?* In this big house? All by herself?"

"Correct. Gemma and I don't have any live-in staff. What we do have, however, is this useless old dog which my wife adores. She refuses to put him in a kennel. Says he would pine for his home. Says it's bad enough she's going away and leaving him alone at all."

Ryan thought he detected more than a touch of resentment in Nathan's comments. Maybe all wasn't so well in his marriage to the lovely Gemma. His wife *was* considerably younger. And nothing at all like Nathan.

Where Nathan Whitmore *could* be charming when he wanted to be, Gemma Whitmore *was* charm. And warmth. And true beauty. Sweetness and sincerity shone out from within. Everyone liked her. Even

Ryan liked her. And he didn't genuinely like too
many of the rich wives he encountered during the
course of his work. Mostly they were snobs, or self-
centred, very spoiled rich bitches. In a way, Gemma
Whitmore was too good for her husband, no matter
how handsome and clever he was.

"Couldn't the dog stay with your boys?" Ryan
suggested. "You said they were staying with an
aunt."

"He could, of course. But that would require Jaws
to go in a car right across the city."

"So?"

Nathan's expression was classic. "Jaws has a panic
attack during any car trip," he said, each word dripping with sarcasm. "We even have the vet do house-
calls nowadays because Gemma won't put the dog
through the trauma of a car ride. Says he's too old
for such stress. Truly, you've no idea what I've endured over the years where that mongrel is concerned.
And a mongrel he is. You should see him. Looks like
a cross between an afghan and a donkey. Eats more
steak in a week than I do in a year. But that's beside
the point, I suppose," he muttered. "The thing is the
dog's staying here, with Kirsty his devoted dog-sitter.
For the next week, anyway."

"That certainly could be a problem," Ryan said,
his security brain slipping into action. "If Gregory's
looking for revenge of any kind, and manages to slip
his tail, your home would be one of the first places
he'd come. With Kirsty having changed her name and
appearance she'd have been safer living elsewhere.
But staying in this house is a different kettle of fish
entirely. It'd be impossible to watch over her properly

from the street. Anyone alone in a house this size is asking for trouble.''

''She won't be alone,'' Nathan said drily. ''She'll have Jaws protecting her.''

Ryan hesitated to mention that even the best, most youthful guard dog could be easily disabled. A bait would do it every time. Or a bullet. Given Nathan's wife adored her dog, he kept his silence on that subject. No point in complicating the situation. If the dog died, they would get over it. If Kirsty died, or was even hurt in some way...

Ryan was amazed how that thought affected him.

''I want you to personally protect Kirsty while I'm away,'' Nathan said. ''You, Ryan. No one else.''

''I'd be glad to do that, Nathan. It would probably be a good thing for Gregory to see me by her side if he manages to get within sight of her. But how can I do it without Kirsty knowing the reason? I can't just hang around her all the time like some nutty fan. She'd recognise me and ask questions.''

''I've thought about that and I've come up with a solution.''

''This I'd like to hear.''

''You could date her.''

CHAPTER THREE

RYAN stared at him. "*Date* her?" he repeated, his voice echoing his shock. "Surely you're not serious."

Nathan was momentarily derailed by Ryan's adverse reaction. Maybe his plan for keeping Kirsty safe plus straightening out her personal life at the same time wasn't going to be as easy to put into action as he'd thought it would be.

"I'm deadly serious. Why? What's the problem? Byron says you're footloose and fancy-free these days. And Kirsty's between boyfriends at the moment," he added, deciding at that point it might not be wise to say she'd *never* had a serious boyfriend.

She'd dated quite a bit since leaving home, according to Lenore, but always dropped the guy when he pressed for a sexual relationship. Lenore believed Kirsty's aversion to physical intimacy was an after-effect of the kidnapping, but the girl herself had said no, that wasn't it. She claimed she liked men, and had been attracted to plenty of guys, but found she just didn't like it when they tried to have sex with her.

Nathan couldn't believe that a daughter of his was genuinely frigid, and could only conclude these guys she'd gone out with weren't made of the right stuff.

Not like Ryan. Now *he* was made of the right stuff.

"Look, I'm not asking you to marry the girl,"

Nathan said with a straight face. "All I'm suggesting is that you ask her out while I'm away. That shouldn't be any great hardship. I thought you liked Kirsty."

"I did. Of course I did. She was a real nice kid."

"Well, she's not a kid any more. She's one stunning-looking female these days. Lost all that puppy fat she was once carrying. And she's a blonde now, would you believe? Did it to get this role. And, you know, it suits her."

Ryan's face remained worried. "This still doesn't feel right, Nathan."

"*Right?* What's not right about it? Kirsty turned twenty-three. She's a grown woman with a mind of her own. If she says yes to going out with you, it'll be because she wants to. And I'm pretty sure she *will* want to. She was simply crazy about you once."

"For pity's sake, that was just a teenage crush. And a natural result of my rescuing her. It wasn't real. She would have moved on from that a long time ago."

Nathan shrugged. "Maybe. Maybe not. Look, if she says no, then no harm done. Just watch her as best you can from a distance. Put another man on the job if you have to. If she says yes, no harm done there either. You get to take out a very pretty girl, catch up on old times, have some fun together. Best of all, you'll have the opportunity to drive her home every night after the play and see her safely inside here. That's the part which worries me the most. Her coming home here late at night all alone. Gemma's given her the money to take a taxi back and forth every night, but she'll just be dropped off at the gate. There's no real security in that. Come on, Ryan, what do you say?"

Nathan was irritated when Ryan still looked doubtful. He hated it when his plans didn't go smoothly. Still, it was good to know that the man he was trying to matchmake with Kirsty had a conscience. Bad enough she had him—a bastard—for a father.

"Stop worrying about the damned ethics of the thing," Nathan argued. "Sometimes the end justifies the means. And the end which matters most here is keeping Kirsty safe."

"True."

"I'll double your usual fee," he added. "And there'll be a bonus of fifty thousand if I come back from the cruise to find my daughter happy and unharmed."

Ryan stared at this man who was holding out a carrot which would tempt even the most saint-like of men. And he was no saint. It was ironic that he'd told Leanne this very day that the one thing he wouldn't do for money was have sex.

Nathan *had* to know that dating someone these days invariably led to sex.

Or did he?

Maybe he was old enough—and old-fashioned enough—to think a couple could see each other every night for over a week without going to bed together.

Even if Nathan had his handsome head in the sand, *Ryan* knew what dating Kirsty would lead to. He thought of several good reasons why he should say no to this proposal, including his own precious rules about not sleeping with the same woman more than twice. But he knew he wasn't going to listen to any of them. The bottom line was that dating Kirsty for a while *was* the perfect solution for keeping her safe from the likes of Gregory.

Every other consideration paled when compared with that outcome. But that fifty grand wasn't on, no matter how tempted he was. If he accepted that, he'd be no better than a gigolo. Hell, he had to have *some* standards.

"All right," he said curtly. "But no bonus, thanks, Nathan. Taking Kirsty out a few times won't be any hardship to me. I'd do it for nothing."

Nathan looked surprised, but pleased. "You're sure?"

"Absolutely."

"Splendid. Thank you, Ryan. I appreciate that. You're a good man."

Ryan wasn't so sure about that. His flesh was already tingling at the thought of seeing Kirsty again, now that she was all grown up and he was no longer a married man.

"Now, on to practicalities," Nathan said. "The play Kirsty's in is called Sisters in Love and it's on at the drama theatre at the Opera House. I suggest you go along to see it, then send a message backstage saying you recognised her and want to see her. I'm sure she'll agree to at least meet you for coffee to start off with."

"Mmm. I'm not really the play-going type. She might wonder what I was doing there."

"You can say your boss gave you some free tickets he didn't use."

"Yes. I could do that." Ryan realised Nathan had really thought this all out, the ruthless devil. "So when do you want me to go? Tonight?"

"No, there's no performance on Tuesday nights. And she's not coming here till tomorrow, so tomorrow will do. There is a matinee performance on a Wednesday, but don't bother with that. They always use the understudy for matinees. Go to the night performance. It starts at eight."

"What's Kirsty's new surname?"

"O'Connell."

"Where on earth did she get that from?"

"I have no idea. I think she just made it up."

"I see. And she's a blonde now, you said?"

"*Very* blonde."

He couldn't quite imagine it, any more than he could imagine her with a brunette rinse. She'd been a redhead when he'd known her. Still, she'd be beautiful even if she were bald.

He thought of her eyes, those incredible green eyes. And the way they'd used to look at him. As if he was some kind of god. He'd felt ten feet tall when she looked at him.

He wondered how she'd look at him now. Not the same way, no doubt. As he'd said to Nathan, she'd have moved on since then. There'd probably been a whole host of boyfriends in the meantime—five years of living and loving out in the big, bad world. She might take one look at him and wonder what she'd ever found in him to admire so much. Nathan was being optimistic, thinking Ryan only had to turn up in Kirsty's life again and she would go out with him straight away, that very first night. He was, after all, from the wrong side of the tracks. Unlike herself; she'd been born with a silver spoon in her mouth.

Unless, of course, she'd turned into one of those

rebellious young rich bitches who liked a bit of rough in the sack.

This last thought went against Ryan's grain, but there was no point in pretending. Kirsty would no longer be the same sweet schoolgirl who'd thought the sun shone out of him.

"Anything else I should know about Kirsty?" he asked abruptly.

Nathan thought of his daughter's sexual inexperience, but once again decided not to enlighten Ryan.

"Not that I can think of at this moment. But if I do remember anything pertinent I'll let you know. I'll be calling you from the ship every day for a progress report, so I'll need your various phone numbers. Home. Work. Mobile. Here's a card with my mobile number on it if you need to call me. But please don't, unless it's an emergency. Do you have a business card with all your numbers on it?"

Ryan extracted one of his own business cards, added his unlisted home number, then handed it over.

Nathan slid it into his jacket pocket and stood up. "Thank you again, Ryan. I'm much relieved to see that my daughter will be in such safe hands while I'm away."

Ryan tried not to wince at the compliment. Or look in any way guilty. The man *must* know what was already on the cards. He couldn't be *that* naïve.

Nathan watched Ryan drive off with a much lightened heart and less worried mind. It was gratifying to know that his judgement of character hadn't been off the mark after all. Not many men would have refused fifty thousand dollars. He must still feel quite a lot for Kirsty.

It was to be hoped, however, that Ryan was as skilled in bed as gossip implied. The last thing Nathan wanted to foist on his daughter was a man who didn't know how to make love to her with the finesse and expertise Kirsty deserved. Virgins needed a special touch. You had to be gentle with them, yet masterful at the same time.

Which reminded him.

Gemma would be coming home soon, without the boys.

Maybe he would be suitably rewarded if he told her his good news tonight.

No, far better to wait till they were alone on the high seas in their luxury suite aboard the *Southern Cross Princess*, the newest of the boutique liners to ply its trade out of Sydney harbour. She would be more in the mood for romance then. Tonight she'd be busy packing, and possibly pining for her beloved boys. The last thing she'd want was sex, *or* surprises.

Nathan sighed. Sometimes he wished Gemma wasn't so important to him. The things she'd made him do in the past. The things she was still making him do.

He loved his wife more than he'd ever thought himself capable of loving any woman. But he wanted her to love him back the way she once had. Passionately. Obsessively. Sexually.

Nothing else would satisfy him. And no one else would do.

Nathan wondered if that was what was wrong with Kirsty. No one else would do for her except Ryan.

"If so, then you're about to have your dearest wish granted, darling daughter," he muttered. "And you have your control freak of a father to thank for it."

CHAPTER FOUR

PRE-PERFORMANCE nerves had Kirsty racing to the loo for the second time in ten minutes.

I have to do better tonight than I did on opening night, she thought. *Have* to. If I don't, Josh is sure to replace me with Carla, and I'll be relegated to the role of understudy.

It was her father's fault, Kirsty decided mutinously. If only he hadn't come to the première. If only he hadn't sat there, right in the front row, with that supercilious look on his disgustingly handsome face, waiting for her to be talentless.

And she hadn't disappointed him. Her performance had been wooden. Flat. Josh had taken her aside at the post-première party and asked her what had gone wrong.

What could she say? No one in the theatre world knew that Kirsty O'Connell was really Kirsty Whitmore, Nathan Whitmore's daughter. And no one was going to!

So she'd blathered on about opening night nerves, and being overawed that the playwright of *Sisters in Love* was in the audience, and luckily Josh had accepted that. A lot of people became overawed when her father was around. But Josh had also given her a gentle warning that she had to do better next time.

Kirsty had watched Carla's performance in the matinee this afternoon and she'd been good. Not brilliant, but much better than *she'd* been last Saturday night.

She had to be brilliant tonight, or she was in big trouble.

Kirsty was hurrying back to the dressing rooms when she ran into the director himself. In his early thirties, Josh was tall and thin and ascetic-looking, with long wavy brown hair, sunless skin and intense, heavy-lidded eyes.

"Not too many nerves tonight, I hope," he said, peering down into her own pale face.

"A few," she admitted.

"Now, look here, sweetie, I don't really want to replace you with Carla, and I certainly don't want to add to your nerves, but one of the show's producers is here tonight. He's very astute *and* very tough. If he says you go, then you'll go, no matter what I think. Remember what I told you at rehearsal yesterday. You have to *become* the part, not just act it. Helen is madly in love for the first time in her life. She's sexually obsessed by her older sister's husband. It's a very emotion-charged and passionate part, as are *all* the parts in a Nathan Whitmore play. You can't afford to just go through the motions like you did on Saturday night."

"I know, Josh. I know. I'll do better tonight. I promise."

He curled a hand over her shoulder, giving it an encouraging squeeze. Kirsty knew the director liked her, but it wasn't a sexual thing. Josh Whitbread was as camp as a row of tents.

"I'm sure you will, sweetie. It's not as though

you're not a passionate girl yourself. Playing Helen should come naturally to you. Just tap into how you felt the last time *you* fell madly in love. Or perhaps the first time would be better. Young love can be so much more intense. Now, off you go, you gorgeous thing you, and break a leg. You can do it. I know you can.''

The *first* time she fell in love? Kirsty thought ruefully after Josh left her. The *only* time she'd fallen in love more like it. But, yes, Josh was so right. First love *was* very intense.

She'd fallen in love with Ryan Harris. Not at first sight, but at the first sound of his softly reassuring male voice, the first smell of his wonderfully clean skin; the first feel of his arms wrapping around her, so strong and secure and safe.

She hadn't recognised the emotion for what it was at the time. She had thought it was relief, coupled with gratitude.

It was only later, after she'd panicked at the idea of his leaving her, that she'd begun to suspect the nature of her feelings for him. He'd been supposedly watching over her that first night, but once he'd fallen asleep in the chair by her bed she'd been the one watching him, imprinting every one of his handsome features on her brain and wallowing in the warm waves of sweet pleasure which lapped through her heart every time she looked at him. By dawn she'd known she was deeply in love, and had begun plotting and planning ways to make Ryan fall in love with her too.

He already liked her, she had reasoned. No man would have been so nice if he didn't.

The next day, when she'd found out Ryan was married, she'd been devastated. Even so, she still hadn't been able to bear for him to leave her, not just yet, so she had taken advantage of his compassion to keep him coming back to visit her supposedly traumatised self as long as possible. She'd played the vulnerable victim to perfection, using all her natural acting talent to create a Kirsty who was soft and sweet and endearing. She'd even talked Gemma into giving Ryan a special thank-you dinner after the trial was over, so that he could see her all dressed up. She might have been only seventeen at the time, but her body had been fully developed and she'd known she was pretty.

She hadn't anticipated that his wife would come to the dinner with him—that black-eyed, black-haired witch of a woman who'd taken one look at Kirsty and seen the truth her husband hadn't seen.

That was the last time Kirsty saw Ryan.

People had thought it was the trauma of the kidnapping which had distressed and depressed her for so long afterwards. But it hadn't been that at all. She'd simply been broken-hearted.

When she'd confided her feelings for Ryan to her mother one day, Lenore had told her it wasn't real love she'd felt, just puppy love and hero-worship. And, whilst her mother understood it still hurt, she'd reassured Kirsty that she would eventually get over it.

And she had, she supposed. Though she still believed it was a true, grown-up love she'd felt. There'd been nothing puppyish about it. She'd wanted Ryan as a woman wanted a man. Just one look from him had turned her knees to water. She would have done anything he asked.

Only he hadn't asked anything of her. He'd walked away with the wicked witch on his arm and probably lived happily ever after.

Kirsty was standing there in the corridor, reliving her emotions at the time, when everyone starting pouring out of the dressing rooms.

It was showtime!

Her stomach still churned, but she walked back towards the wings of the stage with renewed determination. She could do this. All she had to do was focus on what she'd felt for Ryan. She'd pretend the character of Alastair *was* Ryan. Whenever she looked into Alastair's good-looking but weak face she'd think of Ryan's ruggedly handsome features. His stubborn chin and long strong nose. His carved cheekbones. And, yes, those sexy ice-blue eyes of his.

Block everything else out, she ordered herself. Don't look at the audience. Don't think about that producer sitting there watching. Concentrate on nothing else but Ryan. Ryan, your dream lover. Ryan, your hero.

I might just make it, Ryan thought as he sprinted from the car park, along the lower concourse and up the escalator two steps at a time. A hurried glance at his watch showed seven minutes to eight. The curtain went up at eight.

The damned traffic from Bondi back into the city had been heavier than usual, courtesy of an accident at an intersection. Under any other circumstances he wouldn't have had to drive back into town. He'd have stayed in the city and just walked the few blocks from his office down to the Opera House. But he couldn't very well front up to the theatre in clothes he'd worn all day, with his body unshowered for the last twelve hours.

Not quite the way to impress Kirsty. She had an aversion to unpleasant smells, he recalled. During their many chats after the kidnapping she'd confessed that one of the things which had bothered her most during her three-day captivity was the stink of the grimy bed they'd bound her to, and the rank body odour of her kidnappers.

As a young man Ryan hadn't been all that fastidious himself about personal hygiene. He'd hardly been set a good example by his parents. But he'd improved considerably on meeting Byron Whitmore, who always presented himself looking a million dollars. Clothes and cologne, Ryan had swiftly found, did make the man. He'd spent his first few paycheques from IAS on his wardrobe. And on a very expensive aftershave.

His ex-wife had been big on both looking and smelling good too, drumming into him that most women weren't at all turned on by grotty clothes and grimy bodies. Tina had insisted on his showering before coming to bed every night.

So of course he'd had to go home to shower and change before meeting Kirsty. He'd also bypassed his conservative business suits in favour of a casually styled single-breasted one-button black number, plus a no-collar black silk shirt. It was a look which suited him. The women seemed to like it, anyway, and that was the bottom line in this exercise, wasn't it? To make himself as physically attractive to Kirsty as possible.

Woman dated guys they fancied. Kirsty might accompany him somewhere for coffee through curiosity, but anything more would require some chemistry sparking between them.

Ryan leapt up the long rise of the Opera House steps, then raced around the right side of the building to where he hoped to find the drama theatre. He'd never been to a show at the Opera House before. Plays weren't his bag. Neither were opera or ballet, or whatever other artistic performances they put on in the various theatres and concert halls inside Sydney's most famous landmark.

Though he didn't like to admit it to anyone, Ryan had never actually been inside the Opera House at all. He'd looked up their website today, to check where to go, using the virtual tour to see exactly where the drama theatre was located. Just as well. The place was huge, with lots of levels.

Good thing he already had his ticket too, having sent the office gofer to purchase it for him earlier in the day.

The foyer was rapidly emptying by the time he pushed through the glass doors. Clearly *Sisters in Love* was close to starting.

The curtain was just rising by the time the usher showed him to his seat on the end of a row about halfway down. Not the best of seats, he supposed, but a man of his height could always see over heads. And there were plenty of heads between him and the stage. The place was packed!

Ryan sank into the seat, his heart racing. Mostly

from rushing—and catapulting himself up all those interminable bloody steps—but partly from the thought of what might happen later tonight. It wasn't every day that you were hired by a father to protect his daughter *and* seduce her.

Or was he wrong about that?

Maybe Kirsty's father thought he was just going to take Kirsty to dinner or the movies every night—that they'd merely hold hands and chat about old times and exchange a chaste peck at the door. Or maybe he pictured them having video and pizza nights together at Belleview, where, after a bit of snogging on the sofa, he'd get up and nobly go home.

If Nathan imagined that, then he was living in the Dark Ages. Life wasn't like that these days. If he thought the movie world was a jungle than he should try the dating scene of today. It was full of predators, both male *and* female, with sex their weapon of choice and satisfaction the prize.

Kirsty had been living away from home and surviving on that singles scene for quite a few years. She was a woman of the new millennium. A career woman. An actress, no less. Whoops, no, *actor*. Whichever, it meant she would be confident, assertive and sexually active. If she decided she still fancied him, then *he* was the one likely to be seduced, not the other way around.

Yet the Kirsty Ryan remembered hadn't had a clue about seducing a man. She'd been nothing like his ex-wife had thought she was. She'd been a naïve innocent, inexperienced in the sort of feminine wiles which Ryan might have found difficult to resist.

Despite knowing about the life Kirsty had been living since then, Ryan found it difficult to believe that she'd turned into a predator. So perhaps he *could* date her for a week without sex being inevitable. All he had to do was keep his mind on the job and above his waist.

A blonde walked out onto the stage and Ryan stared hard. No, he decided, that wasn't Kirsty. Too tall, for starters. Attractive, though. Mid to late twenties, was his guess, with long honey-blonde hair and an arresting stage presence.

She moved about the living-room set, pouring snacks into dishes, then fiddling with the flower arrangement on the coffee-table. She was joined by a man carrying a couple of bottles of wine over to a corner bar. Dark-haired. Slender. Mid-thirties. A real pretty boy.

He turned out to be the blonde's husband. Going by the name of Alastair. She was called Janette. The party was for her twenty-fifth birthday. It was obvious within five minutes that Janette was crazy about her husband, and, whilst he made all the right noises, you were left with the impression that his passion for her didn't quite match hers for him.

"I'd better go up and get dressed," Janette said, pulling reluctantly out of her husband's arms.

"Yes, you'd better. You've only got an hour."

Janette was laughing and skipping up the staircase at the back of the set when the front doorbell rang. She stopped, and threw Alastair a panicky look.

"Don't worry. That'll only be Helen," he told her. "She rang while you were out shopping this morning and offered to come a bit early and help me with the drinks. By the way, she asked if she could stay the night.''

Janette pulled a face. ''You didn't say she could, did you?''

He shrugged. ''I could hardly refuse. She is your sister, after all.''

''I wish you hadn't. I think she has a crush on you, Alastair. It's becoming embarrassing, the way she finds any excuse to come over and spend time with you.''

''Don't be ridiculous. She thinks of me as the big brother she never had. She likes asking my advice.''

''I hope that's all it is.''

''Darling, she's just a kid. Off you go, now.''

Then Janette disappeared and Alastair hurried to answer the door.

Ryan leant forward in his seat, watching the action on stage with even more attention.

The character called Helen entered.

Ryan leant further forward. Right height. Right nose. Right shaped face.

So *this* was what Kirsty looked like as a blonde.

Ryan sank back into his seat, his lips pursing into a silent whistle. Nathan certainly hadn't exaggerated.

There again, just about everything she owned was being shown off in the party clothes she was almost wearing! Her swishy black skirt ended at her upper mid-thigh. Her shimmering purple halter-necked top clearly showed she wore no bra underneath. And her high-heeled strappy shoes wouldn't have looked astray on a street-walker.

Talk about provocative!

Pretty-boy Alastair couldn't take his eyes off her,

and soon his hands. It was obvious to the audience that they had been having an affair.

"Oh, Alastair, Alastair…" Helen pressed closer to him, if that was possible. "I love you so much. Tell me you love me too. Say it like you do when you're doing it to me."

Alastair groaned, and so almost did Ryan. If this was acting, then she was brilliant. If it wasn't—if she was just being herself—she'd eat him alive!

Ryan's earlier speculation that he could handle a week of innocent dating with Kirsty was in danger of total disintegration. His mind was already firmly below his waist. And how!

"Stop it," the pretty boy pleaded onstage, when she rubbed her hips against his pelvis.

"No," insisted his blonde tormentor. "I want to make you hard. I want you to do it to me now. I can't wait till later tonight, Alastair. Janette's busy doing her hair. I can hear the dryer. She'll be ages. I don't have any panties on, you know," she whispered seductively. "You can do it like you did when we washed up together that day. Remember? When Janette had a migraine and I came over to help?"

Alastair groaned again, but let himself be pulled round behind the bar.

By now Ryan's mouth had gone quite dry and the audience was very quiet. Dear God—and this scenario came from the mind of Nathan Whitmore? Any silly idea that Kirsty's father might not be expecting his daughter and Ryan to end up in bed together also hit home deep. The creator of this play and these characters was not harbouring any old-fashioned standards when it came to sexual matters.

"You're crazy!" Alastair was saying on stage, but he still pushed Helen up against the bar and moved around behind her. The audience couldn't see what was going on below chest level, but they could hear the sound of a zipper being undone.

The ringing of Ryan's mobile phone at that precise moment brought some serious glares and mutterings from the people seated around him.

"Sorry," he apologised, and reluctantly crept back out into the foyer.

"Harris, here," he said brusquely, preferring to be back in that theatre, watching that amazing scene. No wonder Nathan Whitmore was as rich as he was and Hollywood had beat a path to his door. Sex always sold—and that was exactly what he was selling up on that stage. Sex!

"Nathan, here, Ryan. Can you hear me? You're a bit fuzzy and crackly."

"Wait, I'll move outside." He pushed through the doors and stood out under the stars. "How's that?"

"Much better. So what happened with Gregory today?"

Ryan got straight down to business. That was what Nathan was paying him for, after all.

"A car picked him up outside the jail right on nine this morning and took him to a house down at Campbelltown. We made enquiries and found out the house belongs to his uncle, John Gregory. He's fifty, married with three kids of his own, and owns a local garage. His reputation and standing in the community are excellent. I imagine he's the one most responsible for getting his nephew out of the clink. If you remember, Gregory was described as a mechanic during his trial. My guess is he's going to be working for and living with this uncle. You never get parole unless you've got a place and a job to go to. We'll know more in a day or so."

"I see. Well, that's good news. I mean, Campbelltown's quite a long way from the city and St Ives."

"That's what I thought too."

"Of course that doesn't mean he might not have unsavoury friends who live closer. I still want him watched. And I still want you on the job with Kirsty."

"I'm at the theatre now. In fact, the play's already started. I had to leave when you rang."

"Sorry. Thought I'd just caught you before the curtain went up. You lose track of time out here on the high seas. So, how much of the play have you seen so far?"

"Just the first few minutes. But I already needed a breather."

Nathan laughed. "That's some opening scene, isn't it? Grabs the audience's attention straight away."

"You might say that."

"What did you think of Kirsty?"

"Her looks, or her acting ability?"

"Both."

"Well, you were right. Being a blonde suits her. As far as her acting is concerned, I'm hardly qualified to judge. I've never been to a play before. But, since you ask my opinion, I find her pretty convincing in the part."

"Really? You're sure you don't just find her pretty? Her performance at the première was barely adequate."

"Maybe that was just first-night nerves."

"Maybe. Look, I can't stay talking too long. I ducked out of the cabin to make this call while Gemma's dressing. She thinks I've having a pre-dinner constitutional walk around the deck. I don't like keeping this matter a secret from her, but I'm sure you understand it's for the best. She'd only worry and want to go back home."

Which was not what Nathan wanted, Ryan guessed.

"I'll call you tomorrow evening," Nathan added. "A little earlier this time. Hopefully you'll have more good news for me. About Gregory. And about you and Kirsty."

"Nathan," Ryan said with sharp warning in his tone.

"Yes?"

"I think you should know upfront that I'm not a kiss-and-tell type of guy. I'll do my job, and keep Kirsty safe, but whatever happens between us on a personal level is our business and our business alone."

"Fair enough. Must go. Speak to you tomorrow." And he disconnected.

CHAPTER FIVE

GEMMA was dressed and ready for dinner but Nathan hadn't returned yet from his walk around the decks. Odd thing for him to do, she thought. Nathan was not given to walking, especially on his own.

Her husband had something on his mind. That was what was up. A couple of times since they'd sailed he'd seemed about to say something, then stopped.

His hesitation to confide in her did not surprise Gemma. She was used to Nathan keeping his own counsel. And it irritated the death out of her.

She reached for her bottle of perfume, then put it down again. No perfume, she decided. No earrings either. And she pulled the diamond drops from her lobes, slipping them back into the top drawer of the dressing table.

Nathan was partial to both perfume and jewellery. In the early days of their marriage he'd lavished her with both. There'd been this one necklace he'd especially liked: a pearl and diamond choker. He'd thought it looked virginal on her when she was clothed, and downright decadent when she wasn't. Back then, she'd liked wearing it for him when she was naked.

Back then, she'd liked a lot of things.

A shiver ran down Gemma's spine and she wished

once again that she hadn't agreed to this cruise. She didn't want to be alone with Nathan for a day, let alone over a week. She didn't want to rediscover the desire for him which had once possessed her. She didn't want him to get what he wanted.

And she knew exactly what he wanted.

Her, loving him again. With wild passion and without reservation. Like the naïve young thing he'd first met. The impressed and innocent young virgin, so eager for his expert lovemaking, so easily persuaded and programmed to satisfy his every sexual whim.

The thought that she might surrender to those old feelings in this romantic environment was a real worry.

Nathan would undoubtedly interpret any such behaviour as a reconciliation on her part. And she was not ready to forgive him. Not yet. Maybe not ever.

It never ceased to amaze Gemma that Nathan imagined she would get over what he'd done. Fancy having a vasectomy without even consulting her, and then calling her foolish for minding. He knew her greatest wish in life had been for a large family, and he'd snatched that wish away from her, all for his own selfish reasons. He'd claimed he'd done it for her, but she knew differently.

He'd done it for himself.

A frost had descended over her love for him that day, a frost which rarely melted. Only occasionally, in bed, when he caught her at her loneliest, did he succeed in temporarily heating up her ice-encased feelings. But even then her responses were nothing like he'd once evoked. Where once she had fizzed like champagne under his hands she was now like flat lemonade, with only the odd bubble left.

But she was only human, and it worried her that here, in this luxurious setting, with some real champagne fizzing through her blood every night at dinner, she might fall victim to Nathan's practised charms once more. He was so good at sex. So wickedly, wickedly good.

She shuddered, then stared at herself in the mirror once more. Maybe she shouldn't have put her hair up. Nathan liked it that way. There again, he liked it down too. She couldn't win, really. The truth was her husband liked everything about her looks. She was his type, obviously. A feminine woman, with big brown eyes, long lustrous brown hair and an hour-glass figure which having children seemed to have enhanced rather than destroyed.

She supposed she should be grateful that her full breasts hadn't sagged, that she still had a waist and that her stomach wasn't covered in stretch marks. It was silly of her to resent Nathan's compliments about her so-called beauty.

But she did resent them. Fiercely. They always evoked old doubts in her mind, of a time when she'd been sure he hadn't been in love with her at all, that his feelings for her began and ended with the physical.

If she was brutally honest, down deep, she still harboured those doubts. After all, what had Nathan ever really needed her for, except sex? Certainly not intellectual stimulation and companionship. He got that from his cronies in the theatre world. Gemma hated being anywhere near that arty lot, and surreptitiously avoided any invitation which forced her into tolerating their often condescending company.

Nathan didn't even really need her as a housewife. Sure, she ran Belleview very efficiently, but he could just as easily hire a housekeeper and cook. He was rich enough.

As for having his children…

Gemma knew Nathan loved Alexander and Richard now they'd arrived, but becoming a father had hardly been a unique experience for him. When they'd met he'd already had a child by Lenore. A much loved daughter. Kirsty.

Gemma would have dearly loved a daughter of her own.

Tears pricked her eyes as she thought how devastated she'd been when Nathan had told her there would be no more children at all, let alone a daughter.

She could still see the amazement on his face when she'd burst into tears. He'd actually thought she'd be relieved by his news. And grateful. The man had no idea!

Gemma reached for a tissue and was dabbing at her eyes when she heard the doorknob turning. Quickly, she disposed of the tissue and picked up her comb. She didn't turn round from the dressing table when Nathan walked in. She pretended to be finishing her hair, though she did give him a surreptitious glance in the mirror.

It appalled her that her heart actually gave a little jump at the sight of him.

Not that she could blame herself. He really was an incredibly handsome man, with a magnetism and charisma usually reserved for movie stars. He only had to walk into a room and all eyes were drawn to him, both male and female. The female ones lingered, however, and longed, and lusted. It was testament to the power of Nathan's feelings for her—whatever they were—that Gemma was confident her husband had always been faithful to his marriage vows.

''It's cool outside on deck,'' he said as he finger-combed his golden waves back into place. ''You'll need that wrap.''

He nodded towards the armchair, where she'd earlier draped her lavender satin wrap. It matched her strapless evening gown—both chosen by Nathan, of course.

That was one thing they still did do together occasionally. Clothes-shopping. Possibly because Nathan was afraid if he didn't go along with her she'd pop out her old sewing machine and make her wardrobe instead of decking herself out in the designer dresses his wealth and status demanded she wear.

''Though it would be a shame to cover up these lovely shoulders of yours,'' he added as he came up behind her and bent to kiss her neck.

Gemma stiffened under the touch of his lips.

Nathan's head lifted and their eyes met in the mirror. It was a struggle to keep hers cool. But she managed.

His narrowed. ''How long are you going to punish me, Gemma?''

She winced at his tone, and at the truth behind his accusation. Because that was exactly what she'd been doing, wasn't it? Punishing him.

He straightened and glared at her in the mirror. ''I'd rather you divorce me than keep acting like this,'' he went on curtly. ''Ours isn't a marriage any more. It's a war. A cold war. I've put up with five long years of your freezing me out and my patience is wearing very thin. I thought your agreeing to this cruise meant you were prepared to finally forgive me. But I see I was deluding myself.''

''Yes, Nathan,'' she agreed with a brave uptilt of her chin. ''You were.''

He blinked at her with disbelieving eyes. ''Do you really mean that? Are you saying you're never going to forgive me?''

She stood up and turned to face him, her stomach tightening as she gathered herself to say what had to be said. ''I'd like to, Nathan. I really would. But I don't seem to be able to. It festers inside of me, what you did. Going ahead with an operation to make yourself sterile without even discussing it with me was unforgivable.''

''But, Gemma, darling, I told you—I only did it because I love you so much and I was afraid I'd lose you. It didn't occur to me that you could bypass any danger by having a Caesarean. When that stupid doctor told me you almost died giving birth to Richard, I just presumed that having any more children was too great a risk.''

''I would have dearly liked to try for a daughter,'' she choked out.

''Yes, yes, I know that—*now*. Look, I did what I did back then because I honestly thought it was for the best. You've made it perfectly clear to me how you feel about that decision. That's why I—''

''Please don't try to justify yourself *again*, Nathan,'' she cut him off angrily. ''That's what you always say. That you do things for the best. That's the reason you give every time you make a decision without consulting me. But it's not a good enough reason, Nathan. It's just an excuse. An excuse to control everyone and everything around you, but especially the people you supposedly love. Kirsty was right when she called you a control freak, because that's exactly what you are. The truth is you think you know better than everyone else. You think you're wiser and cleverer, but you're not—not in your dealings with me or your family. You can't ride roughshod over all of us for ever without our eventually bucking you off and out of our lives. So, yes, Nathan, maybe we *should* think about a divorce."

"Just like that?" he bit out, his handsome face tight with fury.

"*You* suggested it."

He groaned. "I didn't mean it. Dear God, Gemma, you know I didn't mean it. I wouldn't want to live without you as my wife."

Gemma stared at him, and knew he was speaking the truth. Whatever his feelings for her, they were very intense. All Nathan's emotions were always very intense. It was what made him such a great writer. There were never any half-measures with Nathan.

She sighed. "I guess I didn't mean it either. You know I don't believe in divorce, except in cases of abuse."

Saying as much made her realise she could not go on the way she had been. Even if she couldn't forgive Nathan totally for that vasectomy, she had to try to forget it and move on. For her own sake and the boys' sake. They loved their dad. Whether she still loved

Nathan and whether he'd ever really loved her were not the issues here. He was her husband, till death did them part.

"You're right," she went on wearily. "I have been punishing you. And I'm sorry. But you have to appreciate how much that decision of yours affected me, Nathan. And how much it hurt me."

He reached out and caressed her shoulders with his hands. "I did realise that, Gemma," he said softly. "*Afterwards*. But at the time I kept thinking of how close you came to dying. Like I just said—if I ever lost you…"

"If you seriously don't want to lose me, Nathan, then don't ever—and I mean *ever*—do anything like that again."

"Well, I can hardly do anything like that *again*," he pointed out, though he looked taken aback by her tough stand. And perhaps a little surprised.

For her part, Gemma felt almost exhilarated at having the courage to speak up. This was what she should have done years ago, instead of just sulking, playing the poor, put-upon wife.

Way back before Alexander was born she'd had occasion to stand up to Nathan quite strongly. And he'd respected her for it. Her self-esteem had blossomed. In the years between Alexander and Richard she and Nathan had been very close, and their relationship very passionate.

But his doing what he'd done after Richard's birth had changed everything. She'd become very depressed, her self-confidence had faded, and she'd fallen into the habit of being a yes-wife. Staying at home most of the time hadn't helped, and her ability to really stand up to Nathan had gradually sunk to zero. She hadn't even had the nerve to say no to him in bed. She might not have responded too often, but she'd still let him do it to her without a word of protest.

But no more!

"When *anything* comes up that affects us, our marriage or our children," she swept on boldly with new resolve, "it is be discussed *between* us. You're not to just make decisions all by yourself, without consulting me. I want our marriage to be a partnership, Nathan. A true partnership. I'm twenty-eight years old. I'm a grown-up woman, a wife and a mother with a lot of common sense and experience. I'm not the twenty-year-old ninny from the back of Burke that you married."

"You were never a ninny, my darling," he said with softening eyes. "Even back then."

"I was where you were concerned. I let you get away with blue murder, Nathan. All because I was blindly in love with you. And because you were so darned good in bed."

"I'm still pretty good in bed," he purred, drawing her against him, "If only you'll let me show you."

"I'm sorry," she said stiffly, pulling out of his arms and coming to another decision. "But you won't be showing me any such thing. Not for the next few days anyway. I have my period."

"Mmm. That was a bit of bad planning, wasn't it?" he said irritably.

"I didn't *plan* this cruise, Nathan. *You* did. If you recall, it was all booked and paid for before you even told me about it."

"True," he said, a bit sheepishly. "But you're not sorry you came now, are you?"

"No. It's given us the opportunity to straighten things out. And to talk."

"Talk! I was hoping to do a lot more than talk. Look, your period's no real problem, is it? There was a time when we got around that easily enough."

"*We*, Nathan?" she threw up at him, even more determined now to stand her ground. "Don't you mean *me*?"

"Actually, no," he said with a wickedly sexy glint in his eye. "I wasn't just referring to that. There are many alternative ways of making love, Gemma. You ought to know. I showed you every one of them. And you *enjoyed* every one of them."

Her blush was fierce. "That...that was some time ago."

"You mean when you were still madly in love with me?" he said ruefully.

She turned her face away from him, her heart pounding, her memory flooding her with images— wild, erotic images of lovemaking which had known no bounds.

"You can't have forgotten what it was like," he insisted, taking hold of her shoulders from behind and drawing her back against him.

She hadn't. Of course she hadn't. It had been incredible.

"It could be like that again," he promised, his breath hot against her ear, "if only you'll let it."

Oh, God. Did he have to tempt her like this?

He cupped her chin and turned her face to meet his descending mouth.

Gemma gasped, then groaned. Because Nathan
didn't just kiss. He possessed. Seduced. Corrupted.
His other hand found one of her satin-encased breasts
and it immediately swelled to the heat of his palm,
the nipple hardening and distending. She moaned a
moan of dismay, and desire, then wrenched herself
away.

"No, Nathan," she blurted as she spun out of his
arms and staggered away from him, her heartbeat still
thundering like an express train. "I need you to love
me in more ways than sexually," she pleaded, putting
what she hoped was a safe distance between them. "I
need you to respect and understand me. *Me*—Gemma
the person. Not Gemma your own personal sex
slave."

His eyes narrowed and she wished she knew what
he was thinking. But that was one skill she'd never
learnt, reading Nathan's complex mind.

"I have always loved and respected you," he said,
"even if you don't seem to believe that. But I'm not
sure some men and women will ever understand each
other. Maybe the only way they *can* communicate
sometimes," he added ruefully, "is in bed."

"I don't believe that. And if you do then perhaps
we *should* get a divorce." It was a bluff, but then…he
didn't know that.

"There will be no divorce," he said coldly.

"In that case there will be no sex till my period
has finished," she said firmly, hoping he didn't realise
that was a bluff too. "Even then it will be nice sex.
Loving sex."

His eyebrows arched. "And how do you define
loving sex? The missionary position? With candles

around the bed and love songs playing in the background?''

"Don't mock me, Nathan."

"Then don't be such a little hypocrite. The missionary position was never your position of choice. You find it difficult to come that way."

She could feel herself blushing again. "Loving someone is not all about orgasms!"

He laughed. "Come now, Gemma, that *is* being naïve. If more wives had more orgasms, there'd be far less divorces."

"Really? Then why did Lenore divorce *you*? I'm sure she had squillions of orgasms with you in her bed."

He smiled. "You're still jealous of Lenore. That's a good sign. You must still love me."

Gemma rolled her eyes. The ego of the man! She snatched up her wrap and flicked it around her shoulders with a flourish. "If we don't go, we'll be late for dinner. If you recall, we were invited to the Captain's table tonight."

"Oh, well, far be it from me to deprive the good Captain of your very beautiful presence." He took her elbow as she tried to brush past him and steered her with his usual forcefulness towards the door. "Just don't flirt with him too much, darling wife. I saw the way he looked at you when we were introduced this afternoon and I know exactly what was going through his mind."

Gemma pulled her arm away and glared up at him. "And that's another thing I can't stand. Your being jealous and possessive of me. I hate that almost as much as your not discussing things with me. Which reminds me. What is it that you were going to tell me earlier today but changed your mind over?''

His face went totally blank, his eyes puzzled. "I've got no idea what you're talking about," he said with seeming sincerity.

She still eyed him suspiciously. "Are you sure, Nathan? You're not keeping things from me again, are you?''

"What a suspicious little mind you've got. I suppose I was a bit worried over how I was going to put you in the right mood for romance. But that's not a crime, is it? This is supposed to be a second honeymoon."

Gemma sighed. She should have guessed. He'd been thinking about sex. What else?

"You have a one-track mind, Nathan Whitmore."

"A hazard when I'm not writing. You know that." His eyes dropped to her mouth, which still felt puffy and tingling from his kiss. "How many days did you say it would be before I could claim my conjugal rights?''

"Four."

"Four!''

"Well, maybe only three."

"I think I might have to go in search of a laptop," he muttered. "Then find a quiet cupboard somewhere and hole up writing till then.''

"Over my dead body!''

"I'd prefer your live body.''

"Oh, do shut up.''

Nathan shut up, his thoughts revolving as he escorted Gemma to dinner. No way could he tell her now that he'd had his vasectomy reversed while he was in New York recently. She'd be livid.

When and if she finally fell pregnant, he'd just have to act all shocked—but pleased—about the news. He'd let her think that the first surgeon had done an inadequate job. Such things had happened before.

A miracle! he'd exclaim happily.

Not that she'd be getting pregnant on this cruise, he realised. Which had been his original intention, damn it. He hadn't even thought about her period, which was remarkably stupid of him. Still, he'd hardly been having sex with her a lot lately. None at all since his return from New York. He was no longer familiar with her cycle.

But that was all going to change, come the end of this week. As soon as the coast was clear, she was going to be giving him all the sex he wanted.

No matter what she said, her body didn't lie. It had wanted him just now and it would want him again. It was just a matter of being patient. And pretending to give her what *she* wanted.

Talk, he thought wryly.

Women *did* like to talk. Men preferred to act.

God, if he hadn't been prepared to act instead of just talk, Kirsty's kidnapping might have ended very differently indeed.

Nathan suppressed a groan. That was another thing he didn't dare tell Gemma. What actions he'd taken to protect his daughter.

She'd hit the roof if she ever found out. And so would Kirsty. Thank heavens Ryan was the sort of man to keep his mouth shut. Otherwise there would be hell to pay all round.

CHAPTER SIX

THE curtain came down to dead silence, eventually followed by a burst of rapturous applause. This was not uncommon at the end of a Nathan Whitmore play. It often took the audience a few seconds to snap out of the other world they'd been transported to.

When each member of the cast was presented to the audience individually, Kirsty's applause seemed to be longer and louder than everyone else's. She beamed her happiness, not caring when Carla gave her a sour glare. At least Mimi, who played her older sister Janette, was nice about her improved performance. And so was Peter.

"Wow, honey," he said, sidling up to her when the audience finally let them go. "I didn't know you had it in you. Care to come back to my place for a drink to celebrate?"

Kirsty glanced up into his pretty-boy face and thought it was no wonder Josh had picked him to play the part of Alastair. He was only playing himself, the womanising sleazebag. He'd taken Carla back to his place for drinks last week. And the week before that it had been Mimi.

"Sorry, Pete. I already have a date." With a certain dog named Jaws.

"Lucky fellow."

"Probably some sugar-daddy," Carla said nastily. "The one who buys her all the fancy clothes. She certainly couldn't afford her wardrobe—*or* her jewellery—on her acting career so far." And she sashayed off, leaving both Mimi and Peter giving Kirsty eyebrow-raised looks.

Kirsty decided it was pointless to defend herself, and was grateful when Josh came over.

"That was fantastic, everyone. And especially you, sweetie," he directed at Kirsty after the others started to move off. "I knew you could do it. You don't have to worry about being replaced now."

"Thank heavens."

"By the way, this came for you during the last act," he said, and pressed a white business card into her hand. "I promised to give it to you personally straight after the show."

Kirsty stared down at the business card, then sucked in sharply at the message written on the back.

Wow! What a performance. I'll wait for you on the main steps outside. We'll go for coffee somewhere and catch up on old times. Ryan.

Ryan! This was incredible! All the time she'd been fantasising on that stage about Ryan tonight he'd actually been there in the audience, watching. It sent shivers up and down her spine just thinking about it.

"I take it you're already acquainted with this fellow from IAS?" Josh asked, curiosity and speculation on his face.

"What? Oh, yes. He's an old friend."

"Mmm. I've heard about that company. They're

not just private investigators. They also do security work for the rich and famous. They provide bodyguards for presidents and pop stars. That kind of thing.''

"So?"

"I was wondering how your paths crossed. I heard what Carla said a minute ago about your clothes, and she's dead right. I know clothes, sweetie, and I recognise designer wear when I see it. Are you sure you aren't the secret mistress of some billionaire business man, and this guy is your personal bodyguard?''

"Truly, Josh, what a warped and twisted mind you have. Even bodyguards to the rich and famous have normal families and friends. As far as my clothes are concerned, haven't you ever heard of second-hand designer wear? Sydney's full of shops selling last season's discards of society's darlings for a fraction of what they're worth. Mistress of a billionaire, indeed! I wish.''

"Well, you could snare yourself a seriously rich guy if you wanted to. You've got the right looks. And all the right moves. You even had *me* getting hot under the collar tonight.''

She laughed. If only he knew! She hadn't been to bed with anyone, let alone some billionaire businessman. "I'll take that as a compliment, Josh. Now, I must fly.''

She dashed off to change, her mind racing almost as much as her heart. Fancy Ryan, of all people, being here at the play tonight. Or being at a play at all! He was hardly the theatre-going type. Or he hadn't been five years ago. But she supposed he might have changed in that time.

Maybe—and her stomach flipped over at this thought—maybe he'd also left that awful wife of his.

It was a possibility, because no way would Ryan have sent her that note if he'd been here with that jealous cow. What was her name? Tina. Horrid woman. Sexy-looking, though. Even she had to concede that. But way too old for Ryan. At least thirty, when he'd been no more than in his early twenties.

As Kirsty hurried along the corridor she realised that Ryan's being in the audience was not the only remarkable aspect to this. She was amazed that he'd even *recognised* her. From a distance, too, with stage make-up and short blonde hair. People from her past rarely recognised her these days. She'd sat opposite an old school chum last week in a café for two hours whilst she'd lunched with Gemma and the girl had had no idea who she was. Yet she'd looked her over, as girls looked over their female peers. Kirsty hadn't enlightened her, because she wanted to keep her true identity a secret.

She couldn't help feeling flattered that Ryan *had* recognised her. She was smiling as she burst back into the dressing room she shared with Mimi and Carla.

"My, aren't you looking pleased with yourself?" Carla sneered straight away.

"Oh, do give it a rest, Carla," Mimi snapped. "You're just jealous. Kirsty was fantastic tonight and you know it."

"No, I don't. Tonight was just a fluke. Come tomorrow night she'll be right back to being as pathetic as she was at the première. She probably took something before she went out on stage tonight, by the way she was carrying on."

Kirsty had had just about enough of Carla. She'd been putting up with her snide remarks for ages and had tried turning the other cheek. But that was never the right tactic with bullies. You had to give as good as you got.

"Is that what *you* do, sweetheart? Take something so that you can screw every man you think might help you with your wonderfully successful career? I mean, is there a single male member of this cast and crew who hasn't had you one way or another? Other than Josh, of course. Pity he's gay, isn't it? I hear you have washerwoman's knees as it is. The floors are a bit hard around here, aren't they?"

"You bitch," Carla bit out, her cheeks flushing bright red.

"Takes one to know one." Kirsty whirled away to whisk a few tissues off the dressing-table and start removing her stage make-up. But she could see Carla glowering at her in the mirror.

"I'll fix you, if it's the last thing I do. I should have had that part. You only got it because of your looks."

"Oh, come on, Carla," Mimi intervened on her way towards the door. "That's not true."

"It is. I know it is. I heard Josh say so himself. He said he wanted a blonde who looked sexy, yet innocent at the same time. Like a young Marilyn Monroe."

Marilyn Monroe! Kirsty blinked at herself in the mirror, not seeing more than a superficial resemblance to the famous blonde bombshell.

"Well, so what?" Mimi replied. "Marilyn Monroe could also act, remember? And so can Kirsty. People in glass houses shouldn't throw stones, sweetheart,'' Mimi directed at Carla as she opened the door. ''Do you think you'd have even got the part of understudy if you hadn't been a blonde with big boobs?''

It was a great parting shot, Kirsty thought. Worthy of a Nathan Whitmore play.

She hadn't been great friends with Mimi up till now. Mimi was inclined to keep to herself. But Kirsty liked people who could be fair, and didn't let jealousy or personal rivalry colour everything they said or did.

''At least my blonde hair is real,'' Carla spat at Kirsty once Mimi had shut the door behind her.

''If it is, then it's the only real thing about you,'' Kirsty countered as she continued to clean her face. ''I recognise fake boobs when I see them. Pity you didn't use a decent plastic surgeon. What happened? Couldn't you get one to sleep with you so that you could get them for free?''

Carla's blue eyes narrowed frostily. ''You don't know who you're dealing with. I'm going to destroy you. Piece by pretty piece.''

''I wouldn't bet on that. I'm tougher than I look. But thanks for the compliment. Unfortunately, I don't have time for any more sisterly chit-chat. I have a date.'' And she threw the used tissues in the bin under the table.

''I don't doubt it,'' Carla scoffed. ''Something certainly revved up your hormones. It'll be interesting to see how you go tomorrow night after he's banged your brains out.'' She stormed out, slamming the door so hard after her that the walls rattled.

Kirsty winced, then groaned. Carla was a nasty piece of work, and she really shouldn't take too much

notice of what she said. But it did upset her that Josh
might have only cast her as Helen because she had a
certain look. It would explain why he was so anxious
for her to do well—because he didn't want to appear
a fool. She also worried that her scintillating performance tonight *might* have had more to do with her
pretending Alastair was Ryan rather than any real acting ability of her part.

"Ryan!" she remembered with a gasp. He was
waiting for her on the steps outside. She had to hurry
or he might think she wasn't coming and leave.

All other considerations were pushed aside, because nothing was more important to Kirsty than seeing Ryan again and finding out where life had taken
him during these past five years. She was not under
any romantic illusions that he'd pined for her in any
way since their last meeting, but she was curious
about why he wanted to see her again at all—and,
yes, she was excited by just the thought of seeing his
handsome face again. *Too* excited, perhaps.

Could she possibly *still* be in love with him? Or
were her feelings being exaggerated by what she'd
done tonight, reliving what she'd once felt in order to
give a good performance as the besotted Helen?

Maybe she'd be able to tell where the truth lay
when she saw him again, in the flesh.

Kirsty was used to quick costume changes, but she
must have broken the record for stripping and dressing, because less than a minute later she was hurrying
along the main corridor towards the nearest exit,
wearing dark blue jeans, a scarlet mohair jumper and
black ankle boots. She hitched her black leather bag

up over her shoulder and clutched it to her side as she increased her pace to a run.

Fleetingly, it crossed her mind that her jeans, jumper, boots *and* bag had all been bought in expensive boutiques, not recycled clothing stores. The gold chain she wore around her throat was *real* gold, not gold-plated. The gold studs she wore in her ears likewise. And the opal dress ring decorating her right hand was a solid opal, not a cheap doublet or triplet.

It had been a birthday present from her father, as were the diamond pendant and earrings she'd stupidly worn to the post-première party the other night. She hadn't stopped to think that diamonds like that would naturally cause speculation when worn by a supposedly struggling actor.

The thought that people might find out one day that she was Nathan Whitmore's daughter worried Kirsty. She wanted to succeed on the stage in her own right, and was proud that she hadn't taken a cent from her dad since she'd told him where to stick his money that awful day.

True, she did accept some help from her mother and Gemma and Aunt Jade. They all occasionally took her clothes shopping and bought her the odd lunch or two. But that was not the same as living off her father. Or using his influence in the theatre world to get parts.

Josh's speculation that she might be some billionaire's mistress was way off the mark, given she was still a virgin. But she *was* a billionaire's daughter. Or almost. Kirsty wasn't sure of her father's total wealth, but she knew he'd inherited a fortune from his biological grandparents, and Hollywood had paid him

buckets of money for the film rights to his plays. One
in particular, *The Woman in Black*. The family had
always believed the publicity he'd received from that
deal had led to her being kidnapped.

Thinking of the kidnapping swung Kirsty's mind
straight back to Ryan.

She burst through the exit out into the cool night
air, and was hurrying towards the main steps with her
heart in her mouth when suddenly she saw him, standing down at the quay end of the top step, his hands
slid deep into his trouser pockets, his gaze directed
towards the lights of the city and the bridge.

Kirsty skittered to a halt and just stared at him. And
stared. And stared.

He'd changed as well, she conceded.

His hair was short, for starters. Very short. But still
coal-black. As were his city-smart and very trendy
clothes. The Ryan she'd used to know had never worn
a suit. He'd been a jeans and leather jacket kind of
guy.

Perversely, and in spite of his new sophistication,
he looked tougher. Tougher, but even sexier, if that
were possible.

''Ryan,'' she called out, her voice not quite steady.

He turned, slowly, and their eyes met.

Kirsty's knees went to water, as they had five years
ago, and she knew the truth.

She did still love him.

Just as much as ever.

He didn't move, or say a single word. He just
looked at her. In the end she began walking towards
him, all the while fiercely aware of those sexy blue
eyes of his, watching her. He eased his hands out of

his pockets as she approached, his gaze finally dropping away from her face to run down her body, then travel slowly back up again, taking in everything about her.

Her new slenderness. Definitely her bralessness.

Kirsty swallowed. At that moment, with Ryan's eyes on them, her breasts felt not just braless but exquisitely naked, the nipples peaking hard into the softness of her jumper. A wave of heat flooded her body, flushing the surface of her skin and drying her mouth.

Kirsty could not recall having *this* kind of physical response five years ago. Oh, yes, she'd wanted Ryan to make love to her, even at seventeen. She'd thought about it endlessly. Dreamt about it every night. But those dreams and desires had been of the sweetly romantic variety.

Her desires were different now, it seemed. Very different. There was nothing sweet about what she was feeling at that moment. She was all fire, and heat, and need.

Kirsty realised she wasn't just still in love with this man. She was now in serious lust as well.

Oh, God, she thought. Let him be divorced, please. Let him not just want to have coffee and a chat. Let him want me as I want him.

Kirsty plastered a bubbly smile on her no doubt very flushed face, walked up to him and gave him a hug. Not so much because she was desperate to touch him—though she was—but to hide herself against him for a few more moments.

He seemed startled for a second, but then hugged her back. Quite strongly. Kirsty closed her eyes against his shoulder and wished she could stay in his arms for ever.

But of course she couldn't. Not yet, anyway. But she could hope, couldn't she?

"Well, fancy you coming to a play!" she exclaimed, eventually drawing back, eyes bright and heart racing more madly than ever.

"And fancy you being in it," he returned with a wry little smile. "But you were marvellous, Kirsty. And you *look* marvellous, too. Blonde hair suits you."

"And short hair suits you," she returned truthfully.

He shrugged his broad shoulders. "It's low maintenance."

"I can't imagine your wife liking it," she said, her chest tightening. The night Ryan's wife had come to dinner with him at Belleview she'd spent half the night touching his collar-length hair, as if he was a prized dog, to be stroked and petted all the time.

"Tina and I are divorced," he said, and his eyes locked with hers.

Kirsty could hardly breathe.

"How...um...how long ago?" she managed to get out.

"A year or two."

The realisation that he hadn't come looking for her the moment his divorce was final only confirmed what Kirsty already knew. She might have been secretly pining for him all these years, but he hadn't lost any sleep over her. Still, he was here with her now, *and* looking at her the way men looked at her a lot these days.

Kirsty had no intention of wasting such a golden opportunity.

"You said something in your message about going for coffee together?" she reminded him, trying to sound cool and casual. She didn't do too badly either.

"We could go for a real drink, if you'd prefer. There are plenty of bars nearby in the city."

Kirsty would have dearly loved to sit with him for hours in some dimly lit bar, especially one which had a dance floor, but she'd promised Gemma to go straight home each night after the show—especially tonight, the first night Jaws's precious owner was away. The dog adored Gemma, and would pine terribly for her if he didn't have familiar company—and regular lashings of steak—to comfort him. No matter how crazy she was about Ryan, Kirsty knew she'd worry if she didn't go home to Belleview soon and feed the big lug.

"Would you think me forward if I suggested you come home with me and have coffee there?" Kirsty asked.

Ryan laughed. "It's no more than I would expect from a girl who can play that Helen creature with such conviction."

Kirsty tried not to look guilty or blush. "Oh, that's just acting," she dismissed. "I'm nothing at all like Helen. Which reminds me—what on earth *were* you doing, going to a play? And all alone too. I wouldn't have thought a hunky guy like you would be alone for long. You did say you'd been divorced for a while, didn't you?"

He shrugged, as though his divorce was not worth talking about. "I prefer to live alone these days. It

fits in better with my workaholic lifestyle. Serious
relationships are extremely time-consuming. And
complicated, I've found. I do date occasionally, but
I'm not seeing anyone at the moment. When my boss
gave me a couple of free theatre tickets I wasn't going
to go by myself, but someone said how great the play
was, so I thought, What the heck? I might as well.
And I'm sure glad I did.''

"I'm glad you did too,'' she agreed, beaming her
delight up at him.

"Right,'' Ryan said, smiling back and tucking her
arm through his. ''Shall we get going to your place
for coffee, like you said? Because it's chilly standing
out here. My car's just down this way, in the car
park.''

Kirsty walked with him down the stairs, wondering
all of a sudden if he thought her asking him home for
coffee equated with her asking him home to bed. Men
did presume a lot these days.

"So why is it that a girl with your looks doesn't
have a steady boyfriend?'' he asked as they made
their way towards the underground car park.

"How do you know I haven't?''

He slanted her a rueful smile. ''I'm presuming that
the nice girl I used to know is not the type to ask me
home for coffee when she already has another guy in
tow.''

So he *did* think some kind of sex was on the
agenda! His just having coffee and a chat with her
would hardly constitute two-timing.

The thought of Ryan even kissing her suddenly sent
Kirsty's head into a whirl.

She worried now about what answer to give. She

didn't want to tell him that she'd never really had a boyfriend. She certainly didn't want him to guess she was a virgin. Ryan had a look about him these days which suggested virgins were not his date of preference. He'd probably run a mile at the first hint of her being sexually inexperienced.

Lord, what a pickle!

"I've been giving men a miss for a while," she hedged.

"Oh? Why's that? Last one do the dirty on you?"

Kirsty gnawed at her bottom lip. "He...er...he had a wife," she said, without looking at him.

"Oh. I see," he replied drily, not seeing at all. "Did you know he had a wife all along? Or was she a nasty surprise?"

"She was a *very* nasty surprise."

"Poor Kirsty. Were you in love with him?"

"Terribly."

"I hope you're not one of those naïve females who hang on, thinking their lover is going to leave his wife and marry *them*."

"Oh, no. I never thought that. Not for a moment."

When Ryan stopped next to a sleek black Porsche Kirsty stared, first at the car, then up at him. "Is this *your* car?" she asked.

"Yes, why?" He clicked the door locks up, then opened the passenger door for her.

Kirsty just shook her head. "No reason. Just surprised." But as she climbed in she made up her mind. She definitely wouldn't be telling him she was a virgin. Divorced men who looked like Ryan and drove black Porsches didn't sleep with virgins. They slept with sexy girls like Carla.

Carla's earlier crude words popped back into her mind.

It'll be interesting to see how you go tomorrow, after he's banged your brains out all night.

Kirsty glanced up at Ryan as he gallantly closed the passenger door. "Thanks," she said, using a quick smile to mask her growing inner panic.

Was that what he *was* expecting?

Kirsty knew it wasn't uncommon for guys these days to expect sex on the first date. She'd been out with quite a few males with octopus hands and wild presumptions that she'd do everything from give them blow jobs on the way home in the car to wall-to-wall sex once they got there.

And, whilst she'd honestly thought she was physically attracted to these men at the time, the reality was, when it came to the crunch, Kirsty always recoiled from being that intimate with men she didn't love.

She knew she was an anachronism in this day and age, but she couldn't seem to help it.

Ryan, of course, was a different story entirely. Ryan, she loved. Kirsty could think of nothing more exciting than for him to take her to bed.

At least…in theory. But in reality?

Kirsty watched Ryan walk around the front of the car and climb in behind the wheel, her eyes glued to his broad shoulders and incredibly macho body. He would be beautiful naked, she knew. And he'd be good at sex. He had always been good at all things physical.

But she had an awful feeling she might be hopeless. Suddenly her stomach was churning, and she began hoping, contrarily, that Ryan wouldn't want to sleep with her tonight. Which was perverse. Ryan making love to her had to be her second most persistent fantasy, right after his declaring his undying love for her.

"So where's home?" he asked as he put the key in the ignition.

The powerful car growled into life, the vibration throbbing erotically through the passenger seat up into Kirsty's already turned-on body.

"What? Oh...um...would you believe Belleview? And, no, I'm not still living at home." She started babbling. "I left home years ago. Dad's taken Gemma away on a second honeymoon and I've volunteered for the job of house and dog-sitting for the next nine days."

Which was a pity, she thought. She'd have been much safer asking him back to her grotty little bedsit where there wasn't enough room to bang her brains out—not for a man as big as Ryan. Belleview, however, was the perfect setting for sex and seduction. All those big bedrooms and bathrooms, not to mention huge squashy sofas and acres of plushly carpeted floors!

"If it's too far out of your way," she choked out, "you could always put me into a taxi."

"Not at all. At this time of night it won't take long to drive to St Ives."

"You remember the way?"

"How could I forget? I must have visited you there at least a dozen times."

"You...you were very good to me during those awful days, Ryan. Very...kind. I don't think I ever thanked you properly."

"Tina seemed to think you had," he said drily.

"I know."

He frowned over at her. "You *knew* she thought we were having sex the nights I stayed over?"

She nodded, and Ryan's frown deepened.

"How? Did she accuse you too?"

"No. She didn't have to. I guessed when she kept giving me the evil eye the night she came to Belleview to dinner with you."

Ryan shook his head. "You've no idea the things she said that night after we left. It was the beginning of the end for us, I can tell you."

"I'm sorry if I was the cause of your divorce," Kirsty lied.

"It wasn't your fault. I already knew I didn't love Tina, if I ever did. Our divorce was inevitable. But let's not talk about unpleasant topics. I want to know all about Kirsty O'Connell, the new sensation of the Sydney stage!"

CHAPTER SEVEN

SHE was gorgeous, Ryan thought as Kirsty chatted away on the drive home, telling him things he'd already gathered from Nathan, and quite a lot he hadn't.

But she was not quite what he'd been expecting. Especially after seeing her in that play.

Kirsty was right when she said she was nothing like that Helen character. Not even remotely. She was no flirt, for starters. And while she possessed a degree of self-assurance—and a quite striking physical beauty—there was still a naïveté about her which reminded him strongly of the Kirsty of five years ago.

Fancy getting mixed-up with a married man. Now, that was *exactly* what the old Kirsty would have done. She'd have got mixed-up with *him* if he'd allowed it.

Ryan figured Kirsty was one of those girls who, once they thought themselves in love, could easily become a victim. He was glad she'd found out this guy had a wife before she'd got in too deep. As it was, she'd obviously still been to bed with the creep. Her "being off men' told of more than a romantically broken heart. Sexual betrayal would cut deep with a girl like Kirsty.

She didn't realise how very much like her father she was—both in looks, now that she was blonde— and also in her emotional intensity. He could see her temper rising as she relayed the details of the argument she'd had with Nathan before leaving home.

Passion did become her, Ryan thought as he glanced over at her glittering green eyes and flushed cheeks.

"And do you know what he accused me of then?" she said, her lushly mobile mouth pouting provocatively.

"No. What?"

"He said I was lazy. And spoiled! Said I couldn't possibly survive on my own and that I'd come crawling for hand-outs within no time."

"I hope you didn't."

"Never!"

"So how *did* you survive?" he asked. "Surely you didn't land an acting job straight away."

"I wish. No, I got a waitressing job to begin with, and rented this most appalling room in a boardinghouse near Sydney Uni. You've no idea what it was like."

"I've got a pretty good idea. I've lived in quite a few dumps in my time." His dad had spent most of his life on the dole, and they'd moved too much to get a housing commission place. Mostly they'd lived in rented premises which should have been condemned.

She frowned over at him. "You know, I don't know anything much about you, do I? Other than who you work for and who you were once married to."

"You mean your grandfather never enlightened you about my background?"

"No. Why would Pops know anything about your background? I mean..." She shot him a startled look.

"Oh. Oh, I see. You were one of his boys, were you? A street kid. Like Dad."

Ryan almost smiled. "Not quite like your dad. I never did have Nathan's class or talents. But, yes, I was a street kid. *And* a regular inmate of various boys' homes." Boys' homes sounded a lot better than penitentiaries. "Your grandfather helped me when I needed help. He got me a job at IAS, and a room boarding with a nice Italian family."

"But…but what about *your* family? I mean…you do have a family, don't you? Oh, Lord, don't tell me you're an orphan."

His smile turned very wry. "Nope. Can't use that sympathy-getting ploy. I have parents, all right."

"And?"

He shrugged nonchalantly, but inside his chest was as tight as a vice. "The usual. Rebellious male child doesn't get along with his father. His dad tries to keep him under control but once the kid grows big enough to really rebel he leaves home. After I did that, my folks disowned me."

"Even your *mother*?"

Ryan didn't like to think about his mother. He could never make up his mind if his mother was another victim of his father's fists, or just a low-life as well.

"Mum was a drunk, and not capable of helping me on her own. She had to go along with whatever my dad said to do. After I was first arrested and the welfare people called on my parents both of them said that as far as they was concerned I was dead."

Kirsty looked appalled. "But that's dreadful."

"Life can be dreadful," Ryan said pragmatically,

though girls like Kirsty rarely discovered the depths of dreadfulness which other people's lives sank to. The kidnapping had given her a small taste, but it was obvious she was over that. There was certainly no sign of any lasting trauma. A traumatised person would never make the choice to go on the stage, which was a very exposed profession.

Kirsty thought she'd been brave going out on her own. And she had, too. But the reality remained that down deep she knew she could always go home. Nathan and Gemma would welcome her back. And so would her mother, *and* her grandfather. She didn't know how lucky she was.

"I never knew," she murmured, shaking her head. "That's so sad, Ryan."

"No sadder than millions of other people's lives in this world."

"And that's even sadder. That you should think like that. Doesn't it make you angry?"

"Sure, I was angry back then," he confessed. Hell, he'd been a very angry young man. But meeting Byron had shown him that not *every* man was his enemy, that life *could* be worth living if you worked hard and bettered yourself. "But there's no point in clinging to anger. I'm doing pretty well these days. Keith's made me head of security. I own this car, and a great unit at Bondi. I've had nothing to be angry about for years."

His ex-wife immediately jumped into his mind, and his stomach tightened. Tina's maniacal stalking after he'd left her had made him more than angry. He'd feared for his life for a while. Lord knows what might have happened if the police hadn't brought her to her senses.

Still, the experience had left deep scars. If that was the kind of love he inspired, Ryan wanted none of it. Just thinking about what he'd endured with Tina made him shudder. His life was back on an even emotional keel now, and he aimed to keep it that way, no matter what.

Which meant he had to be careful during the next nine days. Because Kirsty did still fancy him. Quite a bit, if he was any judge. And he more than fancied her back.

Frankly, she'd turned into the most desirable young woman he'd ever met—an intriguing mixture of experience and innocence, of passion and compassion, of high spirits tempered with the most beguiling sweetness.

But it was her eyes which still captivated him the most. Her lovely green eyes. Eyes which never lied.

The way she'd looked at him on the Opera House steps had been more than telling. He'd been guilty of some X-rated thoughts as well. Impossible not to be. She was one hot-looking babe.

But sex with her was definitely not on. Especially now that he'd found out she was on the rebound from an affair with a married man. If he took Kirsty to bed she might very well turn her recently unrequited love onto him. And that would never do.

He might have been given permission to use any means at his disposal to protect Kirsty, but what Nathan didn't seem to realise was that when nice girls like Kirsty slept with a man they often fell madly in love with him. Actually, Ryan had had some *not* very nice girls fall madly in love with him after he'd taken them to bed. Which was why he'd made that personal rule of his, limiting his sexual encounters with any individual partner. Because the last thing in the world Ryan wanted was for *any* female to fall madly in love with him ever again.

Ryan glanced over at Kirsty and reaffirmed his earlier decision. As difficult as it was going to be—and it was going to be damned difficult—he was not going to sleep with her during the next week. Not even once. She was too great a risk.

"I still feel angry with my father," Kirsty muttered.

"So I gathered. But you'll have the last laugh, won't you? You've done everything you said you would. Supported yourself and become a great actress."

"Actor," Kirsty corrected him, and Ryan smiled. He'd known he'd slip up there in the end.

"I do have this problem with political correctness," he said. "I guess I'm an old-fashioned kind of guy."

She smiled over at him. "You mean a male chauvinist pig."

He laughed. "Close."

"That's all right," she said, still smiling. "I don't really give a fig if you call me an actress. The other girls don't like it, though. Mimi especially. She's a real stickler for things like that."

"Who's Mimi?"

"The girl who played Janette."

"Ahh. The other blonde. She was good, too. But not quite as good as you."

"Flatterer."

"Not at all. Well, here we are," he said, and swung his car into the driveway at Belleview, braking to a halt in front of the high, decidedly locked iron gates. "Any suggestions as to how we get in?"

"Won't take me a sec." Kirsty was out of the car in a flash, racing over to begin busily tapping a code into the security panel built into the gatepost. Her back being turned towards him gave Ryan the opportunity to have a good look up and down the street.

The kerbside running along Belleview's security wall was deserted, but there was a navy sedan parked directly opposite, a dark figure sitting behind the wheel.

Ryan stared into the rear-vision mirror till he saw the glow of a cigarette being lit—the all-clear signal. He wound down his window and tapped the side of the car, after which the sedan started up and drove off.

Kirsty jumped back into the passenger seat and rubbed her hands. "Gosh, it's cold out there tonight. Just as well I set the heating to come on at ten or the house'd be like a tomb. What time is it now? Gosh. Almost midnight. Poor Jaws won't be happy, left out in the backyard all this time."

"Dogs don't feel the cold like people do."

"Jaws does. He's a house dog. But it's not the cold he hates. It's being alone."

"Mmm. I was thinking that what you need around here," Ryan said, his security hat well and truly on as he drove round to the front steps, "is a proper guard dog." Not some wimpish mongrel afraid of his own shadow. "This is a big place to stay in all by yourself, especially with your folks away on holiday.''

"Oh, not you too," she groaned. "Dad went on and on yesterday about locking everything up tight as a drum before I went to bed every night. I'd forgotten what a fanatic he is in that regard."

"The man's just being sensible."

They both climbed out of the car at the same time, Ryan zapping the locks down whilst Kirsty fished around in her roomy black shoulder-bag. "You would say that," she said, looking up at last with a bunch of keys in her hand. "You're into security."

"And you're not?"

She shrugged and went over to open the front door. "I don't take stupid chances, but I don't live in fear either. You can't control everything and everyone in life. Of course Dad thinks he can. I pity poor Gemma sometimes, being married to him."

"I'm sure Mrs Whitmore doesn't want your pity. She's a lovely lady, your stepmother."

"Yes, she is that. Everyone adores her—especially her beloved Jaws. Come on—come inside out of the cold. See? What did I tell you? Snuggly and warm in here."

Even warmer than it had been the other day, Ryan recalled. Clearly Kirsty liked her creature comforts. Realising that made him appreciate how much courage it had taken for her to leave home and make do, when she was used to the very best of everything.

"What about the gates?" he asked, before Kirsty could move away from the second security panel built into the wall near the door. He'd noted it there the other day, and personally thought it should have been hidden.

She threw him an exasperated glance. "What's the point in shutting the gates when you'll be driving through them again later on?"

"Better to be safe than sorry."

"Oh, all right!" And she marched over to jab a finger on the appropriate button. "Satisfied now?"

Not even remotely, he wanted to tell her, once again thinking how sexy she was when her blood was up.

It was just as well that she *did* intend him to leave. Because Ryan wasn't sure if he could have kept to his resolve if she'd actually been expecting him to stay.

The longer time he spent with her, the more he was attracted. She was different from every girl he'd ever been with—and slept with.

It wasn't just her money. Or her looks. He'd bedded the rich and the beautiful before. It was something else, some indefinable quality about her which had always attracted him.

Kirsty brought out the best in him. And possibly the worst. He wanted to protect her and keep her safe. But at the same time he wanted to—

"Woof-woof!"

Ryan blinked at the deep-sounding bark as it echoed through the house.

"Woof-woof-woof!"

"Jaws," Kirsty said. "Sounds like he's inside, but he isn't. He's got a very loud bark. Come on, we'll go let the poor thing in and feed him."

Ryan remembered Nathan saying Gemma's dog

was a big mongrel. He had to be, by the sound of
him. Pity he was a bit of a coward as well.

"Did you meet Jaws last time you were here?"
Kirsty asked as Ryan followed her along the hall.

"No, I don't think so."

"Dad won't let him go into any of *his* rooms, or
the more formal areas. And never upstairs. But Jaws
rules the roost in here."

She slid back a door which led into a large
L-shaped family room—so large, in fact, that there
were several groupings of furniture and a television
in one corner which matched the huge screens you
found in clubs.

Ryan was pretty sure he'd never been in this part
of the house before. His initial visits to Belleview had
been confined to Nathan's study. Then, after Kirsty's
rescue, he'd spent most of his time in her bedroom,
except for the night he'd been invited here for that
thank-you dinner. But that had been held in the
front—and more formal—rooms of the house. His
knowledge of the pool in the backyard had been
gained by peering down at it through the window in
Kirsty's bedroom.

That was one room he aimed to keep out of this
time.

The sight of a large brown dog standing, panting,
at one of the sliding glass doors which led out onto
the back terrace brought a wry smile to his face. "If
that's Jaws, then we certainly haven't met. I'd have
remembered a dog like that."

He was the biggest, ugliest dog Ryan had ever
seen, with teeth to rival his namesake. Admittedly he
did have soulful brown eyes, which females would

find adorable, and he used them to good effect. At that moment they were fixed on Kirsty and totally ignoring Ryan.

Ryan suspected Jaws was the ultimate survivor, knowing exactly what side his bread was buttered on and who best to turn to for sympathy and attention. The women of the house.

When Kirsty opened the sliding door he bounded in, jumping up with his huge paws resting on her shoulders and his tongue slurping all over her face.

"Oh, yuk, get down, Jaws. Get down."

He got down, but stayed sidled up to Kirsty, his large head rubbing against her left hand till she started scratching him behind his less than show quality ears. "Yes, darling, yes," she said soothingly. "I've missed you, too."

Ryan felt quite jealous of the obvious physical pleasure behind the appreciative little noises the dog was making. As he watched Kirsty, there was a telling prickling in his loins. No, more than a prickling. A stiffening.

Damn, but he hated having to deny himself. And for the sake of what?

Not to protect her. More to protect himself.

He'd become paranoid after Tina.

Yet Kirsty wasn't anything like Tina. She had a healthy self-esteem. And a career she was crazy about. Surely she wouldn't become obsessed with him. Not on the strength of a couple of nights in the sack.

But what if she did?

Better not to take the risk. Concentrate on the job, bozo, not the girl.

But even as Ryan struggled to keep his mind on just that he couldn't stop thinking about what it would be like to have her hands on him, not that stupid dog. To have her pet *him*, caress *him*. He wanted her to scratch *his* itch. He wanted her to do a whole lot of things which even Nathan might not have envisaged.

"Do you like dogs?" she asked Ryan, her hand now stroking the top of the dog's head and smoothing down the hair on his mangy neck.

Ryan shrugged. "Sure."

"Dad doesn't. Gemma says it's because he never had a dog as a child. Did you have a dog as a child?"

"Once," he admitted. "But only for a short while. He died young." Ryan didn't think he should tell Kirsty that his father had kicked it to death. After that he'd never brought any stray puppies home, thinking they would be safer anywhere else but with him, even in a dumpster.

"Come on, Jaws," Kirsty said brightly. "We'll go get your supper."

The dog trotted after Kirsty's heels as she made her way to the kitchen, which was separated from the family room by a very long white breakfast bar, complete with half a dozen white cane stools. The kitchen was very modern and all white, with sleek stainless steel appliances.

Kirsty opened the stainless steel refrigerator, drew out a blue plastic plate heaped with very lean chunks of steak and put it down for the dog. Ryan couldn't see the kitchen floor from where he was standing but he could hear the sounds of eager gobbling.

"They have a strained relationship, Dad and Jaws," Kirsty remarked as she walked over to switch on the electric jug in the corner. "Actually, they can't stand each other." She opened an overhead cupboard and lifted down two white mugs. "Dad tolerates Jaws because of Gemma, and Jaws hasn't actually bitten Dad for years. But the hair on his spine lifts every time Dad walks into the room. They say dogs are an excellent judge of character, so maybe that explains it."

"You're very hard on your father, do you know that? I'm not sure he deserves it."

Kirsty opened another overhead cupboard and brought out a jar of instant coffee. "Dad deserves everything he gets in life. He's a ruthless bastard."

"His ruthlessness got you home safe and sound five years ago, Kirsty. Don't ever forget that."

Her head whipped round to face him. "No. *You* got me home safe and sound, Ryan. Not Dad. *You*." Her voice vibrated with emotion.

"I was just following orders," he said, but suddenly he was back there, on the day of the rescue, seeing himself through her eyes, feeling what she'd made him feel. As if he was ten feet tall. A god, in her eyes.

"Don't say that," she choked out. "I don't believe that. I'll never believe that." Tears suddenly flooded her eyes and she whirled away, clasping her cheeks and shaking her head in distress. "I'm sorry. Don't take any notice of me. You're right. Of course you're right. You were just following orders."

Ryan knew he shouldn't go to her, but how could he not? He'd always hated to see her cry.

He came up behind her, his hands curling over her

shaking shoulders, his fingertips digging into the scarlet wool of her jumper.

"Don't cry," he said, drawing her gently back against him. "There's no reason to cry. What happened back then is irrelevant. You're safe and sound now. And you have the world at your feet, careerwise. You should be celebrating, not crying."

She shuddered, then sighed against him. "I know. I'm acting like a fool, always wanting what I can't have."

"What is it you want that you can't have?"

When she stayed silent, he realised what she might be referring to.

"Forget that married creep," he said brusquely, annoyed with her for wasting her love on some womanising low-life. "There are plenty more fish in the sea."

"No," she cried softly. "No, there's not. Not for me."

"Don't be ridiculous." He spun her in his arms and glared down into her glistening green eyes. "You'll fall in love a dozen times before you're finished. If that bastard divorced his wife and married you, you'd probably end up miserable—because a guy like that won't ever change. Once a womaniser, always a womaniser. I know, honey, because you're looking at one."

"You, Ryan?" She blinked her amazement up at him.

"Yeah, me. You seem shocked. Sceptical, even."

"Well... I... I..."

"You should never have put me up on that pedestal, honey. I was bound to fall off one day. I'm no hero. I'm just a man.''

''You'll never be just a man to me, Ryan,'' she insisted stubbornly. ''And I don't believe you're a womaniser. You're just saying that to put me off you, for some reason.''

How right she was. And how wrong.

''I'm not that noble,'' he muttered. ''Trust me when I say rarely a week goes by without my having a woman. But they have a very short shelf-life with me, honey. *Very* short.''

She gaped up at him with wide green eyes and deliciously parted lips. He stared down at them and thought the wickedest of thoughts, his flesh swiftly following his mind into the fires of hell. What on earth had he been thinking of, taking her into his arms like this? He should have known he wouldn't be able to resist her.

''I did warn you, honey,'' he growled as his mouth began to descend towards hers. ''You really should have believed me.''

CHAPTER EIGHT

KIRSTY was still reeling over Ryan's revelation when his lips contacted hers. Not at all savagely. But lightly. Seductively.

She'd been kissed before. Many times. But never like this. Not as if she was being checked for taste.

"Sweet," he murmured against her mouth. "I knew you'd be sweet."

"Ryan, I..."

"Shh. You know you want this. And if you don't you soon will."

Kirsty could not believe this was her Ryan talking to her like this, acting like this. Her Ryan wasn't some slimy womaniser. He was a sexy man, yes, but he was also a good man.

His tongue flicked over her top lip. Then the bottom one.

She gasped, and stared up at him with shocked eyes.

"Relax," he ordered. "I'm not going to hurt you."

She wanted to laugh. Of course he would hurt her. Physically *and* emotionally. She was a virgin, damn it. And she *loved* him.

"Do you want to tell me what you like?" he said thickly as his mouth trailed with tantalising slowness from the corner of her mouth over to her right ear. "Or do you want me to play this by ear?"

When she remained speechless, his tongue-tip traced the outer swirls of her ear before sliding inside.

She sucked in, then shivered.

"I had a feeling you'd like that," he said, his mouth lifting away, leaving her longing for him to do it again. "And this..." He turned her round in his arms and slid his hands up under her jumper, stroking back and forth across her naked ribcage till her head tipped back against his shoulder and she stopped breathing entirely. Her breasts he ignored, yet soon they were twin mounds of tortured flesh, her nipples tight and tingling.

Touch them, she urged frantically with her mind. Oh, God, touch them.

He touched them, and she cried out.

And then so did he.

"Christ!" he exclaimed, letting her go so abruptly that she fell forward across the kitchen bench.

Kirsty's befuddled brain eventually took in what had happened. Jaws, thinking perhaps that Ryan was hurting her, had come to her rescue and was now clamped to his trouser leg—not his actual leg, by the look of things—shaking it vigorously, growling ominously at the same time.

"Let me go, you stupid dog," Ryan commanded irritably. "I wasn't hurting her. She was *liking* it."

Kirsty couldn't help it. She burst out laughing. Who would have thought that Jaws— whose cowardice was well known—would have the courage to take on someone as formidable-looking as Ryan?

"This isn't funny," Ryan muttered, clearly doing

his best to stay calm and keep his leg still. "Can't you do something before he rips my trousers? They cost me a small fortune and I might never get another pair to match the jacket."

Kirsty just stood there and crossed her arms— partly to hide her still fiercely erect nipples, and partly because she wasn't going to let him off that easily. How dared he turn up in her life again and de-myth his hero status in her eyes? How dared he assume she was some little tart who'd just let him do what he liked with her? "Serves you right for turning into a sleazebag."

"I'm not a sleazebag. I always tell my ladyfriends exactly where I'm coming from. And the rules I live by."

"I don't recall hearing any rules," she said haughtily, her arms still firmly crossed.

"You will. Afterwards."

"After what?" she snapped.

"After you get this bloody dog off my leg!"

Kirsty flinched. Ryan in a temper was not a nice experience. She much preferred him when he was playing the hero, or even the womaniser. Dear heaven, but he knew how to turn her on. Without doing much either. She'd been beside herself in a couple of minutes flat. Imagine what he could do in bed, with their clothes off!

Kirsty decided then and there that, despite *not* being a little tart, she was going to find out. Be damned with worrying about her virginity. Or losing her heart—plus her head—over him again.

A girl had to do what a girl had to do.

Kirsty hunched down next to a by now near-rabid Jaws and wondered where to start.

Attacking Ryan's trousers seemed to have set off very bad memories in the poor dog's head. Kirsty wondered which other trousers had been on the end of this rarely seen aggression. Her dad's, of course. Had he done something to Gemma once? Hit her, perhaps? Kirsty wouldn't put it past her father doing something like that. She'd heard rumours that the early days of his marriage to Gemma had been very stormy. It wasn't wonderful at the moment either. Gemma hadn't confided in her what was wrong, but Kirsty knew there had to be something. She'd caught Gemma looking so sad sometimes, for no apparent reason.

Pity she didn't divorce the bastard. No wonder Jaws hated him.

"Jaws, darling," she began in the same soft sweet tone Gemma always used with dogs and small children. "Let the nice man go. He's not really a baddie. Just a sleazebag and a sex maniac. I'll give you some more food if you let him go. Food?" she repeated, and nodded towards the fridge.

His favourite word seemed to register, a light popping on in his big brown eyes. Jaws stopped shaking Ryan's trouser leg, then reluctantly let go. The expensive black material, however, looked irretrievably damaged.

Tough, she thought, and waltzed over to get Jaws his breakfast, which was already defrosted in the fridge, awaiting the morning. No matter. She could easily defrost a new lot before then. Gemma had left dozens of prepared meals ready for her adored pet in the freezer.

"I'll just take him out into the garages," she said, using the plate of steak to entice Jaws down the hall which led off the kitchen, past the laundry and old servants' quarters and ending up at the garages. "Then I'll be back to hear all about those no doubt very nice rules of yours," she threw caustically over her shoulder.

"Fine," he called back. "And I'm *not* a sleaze-bag."

"Didn't deny being a sex maniac, though," Kirsty muttered under her breath as she settled Jaws in the garages with his food.

He'd be okay in here for a while, she thought, glancing around the extremely large area. It could, after all, accommodate six cars, but there were only two in there at the moment. Her father's dark blue BMW and Gemma's white Astra. Kirsty didn't own a car. Couldn't afford one.

But maybe she would be able to soon.

Still, she had more on her mind at the moment than buying a car, and he was waiting for her back there in the kitchen, a six-foot-four tower of threatening testosterone.

Ryan had moved into the family room by the time she returned, draping his big macho body over one of the armchairs which faced the television. He'd turned it on as well, she noted, and was watching some golf game from somewhere on the other side of the world.

"I see you have cable," he said, his eyes not leaving the screen.

"Dad and Gemma have cable," she corrected him.

"Not me. So, is this what you're going to do now? Watch television?" She couldn't believe it. A minute ago he'd been making hot love to her and now he was seemingly engrossed in a golf game.

"Kissing you was a mistake," he said matter-of-factly.

Kirsty took a second or two to recover from the shock of this blunt announcement. "Why?" she finally asked.

"Rule number one," he said, his expression uncompromising as his eyes turned away from the screen onto her. "Never make love to a female who's vulnerable."

Kirsty blinked her surprise. "You think I'm vulnerable." Now *that* was first. All the men she'd ever dated had thought she was a bitch. A frigid bitch.

"I *know* you're vulnerable."

She walked over and sank into the armchair across from him, crossing her legs and placing her arms on the armrests, her hands curling perhaps a little too tightly over the end. It took an effort of will to relax them and to appear cool, especially when inside she was bubbling away with a dozen mixed emotions.

"Define vulnerable," she said through gritted teeth.

"In your case it's simple. You've had your heart broken recently by some married creep. That makes you vulnerable. I don't want you falling in love with me, Kirsty. And you might, if we have sex."

"Trust me when I say that won't happen." Hard to fall in love with someone you already love.

"Why? Because you're still in love with the creep?"

"Yes." And he's not really a creep, she wanted to add, but decided not to.

"You only *think* you are. You're young. You'll get over him soon enough. Young girls fall in love a lot."

"That's a matter of opinion."

"Maybe, but it's *my* opinion. And that makes you a risk in my eyes. I don't sleep with risks."

"Really. And is there a rule number two?"

"I don't sleep with the same female more than twice."

Kirsty was totally taken aback. "Goodness. Why's that?"

"Because that makes her a risk."

"A risk of what, exactly?"

"The same thing. Her falling in love with me."

"My God, you're paranoid!"

"Perhaps. But that's the way it is."

"What's so terrible about a woman falling in love with you?"

"It leads to complications."

"Huh! You mean it leads to commitment. That's what you don't want, Ryan. Why don't you just admit it?"

"All right, I admit it. I don't want commitment. I've been there, done that, and I didn't like it."

Kirsty wanted to ask him for more details of his failed marriage, but something in his face stopped her.

"So, on the strength of one bad marriage you opt out of relationships altogether and just sleep around, having one-night—oh, pardon me—*two*-night stands. Did I get that right?"

"Spot-on."

"So where do you usually conduct these wonderfully romantic encounters of yours?"

"In hotel rooms."

"I should have guessed."

"That's another of my rules. I never take women back to my place."

"Oh, yes. Of course. We wouldn't want the poor darlings getting the wrong idea." Exasperation with his ridiculous rules put some real acid in her tone. "For crying out loud, Ryan, what kind of pathetic way is that to live?"

He did, finally, look a bit uncomfortable with his personal lifestyle. "I'm just trying not to hurt anyone."

"No, Ryan, what you're doing is trying not to *get* hurt. But the way you're going about it…it's not right. And it's changed you."

"We all change, Kirsty," he returned coolly. "Life changes us. *You've* changed."

"Me?"

"Yes, you. You're much tougher than the girl I rescued."

She smiled. "You called me vulnerable a minute ago. Make up your mind."

"That's what I mean. You stand up for yourself these days with all the tenacity of a street fighter. The girl I rescued was a far softer creature."

"The girl you rescued was a figment of my romantic imagination. I created her, Ryan, because I thought you might fall in love with her. I knew you couldn't possibly fall in love with the difficult, prickly, rebellious, *non*-vulnerable me."

He stared at her for a few seconds before smiling

a slow, wry smile. "You naughty girl. So Tina was right about you all along."

"In a manner of speaking. Whatever she imagined I was doing to you, I certainly was doing in my mind."

He laughed, but the sound had a dark, cold edge to it and not a scrap of humour. "Oh, no, you weren't. Not even in your mind. You wouldn't have even known such things existed back then. Of course, now is a different story. I dare say you know a lot more about men these days..."

His eyes narrowed on her lips and her whole mouth went dry.

"But that's beside the point," he went on abruptly. "You're still on the rebound, and I don't have sex with females on the rebound. Rules are rules. I'd better go."

It took all of Ryan's will-power to force himself up onto his feet. It would have been a lot easier to stay and do what his body was still aching to do. But he knew that would be a huge mistake. Ryan took pride in the fact that at least he learnt from past mistakes.

Kirsty stood up also. "But you haven't had your coffee yet."

He hesitated.

"Come on," she said with a saucy little smile. "I promise not to jump on you. One cup. Then you can go home."

He sighed and sank back down. "One cup. Then I *am* going home."

"Of course you are," she said sweetly. *Too sweetly.*

Ryan shook his head as he watched her walk off with a wiggle in her hips. He knew women. Kirsty thought she could get him to change his mind. But she was wrong. The danger of his succumbing to his dark side tonight had passed, and would remain passed, provided he didn't touch her again.

That was what had been his undoing earlier. Taking her into his arms. If he hadn't been stupid enough to do that he wouldn't have kissed her in the first place, or started fondling her beautiful and exquisitely responsive body.

Hell, don't start thinking about that.

"How do you take your coffee?" she called out from the kitchen.

"Usually not at all. Coffee's bad for you."

"Live dangerously for once, then. How about cream with two sugars? Go on. I dare you."

"Whatever. I'm still going home straight afterwards."

"That's fine by me," she said happily when she walked in, carrying the two white mugs she'd taken out earlier. She handed him one then sat back down, cradling the other in her hands. "I'll have you know I have rules of my own when it comes to men and sex."

"Dare I ask what?"

"Rule number one. I never have sex on the first date."

"How commendable of you." He lifted the mug to his lips. The creamed coffee looked rich and delicious and wickedly more-ish, just like the girl who'd made it.

"So what are you doing tomorrow night?" she asked, just as he went to take a sip.

He gulped down a far too large mouthful, burning the roof of his mouth and half of his gullet.

He ignored the pain, however, and laughed. "Don't you know how to take no for an answer?"

"Not when the no is based on a false premise. I told you. I'm not going to fall in love with you. You're worrying for nothing. Besides, you don't have to have sex with me if you don't want to. I still want to see you again. So, I repeat, what are you doing tomorrow night?"

Ryan was torn between the devil and the deep blue sea. He'd be stupid to say no. It would be far easier to protect her up close and personally than from a distance. That was why her father had suggested the dating idea in the first place.

And Kirsty was right. He didn't have to make love to her if he didn't want to.

The trouble was he wanted to. Terribly.

"How about meeting me at the same time, same place?" she suggested. "I'll make sure the dog has been well fed and watered before the play. Then we could go out somewhere for a drink after the show, before coming back here."

"You want me to come back here with you again?" he quizzed, frowning.

"Well, you won't take me back to your place, will you?" she quipped teasingly. "Look, put away your paranoia for a while, will you? I'm not asking you to stay the night. I just thought you might be nice enough to drive me home afterwards. If it bothers you that much, I'll take a taxi."

Ryan knew he couldn't let her do that. He had a job to do. He'd have to see her safely home. Even safely inside. The trick would be getting himself out-side again without complicating everything by doing what she obviously wanted him to do—despite her protests and denials. Ryan knew when a woman wanted him. And Kirsty wanted him. Being a typical woman, she'd pull out all the stops tomorrow night to get what she wanted too.

Still, forewarned was forearmed. Ryan knew what to expect next time, as opposed to tonight, when the situation had been a bit of a fishing expedition.

"I have no problem with driving you home," he said coolly, his eyes locking with hers as he went back to sipping his coffee. "Okay. Same time, same place. Tomorrow night."

Kirsty could not believe she'd done what she'd just done. Not only asked Ryan to take her out, but wan-gled it for him to bring her back home here again—virtually giving him permission to stay the night if he liked.

And he *did* like. She'd seen it just then in his eyes.

Kirsty was grateful her spine had been pressed firmly up against the back of the armchair at the time, or she might have spilled her coffee. As it was her fingers had gripped the mug as if it was a life raft and she was being dragged down under a stormy sea for the tenth time.

With a supreme effort of will she relaxed her body, then tapped into her acting skills.

"Great." She threw him a smile, deciding this was how she was going to play it from now on. Cool and casual. Woman of the worldish. Definitely not vulnerable. "Would you mind my asking you a teensie-weensie question about your rule number two?"

He smiled a wry little smile. "Shoot."

"When you say you only sleep with the same female twice, do you mean two separate dates or two actual acts of intercourse? I mean, if you had sex twice on the one night, is that it? *Finito?*"

His smile widened, sending another sexually charged quiver rippling down her spine. Damn, but she wished he would stop doing that. It scattered her wits, and she needed her wits.

"I thought you said I didn't have to have sex with you if I didn't want to."

"What? Oh, yes. Yes. Absolutely. No sex necessary. I was just curious." Was he kidding her? The guy who'd just been making hot love to her in the kitchen was not going to knock her back a second time. Why agree to come out with her at all if that was his intention?

"In that case, I meant two separate dates," he said. "When I'm in the mood, once is rarely enough for me."

Kirsty gulped. "Really? Right."

Which meant that tomorrow night, in this very house, Ryan *was* going to bang her brains out. Unless, of course, he found out she was a virgin first. Then he would run the proverbial mile. Because virginity would equate with vulnerability in his mind.

"Kirsty?"

"What?" She blinked at him.

"What's going through that devious little head of yours?"

She swiftly adopted a suitably enigmatic expression. "I was just thinking."

"What about?"

"Nothing to do with you, Mr Paranoid," she lied, all the while wishing she'd slept with at least one of those sex maniacs she'd gone out with. Then there wouldn't be anything to panic about.

It was to be hoped that all those years of tampon-using had done the trick. Or all those summers of horse riding during the school holidays. Pain she could hide. But blood and gore would rather give the game away.

He put down his largely undrunk coffee and stood up. "If you have no more interesting questions, I'll be going."

"You haven't finished your coffee," she pointed out, even though her own mug was still half full.

"I know. But coffee keeps me awake."

"Well, we wouldn't want that, would we?" she said, and, dumping her mug down next to his, she jumped to her feet. "We want you all bright-eyed and bushy-tailed tomorrow night."

He looked startled. "My God, you certainly have changed, haven't you?"

His remark rather annoyed her. What had he honestly expected? That she would be the same soppy, snivelling, shy nincompoop she'd become for a while after the kidnapping?

Kirsty had to confess that not *all* her behaviour back then had been pretence. She *had* been a bit traumatised at the time. Hell, who wouldn't have been? But life did go on. And life brought change, as Ryan himself had said. So why did he act sometimes as if he preferred the girl she'd been rather than the girl she was now? Kirsty thought she was a much more interesting person at twenty-three than seventeen. And certainly sexier.

Her responses to Ryan's touch earlier this evening had been electric. She suspected she just might be pretty good in bed—with him, anyway—if only she could get around the physical reality of being a virgin.

There had to be a way. Surely.

And then it came to her!

Why hadn't she thought of that solution before?

"I'll walk you to the door," she offered brightly, hooking an arm through his. "And open the gates for you. *And* close them afterwards," she added, before he could open his mouth.

"Make sure you do."

Kirsty rolled her eyes up at him. "Don't get like Dad, Ryan. I couldn't stand it."

"Maybe I'm programmed to protect you," he said, and she laughed.

"Oh, please. The last thing I want you to do is protect me. Now, go home, get your beauty sleep and I'll see you tomorrow night!"

CHAPTER NINE

As soon as Gemma left to have her hair done at the on-board salon, Nathan dashed out onto the balcony to ring Ryan. Not being able to make love to Gemma—or write—hadn't left him much distraction from his worries over Kirsty, and he was anxious to find out what was going on back in Sydney. Since it was only mid-afternoon on a Thursday, Ryan should be in his office, Nathan worked out, and dialled his office number.

"Ryan Harris," Ryan answered on the third ring.

"It's Nathan. How are things going?"

Did the man hesitate? Or was he imagining it?

"Everything's fine at this end," Ryan reported brusquely. "Gregory hasn't put a foot wrong. Didn't go anywhere last night. Went to work today at his uncle's garage. Started at eight. Didn't even leave the place for lunch. His aunt must have packed him one. He's still there. Probably won't knock off till four or five. Don't worry. We watch him every second. I'm also having Belleview watched every night while Kirsty's at the play to make sure there are no nasty surprises when she gets home."

"Did you drive her home last night after the play?" he wanted to know. He'd thought about Ryan and

Kirsty as he'd lain awake last night, wondering if all his plotting and planning had borne fruit.

If Ryan was half the ladies' man his reputation suggested, he wouldn't let the grass grow under his feet. Kirsty was, after all, a real looker these days.

"Nathan, I told you that—"

"Look, I don't want any details. Just did you or did you not drive her home? Surely I'm entitled to know that much. She's my daughter, damn it."

"I drove her home," he admitted, but his voice was tight, as if he hated admitting even that much. "But I went home to my own place half an hour later," he added.

Mmm. Didn't sound as if things were going too wonderfully in that department. Maybe he'd got it all wrong between those two.

"And tonight?"

Dead silence.

"All right. All right. I won't ask. I'm just worried about her."

"I wouldn't worry about her too much if I were you, Nathan. There's one girl who can look after herself."

"Really?"

Nathan couldn't contain his surprise. He didn't think *any* female under forty could look after herself. They liked to think they could, but they couldn't. Why? Because on the whole they were too darned nice. And too darned trusting.

Still, maybe Kirsty had grown up like him. Not at all nice. And without a trusting bone in her body.

"I'm glad to hear that," he said. Though that didn't solve the girl's sexual problems, *or* his wanting her to be lovestruck, not stagestruck. A thought suddenly crossed his mind which could explain several things.

"You don't think Kirsty's a lesbian, do you, Ryan?"

The other man's laughter put paid to that theory. It also sounded as if Ryan was laughing from experience—which was good. Very good.

"Sorry, Nathan," Ryan said a bit sheepishly. "But were you asleep when you watched her in that play the other night?"

Damn and blast, Nathan thought. Ryan hadn't been to bed with her after all. He just believed, like a lot of people, that when an actor played a part they *were* that part. It was a common misconception.

"The only thing Helen and Kirsty have in common," Nathan said irritably, "is that they both fell in love with married men."

"Hell. You know about that, do you?"

"Well...yes. Of course." Hadn't he told Ryan himself the girl had been crazy about him?

"I thought you and Kirsty weren't talking," Ryan said in a puzzled tone.

Nathan felt a bit confused himself. "We aren't. In the main. But I still hear plenty about her via her mother and stepmother."

"I see. No, I don't see. You should sound angrier. I mean...I know Kirsty didn't know the man was married when the affair started, but still...most fathers would have been spitting chips."

The penny dropped for Nathan and he wasn't just angry. He was flabbergasted! "Are you saying Kirsty's been having an affair with a married man? *Recently?*"

"Well...pretty recently. I'm not sure exactly when she broke it off. For pity's sake, Nathan, I thought you already knew about the affair after what you said about her and Helen both being in love with married men."

"The married man I was talking about was *you,* you idiot. I thought the girl was still a bloody virgin!"

Nathan instantly regretted calling Ryan an idiot, but Christ, the thought of Kirsty being seduced by some married, womanising scumbag made his blood boil.

"Sorry, Ryan," he muttered. "You're certainly no idiot. And you're quite right. I *am* spitting chips."

"I'm sorry to be the one to disillusion you further, Nathan, but, like I told you the other day, your daughter got over me years ago. Someone's been telling you little white lies here, I think."

Nathan practically ground his teeth. That lying, sanctimonious little witch! She'd been telling Gemma and Lenore a whole load of crap.

But it certainly put a new light on how she'd got that part. Probably slept her way into it.

"So who is this married man? Do you know?"

"She didn't say. And I didn't ask."

"If it's that bastard who's producing the play, I'll kill him. Or sue him. Or ruin him!"

"Hey, hold it there, Nathan. I seem to recall you telling me that your daughter was a grown-up woman with a mind of her own. And a life of her own. She can sleep with who she likes and, really, it's none of your business."

"My daughter will always be my business. And who she sleeps with will always be my business."

"I don't agree."

"Why? Because *you're* sleeping with her now?"

"I think we'd better terminate this conversation before it gets out of hand."

"Maybe we should. You can send your daily report by text message in future. You have my number."

"If that's what you want. You're the client."

"Which you'd do well to remember," Nathan snapped, and hung up.

Ryan stared down into the dead phone, stunned by what had just transpired. Suddenly he saw what Kirsty had been getting at where her father was concerned. The man was into control in a big way. And when it slipped out of his grasp, even momentarily, he couldn't handle it.

What staggered Ryan the most was that Nathan had hired him to protect Kirsty, and suggested the plan of his dating her, *believing* Kirsty was a virgin!

What kind of father did something like that?

Ryan shook his head as he dropped the receiver back into its cradle. Maybe he was misjudging the man, but he didn't think so. Nathan had *expected* him to seduce Kirsty. Hell, he'd even tried to *pay* him for the privilege, with a huge bonus thrown in.

Why, for God's sake?

Did he think that once they were lovers he'd protect her more vigorously? That a personal connection would always be stronger than a professional one?

Ryan was in awe of such ruthlessness. Nathan had really meant it when he'd said the end justified the means. He'd been prepared to sacrifice his daughter's so-called virginity—and possibly break her heart—to keep her from physical harm.

Ryan wasn't sure if he respected the man or despised him.

He was certainly a different type of father than any he'd ever known.

What also amazed Ryan was why Nathan should have entertained the concept that Kirsty was still a virgin in the first place. Okay, so maybe Gemma or Kirsty's mother had said she was, but, truly, you'd have to be naïve to swallow that one.

And naïve was the last thing Nathan was.

Perhaps when you became a father you lost your natural judgement and thought your offspring were better than other human beings. Sweeter. Purer.

No, no. Ryan couldn't cop that. Nathan had been almost scathing about Kirsty's behaviour. He'd called her difficult and stubborn and stroppy. Which she could be, at times. Nathan did not wear rose-coloured glasses when it came to his daughter.

Clearly someone had fed him a convincing line of bullshit, because Blind Freddie could see that Kirsty being a virgin was as likely as a politician being honest. Twenty-three-year-old girls who looked like Kirsty were never virgins these days. Not unless they'd been locked in a convent all their lives, or converted to some strict no-sex-before-marriage religion before their hormones kicked in.

Which Kirsty hadn't. She'd been living alone and mixing with theatre people for the last few years, probably cutting her sexual teeth on managers, actors, producers and directors. Ryan had no doubt that she'd slept with a good few of them, not just one.

But so what? She was young. And beautiful.

And highly sexed.

Ryan's mind swept back to last night, and the way she'd responded to him. He'd known after seeing her in that play that she'd be passionate. But she'd been more than passionate. She'd been almost mindless with desire. If that damned dog hadn't interrupted them, Lord knows what would have happened, right there in that kitchen.

More surprisingly, by the time he'd touched her breasts he'd been close to being out of control himself. Which was not like him at all. Ryan prided himself on never losing control with any woman.

But then Kirsty wasn't just any woman. She was an original.

And tonight, if he wanted to, he could make love to her. She might still be in love with some other man, but that didn't stop her wanting *him* to make love to her. Not just once, either. That was what had been behind her questioning him about his rule number two.

The thought was incredibly corrupting. Even more was the knowledge that he was more than up to the task. He was a regular robot when it came to sex. Superbly programmed and extremely well practised, courtesy of his ex-wife.

When he'd first met Tina he'd been absolutely hopeless in bed, a graduate of the wham-bang, thank you, ma'am school of sex. His older and very experienced new girlfriend had taken his inept but very willing male body and taught him everything she knew—and everything *he* had to know to please her. She'd tutored him in every position she liked, and every type of foreplay she liked.

And she pretty much liked everything there was.

The kinkier the better. She had shown him how to exert control over his body, how to hold on and on till he went through the pain barrier, programmed him not to come till she'd climaxed at least twice. Even then he'd been expected to be ready for more within minutes. No rest for the wicked.

Once they were married and living together she'd wanted him to service her a couple of times every morning, and every night, and most of the weekend. She'd even picked him up in his car during her lunch-break sometimes, for a quickie in the back seat, or whatever other activity she'd had in mind. For a while after the wedding he'd thought he'd found heaven, where in fact he had already been on the rocky road to hell.

When he'd finally left her, not long after he'd res-cued Kirsty, Ryan had thought the hell was over.

But it had only just begun.

Kirsty had accused him of being paranoid about women falling in love with him. Yeah, well, he was. But he had every right to be. Kirsty simply didn't understand.

She'd also accused him of protecting himself more than the women he slept with. Which perhaps was true most of the time. But not this time. This time the person he was protecting was Kirsty.

Sure, he could take her to bed, as she wanted him to. Kill two birds with one stone—do his job, have some great sex on the side, then dump her at the end of this assignment. She wouldn't go nuts as Tina had gone nuts. He'd already worked that out. Kirsty wasn't of Tina's ilk. She wasn't a fruit loop.

But she would be hurt. Very hurt.

Her knowing his pathetic rules in advance would not change that.

Ryan could be a cruel man at times. But he wasn't deliberately cruel. He wasn't like his father.

So there would be no sex tonight. No doing what Kirsty wanted, regardless of how provocative she was.

But, by God, it was going to take every ounce of self-control he owned to resist her. He had never felt this frustrated. Not in years. Not ever!

Ryan shook his head and glanced up at the wall clock. Only three. He felt like getting out of here, but it was still a couple of hours before he could finish up and go home. He had to stay in the office till all his operatives had checked in. And plan the rosters for the following week.

Thankfully, their workload at the moment was on the light side. It usually was in the winter months. There weren't so many high-profile visitors to Sydney. Nor as many concerts. Or conferences. Or parties.

He pushed paper around the desk for the next hour, and took a couple of calls, grateful to hear that Gregory was still behaving himself like a candidate for citizen of the year. Finally, he just couldn't stay there any longer. He threw down his pen and leapt to his feet, scraping his chair back from his desk. With a flourish he whipped his suit jacket from the back of the chair and shrugged himself into it. Five seconds later he was striding past his startled secretary.

"Have to go," he told her curtly. "Emergency. Direct any important calls to my mobile."

He was gone before Bronwyn could do more than

raise her eyebrows and wonder what the hell was the matter with her boss today. He certainly wasn't his usual cool self.

Ryan simply could not sit there any longer in that claustrophobic office. He would go home, change and go jogging. He'd run up and down along the promenade, then do the same along the water's edge. He'd run and run till he could think of nothing but his pounding feet and the sea breeze in his face.

And when he was suitably exhausted he'd go home, have a long cold shower, then listen to some soothing music or watch some suitably mindless show on TV. Around ten he'd dress and drive into town, and meet Kirsty as they'd arranged. If things proved unbearable tonight, he'd say bye-bye permanently and get another operative to watch her from a distance. Gregory certainly hadn't proved to be much of a threat so far. He doubted Kirsty was in any real physical danger from him.

He was the danger.

He'd do his level best to keep his hands off her tonight and just do his job. But he was still worried.

Worried? He was bordering on panic-stricken, his body betraying his good intentions at every turn. He'd had a hard-on all day, damn it!

"If Kirsty gets hurt tonight," he muttered under his breath in the lift ride down to the basement car park, "then it's all *your* bloody fault, Nathan Whitmore. You set this in motion. You, with your 'means justifying the end' philosophy. Kirsty's right. You're nothing but a control freak and a ruthless bastard."

CHAPTER TEN

SHE spotted him waiting for her exactly where he'd been waiting the night before, watching the city lights and wearing another superb suit. Charcoal-grey this time. He swung round at the sound of her hurried footsteps, his jacket flapping open, revealing a polo-necked top underneath. It was black, as were his belt and shoes.

Kirsty was wearing jeans again. Designer label, and made of stretch denim which hugged her body like a second skin. Her sweater was cream-coloured, a very similar shade to her hair. It was equally soft and fluffy, with a deep V neckline which showed off her rather impressive cleavage. She was wearing a bra, unlike the previous night, a white satin half-cup number which pushed her breasts up and together, creating a valley into which her gold chain was in danger of disappearing. A matching white satin G-string rather inadequately covered her bottom, the narrow strip between her buttocks making her hotly aware of her female body underneath the tightly stretched denim.

She'd spent all afternoon preparing herself, as she imagined the concubines in a harem might prepare themselves for a night with the Sheik, making sure every inch of her flesh was prettily perfumed and absolutely perfect.

Unfortunately, the one thing she should have done she hadn't done. But when she'd unwrapped that *thing* she'd hastily bought in that creepy adult shop this morning she'd shuddered in revulsion, then shoved the offending item in a drawer.

Which left her still as physically virginal as she'd been last night.

Kirsty had started worrying about that fact again during the play tonight, and her performance hadn't been nearly as scintillating as the night before.

But as soon as she saw Ryan again she was glad she hadn't taken that route. To use a piece of plastic on herself would have been a sacrilege. She wanted to experience the romantic fantasy of Ryan being her first, in every way. With a bit of luck he wouldn't notice anything, but if he did then hopefully, by then, he'd be too aroused to stop or care.

The way he was gobbling her up with his eyes was certainly encouraging. Kirsty battened down her nerves, determined to keep herself in non-vulnerable mode.

"You turned up," she said teasingly.

He smiled a wry little smile. "You were worried I wouldn't?"

"Not really." And she reached up on tiptoe to kiss him on the cheek. "You look marvellous in black."

"And you look marvellous in anything," he returned drily. "You were also wonderful as Helen again tonight."

She was taken aback. "You went to the play again?"

"Half of the second half. I got in here a bit early and thought I might as well go in, rather than stand outside in the cold."

"I wasn't too bad by then. But I can't say I was all that wonderful in the opening scenes."

"I'm sure you were fine. Don't be so hard on yourself."

"At least I was better than Peter," she said with a little laugh.

"Peter? Which one was Peter?" Ryan asked as he took her elbow and started steering her down the steps.

"He plays Alastair. When he arrived tonight he was so stoned Josh threatened to take him off. Josh is the director, by the way. The man you gave your card to last night."

"The gay guy?"

"Yes, that's him."

"So the play's director isn't your married lover?"

Kirsty stopped, puzzled by Ryan's comment. "Why would you think he was?"

Ryan shrugged. "It just seemed likely you'd become involved with someone connected with the play. A producer. Or director. I can well imagine you falling in love with some clever creative guy."

"Well you'd be wrong," she said stiffly, nerves over her lack of *any* lover gathering once more.

"Not someone in the theatre world?"

Kirsty thought they'd better get off that subject. "I really don't want to talk about him, thank you, Ryan."

"Sorry. Didn't mean to pry. So where do you want

me to take you first? Or are you one of those girls who likes the man to decide everything?''

''Certainly not. There's a very nice cocktail bar on the ground floor at the Regency Hotel. The public are welcome, not just the guests. I'd like to go there.''

''The Regency,'' he repeated with a frown.

''Too expensive?'' she queried.

''No. Not at all. The Regency it is.''

''We could walk there, if you like. It's not all that far from here.''

''No. We'll drive. Save the walk back.''

''What about parking?'' Kirsty asked. The Regency was tucked in a narrow side street near the quay, where parking was at a premium.

''They have valet parking.''

They certainly did. And the valet knew Ryan by name.

''He knew who you were,'' a startled Kirsty said as the Porsche was driven away down the ramp.

''I come here quite a bit,'' Ryan said, taking her arm once more and pushing through the revolving glass doors into the hotel's foyer. ''The Regency has a lot of celebrity guests who require minders.''

''Oh, I see,'' she said, breaking into a relieved smile. ''You come here a lot for your *work*.'' For a moment there she'd thought something else.

''And you?'' he asked. ''Do you come here a lot? To the cocktail bar, I mean,'' he added on a droll tone.

''Hardly ever,'' she replied truthfully.

The Regency was one of the most expensive hotels in Sydney. Kirsty was acquainted with it—and its cocktail bar—not because the hotel was part of her present social life—the drinks were far too expensive for her current income—but because she'd celebrated her eighteenth birthday there.

The Regency had been the setting for a lot of Whitmore celebrations over the years. Although not old in years, its decor had a grandeur reminiscent of the famous old London hotels. It abounded in wood-panelled walls, crystal chandeliers and gilt-framed everything. Her grandfather leased one of the exclusive shops which fronted the spacious marble-floored foyer, the elegantly styled boutique selling exquisite pieces of opal jewellery to wealthy tourists and visitors to Sydney. The word "Whitmores' was synonymous with top-quality opals in Australia, their speciality being the black opal.

"That's Pops's opal shop," Kirsty said, pointing to the place in question as they walked past.

"Yes, I know," Ryan replied, and directed her towards the archway on the right which led into the cocktail bar.

"Oh, yes, I forgot you were well acquainted. Did you also know that he once held a ball in the ballroom here and auctioned off a multi-million dollar opal as part of the entertainment? There was an attempted robbery and a shooting and Lord knows what else. The newspapers and gossip columns had a field-day for ages."

Ryan nodded. "I actually do remember that. Caused a real ruckus at work, because we had the security job that night. Heads rolled afterwards, I can tell you."

"You were *there*?"

"Not me, personally. I wasn't into security work

back then. I'd not long been promoted from office boy to apprentice PI, doing hack work. You know the kind of thing. Hiding in the back of a van for hours at a time, surrounded by takeaway food. Videotaping insurance fraud suspects and adulterous husbands.''

"Yuk."

He laughed. "It had its moments. Now, do you want to sit up at the bar?''

Kirsty glanced around the dimly lit and decidedly hazy room, which had been revamped since her eighteenth birthday and now had a name: Rendezvous. Where before it had resembled an English gentlemen's club—all carved-leg tables, bronze ashtrays and studded leather chairs—it now wouldn't have looked out of place in a French bordello.

The carpet was a deep plush red and the walls were covered in red and gold embossed wallpaper. The stools at the black lacquer-topped bar were anchored to the floor by shiny brass poles, and their seats were covered in gold velvet. Red velvet swags with gold fringes and tassels decorated the tall narrow windows through which the harbour lights winked.

A shiny black grand piano perched up on a red-carpeted stage in a far corner, with a small parquet dance floor in front of it, flanked by some sexy-looking booths. They were built into the walls, semi-circular and very cosy, with strategic greenery providing perfect privacy between them. The tabletops were black lacquer—same as the bar—and the seats were covered in the same gold velvet as the bar stools. Each would hold four people at a pinch. Most were presently occupied by couples, dripping all over each other with untouched drinks in front of them.

It had become a place for lovers, Kirsty realised with a small quiver of delight.

"I'd prefer one of those booths," she said, thinking if she was going to live out a romantic fantasy, then why not go the whole hog? It was a pity, though, that there wasn't a piano player, plus one of those torch singers lying atop it, with a long cigarette holder in her hand.

Kirsty had a thing for the *films noir* of the forties. She enjoyed the way they suggested sex, as opposed to the explicitness of more modern movies. Or the in-your-face eroticism of European movies.

Her great-aunt Ava was addicted to Italian movies, but Kirsty felt confronted by the directness of the Italian directors. She liked her sex dished up with more subtlety, yet with a slightly dangerous edge. She thrilled to the bad-girl heroines of those forties movies, the ones with sexily styled hair draped over one eye—blondes, usually, mysterious women who wore slinky dresses and delivered drily taunting dialogue.

Lord knows why. They weren't virgins, *those* blondes.

Maybe it was because they were what she'd *like* to be.

As if she'd conjured her up, a tall blonde in a very slinky black dress emerged from the ladies' room in the corner, undulated her decidedly feminine form across the dance floor, mounted the two steps which led up onto the stage and seated herself at the piano. She wasn't young. Or all that attractive, facially. But she had a presence, and she knew it.

After a voluptuous stretch of her arms and a knuckle-cracking flex of her fingers, she began to play *and* to sing, a sultry, bluesy number which complemented the sensual atmosphere of the room and didn't intrude on one's conversation.

It wasn't exactly the scenario Kirsty had dreamt up in her imagination, but it came a close second.

"What would you like to drink?" Ryan asked after she'd slid into the first empty booth they came to. There weren't many empty ones. The place was reasonably full, despite it being a Thursday night.

Kirsty picked up the cocktail menu and examined all the exotic drinks on offer. They had French names, each fortunately followed by a description of the ingredients.

"I'll have the third one down," she said, pointing. It was gin-based.

"Really? Okay." He shrugged. "I'll try one too."

"Don't forget you have to drive me home."

The corner of his mouth quirked into a very small, very dry smile. "I won't forget that. Don't worry."

Their eyes met and Kirsty quivered inside.

"I'll go get them from the bar myself," Ryan said. "I don't think there's much staff on tonight."

She watched him walk away, aware that several of the female patrons watched him too. A very watchable man, was Ryan.

Kirsty tried telling herself not to get too carried away with what was happening between them. He'd read her his rules. She knew the score. She had two nights with him, at best.

Unless…

Rules *were* meant to be broken, weren't they?

Kirsty smiled up at him when he returned with two pink cocktails in triangular frosted glasses, complete with decorative cherries speared through by tiny white matchstick umbrellas.

She picked out her umbrella, popped the end into her mouth and slowly sucked off the cherry.

"What?" she said when Ryan's eyes darkened.

"Nothing." He dropped his cherry and umbrella into the bronze ashtray and swigged back a decent mouthful of the pink liquid.

"Maybe you should have ordered a beer," Kirsty remarked.

"Maybe I should have," he countered. "This is definitely a ladies' drink." And he downed the lot.

"You might find it packs a secret punch."

"Even if it was straight alcohol, that itsy-bitsy amount wouldn't touch the sides of a man my size. Don't worry. I don't ever drive over the limit. Can *you* drive, by the way?"

"Of course."

"But you don't own a car?"

"Can't afford one."

"Your father could."

"Yes, but I can't." Kirsty cocked her head on one side and squinted up at him through the hazy air. "Are you trying to pick a fight with me?"

His smile carried a wealth of irony. "Could be."

"Why?"

"It's safer than asking you to dance."

"Is that a hint?"

"Hell, no. I wish I hadn't mentioned it."

She slid out of the booth and stood up. "Come on," she said, and stretched out her hand towards him.

He didn't budge. "What if I said I can't dance?"

"Anyone could dance to this music. All you have to do is shuffle your feet. Don't be a coward, Ryan. Get up and dance with me."

"I want my objection placed on record," he muttered as he reluctantly joined her on the dance floor.

"Your objection is noted. Now put your arms around me and stop whinging. Or is this rule number four? Never dance with a date."

"Actually, no. But it could become one after this. The truth is I've never actually danced with a date before. I wasn't lying when I said I can't dance."

Somehow, Kirsty wasn't surprised. As physical as Ryan was, he was also reserved. Dancing put you on show. He was a quiet achiever, was Ryan.

"It's simple. Look. I'll show you. Here. You put your arms around my waist, I put my arms up around your neck, and you just move to the rhythm of the music."

He had a great sense of rhythm, Kirsty quickly realised. "See? You're a natural." She smiled up at him, but he didn't smile back. Instead, his arms tightened around her waist, pulling her hard against his lower half.

Kirsty gulped, her smile fading.

"You still think it's a good idea I dance with you?" he said huskily.

"Yes," she choked out.

"You don't know what you're inviting."

"Feels good to me."

"You haven't forgotten my rules, have you?"

"Hardly."

"I *will* walk away when it's over."

She grinned. "Not like that, you won't."

He laughed. "No. Not like this. I should have known…"

"Known what?"

"That you'd have your wicked way with me in the end."

Kirsty laughed too. "That's funny." How often did a virgin have her wicked way with a confessed womaniser?

"What's funny about it?"

"Uh-uh." She shook her head from side to side. "Kirsty's rule number two for relationships. Never complain. Never explain."

"I like the first part. Won't say I'm crazy about the second."

"You can't have one without the other. Take it or leave it."

"I'll take it. Can't stand women who complain."

"I'll bet not too many of them complain about you in the sack."

"Don't judge a book by its cover."

"Are you saying size doesn't matter?"

"Does it to you?"

"That depends."

"On what?"

"On its owner."

"Typical female opinion."

"Are you saying all women are the same to you, once the lights are out?"

"I never turn the lights out."

She gulped. "Oh…"

The music stopped, and so did Ryan. But he kept holding her close, his mouth hovering over hers, his eyes narrowed and smouldering.

"You are far too beautiful for your own good, do you know that?" he growled. "And far too sexy."

Kirsty didn't know what to say. Or to think. How could a girl be too beautiful or too sexy in the eyes of the man she loved?

"Kiss me," she whispered.

"Not in a million years," he said. Whirling her in his arms, he cupped her bottom with both his hands and gave her a firm push in the direction of the booth. "You can't have *everything* your way. Just keep it warm for me, honey. I'm going to get myself a cold beer."

It was a breathless Kirsty who slid back into the booth. Breathless and hot. Keep it warm for him? Heavens, she was on fire!

Her hand shook as she picked up the remainder of her cocktail and sipped slowly, doing her best to get herself back into woman-of-the-world mode. She couldn't fall apart now. She had to stay cool, not act in any way virginal. But it was difficult not to be daunted by what she'd felt on that dance floor. It was…impressive.

No lights, he'd said. Oh, Lord!

Ryan was walking back towards her with a beer in his hand when Kirsty realised that one of the other women watching him wasn't just watching him. She was staring at him as if he was a ghost or something.

Ryan didn't seem to notice her at all. Or if he did he ignored her.

"Do you know that woman?" Kirsty asked as soon as he was back.

"What woman?"

"The blonde in that booth over there."

Ryan looked, then muttered a four-letter word under his breath.

"So you do know her?" Kirsty persisted.

"Yes. I know her. Unfortunately."

"She's coming over."

CHAPTER ELEVEN

A DIFFERENT four-letter word escaped Ryan's lips.

Kirsty watched the woman weave her way over. She was obviously drunk. But she had a body to die for, housed in a white wraparound skirt and a glitzy gold top which left little to the imagination. It had long tight sleeves and a crossover bodice which gaped alarmingly as she walked. When she reached them and leant forward, with her hands resting on their table, you could see all of her large but perfect breasts, plus their long dark-tipped nipples.

"You sure have a high turnover, darling," she directed at Ryan, her words slurring. "There again, with your appetite and those ridiculous rules of yours, that's inevitable. Has he told you the rules yet, sweetie?"

"Leanne," Ryan said curtly. "You're drunk."

"Yes, I know. I was supposed to meet Harold here but he stood me up, the bastard. Now I'll have to get a room for the night because I'm too plastered to drive home. Still, they have great rooms here, don't they, darling? And nice big beds. Fancy a threesome, sweetie?" she asked Kirsty.

Despite her shock, Kirsty managed to keep sipping her drink, as she imagined a forties *film noir* heroine might act. "Sorry," she said with quite superb nonchalance. "Some other time, maybe. I want him all to myself for tonight."

"I had a feeling you'd say that. You're in for a treat, but watch yourself. He knows all the right moves and makes love like a machine. But that's his main flaw. He's a machine."

"Goodbye, Leanne," Ryan bit out.

"Bye," she trilled, waving a floppy hand over her shoulder as she wove an unsteady path from the room.

Kirsty noted that the singer happened to start singing something about love at that moment. It was not a happy song. She wondered wretchedly if it ever made people happy, being in love. She looked into Ryan's eyes and saw hardness. Not guilt. Or even embarrassment.

"I did warn you."

He was right. He had. Which made her hurt even more foolish. "You certainly did. So this is your hotel of choice, is it, for your wonderfully romantic encounters?"

"Yes."

"It's expensive," she pointed out.

"It's convenient. Just down the road from my office."

Her eyes widened. "You come here during the day?"

"Does that shock you?"

"It shouldn't?"

"No, it shouldn't," he said harshly. "Where and when did you have sex with your married man? I'll bet it wasn't at night. Or even in a bed. I'll bet it was in all sorts of sordid little places."

She stared at him, hurt pushing her love for him

way, way back into a dark place where hate was just a breath away. But despite all that she still wanted him, with an angry fierceness which demanded satisfaction.

"I want you to get us a room," she blurted out. *"Now."* And she swilled back the rest of her drink.

"You don't mean that."

"I do. I want you to get us a room and I want you to do to me exactly what you did to her."

"Now I *know* you don't mean that. I'm taking you home," he ground out, and, grabbing her wrist, yanked her out of the booth. She just had time to snatch her bag off the seat before she was being dragged from the bar, out into the cooler air of the deserted foyer.

"Stop manhandling me," she demanded, trying to pull out of his grasp, but he was way too strong for her.

"I thought that was what you wanted," he snarled. "To be manhandled."

"Not that way."

"Which way, then. Like this?" And he whipped her round into his arms. His mouth, when it crashed onto hers, demonstrated a blistering hunger.

He might not love me, Kirsty thought dizzyingly as his tongue darted deep. But he sure does want me.

Yeah, sure, honey, came a taunting voice in her head. Like he wanted that big-boobed blonde in there. Like he wants all his women. At the time. But you'll go the way of the rest in the end. He told you so himself. Don't start thinking you're anything special. And don't start thinking this will last. Just enjoy him for the moment. Because that's what he's doing with you.

His head finally lifted to twin gasps. His and hers.

"I'll get us arrested if I keep this up," he said thickly. "Let's go."

Kirsty's head whirled as he shepherded her forcefully through the foyer. She wanted to laugh. Or cry. Or something. Pride demanded she tell him she'd changed her mind, that she didn't want him to take her home and she didn't want to go out with him ever again. But pride had no power against the level of excitement roaring through her bloodstream, so she did nothing, just stayed silent and went along with him.

The drive home seemed endless, and agonisingly tense. Neither of them spoke, and Ryan kept glancing in the rear vision mirror all the time, irritating the death out of her.

"Why do you keep doing that?" she snapped at last.

"Doing what?"

"Looking in the rear vision mirror as though you think someone's following us."

"I think someone is."

"That's ridiculous. Why would someone be following us?"

"I have no idea. But the same car's been behind us since we left the city. I noticed it on the bridge when I changed lanes, and he changed lanes too. He's been behind us ever since."

"He? How can you tell it's a he?"

"I can't. I'm just presuming. I'm going to slow down, see if he'll pass."

Ryan slowed, and the car did pass. The man at the wheel was middle-aged and bald. And didn't even give them a passing glance.

"See? He wasn't following us at all."

"Not necessarily. A professional tailer would pass, if he thought he'd been spotted. Then he'd wait down a side street and join in again later. Or he'd call a colleague to take over."

"A professional tailer! I think you've been doing security work for too long. Or you're being paranoid again. People who are followed like that are criminals, or enemies of criminals. Of which you're neither, I hope. You haven't been stepping on some serious toes lately, have you?"

"I've stepped on quite a few over the years. But you're probably right. I am being a bit paranoid. No one could have known where I'd be tonight. Mmm. No one behind us any more either, I see." He stared in the mirror again before turning his eyes back onto the road ahead.

"So now that we're talking again," he resumed, "why are you so angry with me about Leanne? She meant nothing to me."

"That's what I'm angry about. None of the women you sleep with mean anything to you."

"I haven't slept with you. Yet."

"But you will, won't you?" she countered, her stomach contracting into a tight knot. "And you'll walk away without a backward glance, just like you did with her."

"Not quite like I did with her. You're different."

You don't know *how* different, buster.

"In what way?" she said, wanting to hear his version of "different".

"In that I like you."

Kirsty was both taken aback and touched, despite everything. "Are you saying you didn't like *any* of the other women you've slept with?"

"I didn't really get to know any of them."

"Except in the biblical sense."

"Exactly."

"How on earth do you meet these women who let you use them like that?"

He shot her a dry glance. "What happened to your rule of never complain, never explain?"

"There are exceptions to every rule."

"Possibly. But this isn't going to be one of them. Look, let's keep this simple, shall we, Kirsty? We fancied each other five years ago, but we couldn't do anything about it. We still fancy each other, and now we *can* do something about it. And we're going to. Starting tonight. What we're *not* going to do is become emotionally involved with each other. That's the agreement. Them's the rules."

"Do you think there's even the remotest chance of your getting emotionally involved anyway?" she scorned.

"There's more of a chance with you than any other female I've ever been with. But still…no, Kirsty. I won't be letting that happen. What about you?"

No way was Kirsty going to give him an excuse to back off at this point. She was still on a slow simmer from his kisses back at the hotel. "Oh, for pity's sake, I've already told you. I'm in love with another man. I'm just in this for the sex."

He laughed. "You really have changed, haven't you? But I still like you. I really do."

"Careful. Liking me might make *you* a risk. And that would never do. Remember your rules."

"Trust me, honey, I never forget my rules. They're imprinted in my brain."

And in his body, she suspected. That was why he was like a machine in the lovemaking department. Because he never let his feelings get out of hand. He never lost control.

And yet he'd come close back in that foyer. Maybe that was what he meant about her being different.

"Belleview coming up," he said. "Get ready to jump out and open the gates."

"No need. I brought one of Dad's remote gizmos with me." She dived into her bag and retrieved it. "It opens the gates *and* the garages. You can put your car in there for the night, if you like."

"No, I'll park it out at the front. Let any would-be burglars know you're not home alone."

Kirsty rolled her eyes but decided not to bother protesting. She knew when she was beating her head against a brick wall. He was just like her father. Maybe it was a man thing. Or the result of his job. Or just plain cynicism. Her father was the most cynically minded person she had ever known.

Always believe the worst of people, was his personal credo.

She suspected Ryan subscribed to that same school of thinking.

"I'll feed the dog tonight," he said, when Jaws greeted their entry into the house with some impressive barking. "We need to make friends if I'm going to be around for a while."

"Really? And how long do you intend being around?" she couldn't help asking. "One night or two?"

He slanted her a wicked smile. "That depends."

Kirsty tried not to panic. But she got the message. It all depended on her performance tonight—rather as the run of a play depended on the performance of its players. If she was brilliant, she got two nights with him. If not, he was out of her life in the morning.

"What if you think I'm a dud in bed?" she asked, dumping her bag on the marble console in the hallway.

"I'm sure you won't be."

"Don't be so sure," she muttered under her breath as she glanced up into the mirror and began fiddling with her hair. She had naturally wavy and easily managed hair—which was a plus, the hairdresser had told her, if you were going to consistently bleach it.

Ryan watched her swiftly fingercomb her windswept bangs back into place, his expression annoyingly unreadable. What was he thinking? she wondered. And feeling? Not nervous, that was for sure. She was the one who was nervous. Excruciatingly so.

"Okay," she said, throwing a bright smile over her shoulder at him. "I'm back looking gorgeous. Let's go see you make friends with Jaws. I don't like your chances."

She was wrong. He not only made friends with the dog, but had Jaws drooling over him. Last night had to have been a momentary aberration, Kirsty realised. Bad memories, as she'd thought at the time.

"See?" Ryan said, standing right next to Jaws, stroking the dog's back as he devoured his dinner. "A lamb in wolf's clothing."

"Not like you," she countered drily. "You're a wolf in wolf's clothing."

"And what about you?" he drawled, his eyes all over her suddenly as he closed the space between them. "You're a vamp in vamp's clothing. Have you any idea how sexy you look in those boots and jeans? And that very provocative jumper? This neckline is just wicked." He reached out to lift the end of the gold chain from her cleavage, shocking Kirsty when he bent to lick the spot where it had lain, nestled between her breasts.

"Oh," she gasped, goosebumps breaking out all over the surface of her skin.

He straightened, dropping the chain back into place and holding her gaze whilst he began to lift her jumper from the bottom.

"Arms up," he commanded, and she instinctively obeyed.

The jumper was whisked over her head and duly disposed of, leaving her standing there in jeans, boots, and white satin bra.

Despite the heating, she shivered.

When his hands reached around behind her back, she yelled "No!" and grabbed them. To be naked to the waist before him under the fluorescent lights of the kitchen was just not on, no matter how much her heart was racing and her body zinging.

His eyes searched hers in surprise. *"No?"*

She shook her head. "No. Not down here."

"Where, then?"

"Upstairs. In my bedroom. Would you mind?"

"No. Sounds perfect. Shall I carry you up the stairs, or isn't that on your agenda?"

"Carrying me up the stairs sounds perfect as well." Especially since her legs were going to jelly.

How strong he was, she realised when he scooped her up and carried her easily through the family room, out into the hallway and up the staircase, heading unswervingly for the room he probably knew best in the house.

Kirsty's bedroom at Belleview had undergone several refurbishings over the years. It had been all pretty pink and lace when she was girl, then starkly black and white during her early and very rebellious teenage years. Back to a sedate blue and white around her sixteenth birthday, and finally to a classy peach and cream these days, courtesy of Gemma's personal taste.

The attached bathroom, which had also undergone some recent changes and now serviced the guest bedroom on the other side as well, was totally cream from top to bottom, with gold fittings and peach-coloured towels. The old bath had been replaced by a corner spa in which Kirsty had wallowed for ages today, thinking about just this moment and what it might be like.

Nothing at all as she'd imagined.

Inner panic had returned with a vengeance by the time Ryan opened the door, switched on the light and carried her into the room. He stopped at the foot of the double bed and frowned down at the cream satin quilt and the mound of peach satin cushions which decorated the bedhead.

"It's all different," he remarked, glancing around at the pale peach walls. "It used to be blue."

"Gemma likes to decorate."

"It's very nice. Very…feminine. But I'm afraid I'll have to put you down so I can get rid of all those silly little pillows and that extremely ruinable quilt."

"That's all right, I need to go to the bathroom anyway." Desperately.

"Don't go getting undressed in there," he told her as she scuttled off. "I want to have the pleasure of doing that."

Gulping, Kirsty dashed into the bathroom.

Ryan frowned when she banged the door shut behind her. Surely she couldn't be nervous. Not the girl who played the tarty Helen with such panache. Or the girl who hadn't turned a hair to Leanne suggesting a threesome. Or the girl who'd boldly told him just now that all she really wanted from him was the sex.

He had to be imagining things. Okay, so she wasn't a sexual vulture of Leanne's ilk. But she was far from an innocent little thing. She'd set out to seduce him tonight and, just as he'd feared, he hadn't been able to resist her. Hell, he didn't even want to try any longer. She knew the score. If she got hurt, then it was her own silly fault. Not his. Not even her father's. As Nathan had said, Kirsty was a grown woman with a mind of her own. She wanted him, and she was going to get him. All night long, by the way he was feeling.

Shrugging off any lingering qualms, he threw all the peach cushions onto the cane chair in the corner, then pulled the quilt back over the end of the bed, revealing fresh cream sheets and a cosy cream doona. Four regular-sized pillows still graced the bedhead.

Kirsty must like pillows. He quite liked them himself. Handy things when making love. Pillows.

He heard the toilet flush, then a tap start to run. It stopped, but she didn't reappear. Probably doing her hair again, or touching up her make-up. It was a female thing, he accepted, wanting to look a million dollars despite the fact that soon she was going to be naked and all mussed up.

A man had different priorities.

He wished she'd hurry up.

Frustrated, he ripped off his jacket and tossed it onto the cane chair as well. He walked back to the bed and emptied his trouser pockets onto the bedside chest. Wallet. Keys. Cellphone. Condoms. Some spilled onto the floor. He'd actually brought six with him, which was possibly excessive, even for him. But better to be safe than sorry. Still, six might look bad for the first night. Picking up the three which had dropped onto the plush pile cream carpet, he decided to pop them into the top drawer of the cream-painted bedside chest.

He wrenched the drawer open via the gold handle and his jaw dropped, his normally cynical blue eyes rounding in surprise.

"Good grief," he exclaimed.

Ryan had seen the odd vibrator in his twenty-nine years, but nothing quite like this. It was phallic-shaped, yet slightly curved, made of blue plastic with bubbles all over its surface. It was around the same size as himself, when erect, but where any man might eventually wear out, this little number had batteries built into the base.

With a turn of his wrist, he clicked it on and the head began to rotate in circles. A startled Ryan was watching its amazing manoeuvres when the bathroom door opened and Kirsty emerged.

CHAPTER TWELVE

OH, NO. Kirsty groaned once she realised what had happened. Why, oh, why did he have to open that drawer?

When Ryan kept staring at her, in that slightly shell-shocked fashion, Kirsty's embarrassment changed to exasperation. For pity's sake, it wasn't as though he wouldn't have seen similar things before, with the type of women he'd been mixing with. Leanne probably owned a collection of sex toys to rival the Marquis De Sade's!

"I opened the drawer to drop a few condoms in," he explained, "and I found this...er...gadget. I have to confess I didn't think you were the type."

Kirsty winced. When the saleslady in the adult shop had asked what kind of vibrator she wanted, and she hadn't had a clue, the woman—who'd been at least sixty—had suggested this new arrival. With a couple of creepy-looking guys hovering nearby, Kirsty had quickly agreed, paid for it like a rocket and bolted. She hadn't realised the darned thing was so appalling till she'd got it home.

Seeing it in action, though, made it look even worse. The prospect of pretending she habitually used such a large, rampantly aggressive implement on herself was simply not on. It was time for the truth, and be damned with the consequences.

"It's never been used," she told him tautly. "I only bought it this morning."

His eyebrows arched. "With tonight in mind?"

She sighed. What a mess she'd got herself into!

"In a way. Just not the way you're thinking of."

His eyebrows lifted even further. He stared down at the big blue vibrator as it buzzed and twirled. "The mind boggles, Kirsty. What way were *you* thinking of?"

Kirsty closed her eyes for a few seconds and prayed for deliverance from this increasingly complicated situation. If this had been a play, it would have been a farce. If it had been a movie, it would have been described as a screwball comedy. So why didn't she feel like laughing?

By the time she opened her eyes again she'd already accepted that Ryan was not going to be pleased with what she was about to say.

But it had to be said.

"I lied to you," she confessed, feeling sick, yet oddly relieved at the same time. "Not directly. By omission and implication."

He switched the vibrator off, but continued to hold it. "About what?"

"I've never had an affair with a married man. I've never had an affair with anyone. I'm a virgin."

"A virgin!" he exclaimed, blue eyes staring, blue vibrator frozen in mid-air.

"I knew that was the last thing you'd want, so I thought I could eliminate any evidence of my condition. I bought that...that thing there, thinking I could use it and then you'd never know. But I just couldn't.''

His eyes dropped down to the vibrator he was still clutching. "I don't wonder."

"I know it was stupid of me, and I'm sorry." Tears threatened but she kept her chin up—which wasn't easy, considering she was standing there feeling foolish now in her jeans and skimpy satin bra.

His eyes lifted back to hers. "So there is no married man?"

"No. Not any more."

He frowned. "I'm not quite with you."

"You're not married any more," she explained tartly, and waited for his reaction.

His eyes blinked wide. "You mean you meant *me*? You were in love with *me*?"

"Yes."

"But that's ridiculous!" He threw the vibrator back into the drawer and slammed it shut. "Look, I knew you had a crush on me after I rescued you, but that wasn't love, Kirsty. That was just…circumstances. You were grateful to me and—"

"No," she snapped. "It was nothing at all like gratitude." Brother, was she fed up with people telling her that. "I was *in love* with you!" she asserted. "Why do you think I'm still a virgin? Because no man has ever compared with you. Sure, I've found other men attractive over the years. I've dated more than my share. But every time my date wanted sex, I simply didn't want him back enough. Certainly not to do something so…so intimate! Yet I'd have had sex with you in a flash. You could turn me on more with a single look, Ryan, than they could with a million different passes. And that hasn't changed. One look from you last night and I went to water.''

He didn't say a single word. But she could see those rules of his revolving around in his head.

''Am I still in love with you? You're asking yourself,'' she went on bravely. ''Last night, I would have said definitely yes. Tonight, I'm not quite so sure. What I do know for certain is that I want you to make love to me more than anything else in the world. But whether you do or not is up to you.''

Up to him.

Ryan tried to get his head around what Kirsty had just told him, but he was having a great deal of difficulty. All he could think of was that Nathan had been right after all. His daughter *was* a virgin. Worse, she imagined she might be in love with him.

Which meant making love to her *was* out of the question. Hell, it blew his rules right out of the water!

Yet he wanted to. More than ever.

Which was perverse.

''I'm not trying to trap you,'' she babbled on, standing there with her hands clasped—yes, like a virgin—in front of her semi-naked breasts. ''Even if I decide I am in love with you afterwards, I won't start stupidly hoping you'll fall in love with me and want to marry me. I mean…look, don't get me wrong. I wouldn't *mind* if you fell in love with me. But I won't have a nervous breakdown if you don't. If it helps, I'm not interested in getting married at all. Not for a long time, anyway. I'm young, and my career has just got off the ground. The thing is, Ryan, I just want…*you*.''

He looked at her glittering green eyes and softly parted lips and understood exactly what she wanted. She'd been right when she'd said it earlier. Sex. That was what she wanted, and needed. Hell, why not? She *was* young, and healthy, and her hormones had to be raging.

But she wasn't really in love with him. How could she be? She didn't even know him. All she knew was the hero he'd appeared to be at a vulnerable point in her life. She'd woven silly romantic dreams around him, then somehow kept them alive, spurning the attentions of other men in favour of clinging to a fantasy.

Till fate had made their paths cross again. And her fantasy was suddenly within reach. Bingo!

The trouble was, by telling him the truth just now she'd become *his* fantasy.

What man hadn't dreamt at some time about having a beautiful young woman crazily in love with him? A beautiful *untouched* young woman, ready and willing to give him her virginal body to be enjoyed and erotically enlightened. Ryan gazed upon Kirsty's lush loveliness and thought of the satisfaction of being her first lover, of *knowing* he could give her pleasure such as she'd never had before.

Impossible to turn his back on such thoughts, and on her.

"You might want me to make love to you, Kirsty," he said, walking slowly round the base of the bed towards her. "But you do not love me."

He saw her knuckles whiten at his approach, but it didn't stop him. He was way past the point of no return. All his rules, it seemed, were about to be broken.

Ryan found some comfort in the thought that by making love to her he'd eventually show her that her feelings *weren't* love. By the time he'd finished with her she'd be well versed in the power and nature of lust, with its many dark, deceptive faces. Any romantic illusions she held about him would be well and truly dashed.

"It isn't love which makes your heart jump when I do this…"

She gasped when the back of his right hand grazed across her satin-encased breasts.

"It isn't love which lets me undress you." His arms slid around her back and unhooked her bra.

"It certainly isn't love," he said as he tossed the bra aside, "which will find no words of protest for whatever I want to do to you."

In a flash he had her on her back across the bed and was lying beside her, his head descending to where her pretty pink nipples were already straining upwards, round and hard as pebbles. His tongue flicked out over the first one and her back arched off the bed.

She made a sound which was part-gasp, part-moan, part-whimper.

It electrified him more than any sound any woman had ever made, as did the thought that he was probably the first man to do that. There again, he was going to be the first man to do a lot of things.

His body leapt at the thought, as did his mind. Or was it his heart?

Don't be ridiculous, he told himself, even as his

hands became uncharacteristically eager to rid her of
the rest of her clothes. Slow down, he warned himself,
even as he wrenched off her boots and peeled off her
jeans and panties. Stop feeling like this. She might be
a virgin, but basically she's just another female wanting you to screw her.

But she loves you, a seductive voice whispered in
his head. *She's always loved you. She said no other
man compared.*

Just words. Just stupid, bloody romantic drivel. An
illusion. A fantasy. Only a fool would be drawn in
by them. Reality lies in the ease with which you've
stripped her, the wetness between her legs and the
mindlessness of her moans. See, look at the way she's
writhing on the bed, her head threshing from side to
side. Soon she'll come, with just your hands exploring
her. Then, when you go down on her, she'll come
again. And finally, when her mind is gone and her
body is oh, so ready, you'll have no trouble taking
what she idealistically and naïvely imagines she's
saved just for you.

After that she'll be no different from all your other
lays.

Kirsty had never dreamt she would feel like this. So
feverish and frantic. Yet, for all her dizzying excitement, it wasn't quite what she wanted. She wanted
his mouth on her mouth, not her breasts, and *him*
inside her, not his fingers. She wanted to wrap herself
around him and hold him close. She wanted to love
him with all the love she'd been storing up in her
heart all these years.

But her body seemed to have other ideas.

Everything was twisting tight inside her, then tighter. She felt so hot. Her nipples blazed under his lips and teeth; her lower body ignited under his oh, so knowing hands. She began whimpering like some wild animal caught in a trap. Yet it wasn't pain she was feeling. Not quite pleasure either, but a darkly focused tension which was blanking her mind to everything but that moment of release which she knew was coming.

Kirsty was technically a virgin but she wasn't totally innocent—or ignorant of her body. She'd lain in bed alone at night and touched herself, thinking of Ryan. She'd made herself come before lots of times.

But this was far more intense than any of those experiences. Of course it would be. It was Ryan touching her. Ryan sucking on her nipples. Ryan in bed with her at long last.

"Oh!" she cried out.

The orgasm ripped through her, making her hips jerk off the bed. Her mouth gaped wide and the spasms went on and on. Dazedly, she realised Ryan had abandoned her breast and was staring down at her, watching her.

But she didn't care. Oh, Lord, she didn't care!

Finally the spasms began to ease off, and she scooped in a much needed breath. Ryan immediately moved her again, up and around into the bed, with her head on the pillows, her arms flopping wide. His mouth dropped back to her breasts, but it didn't stay there. It travelled downwards, and so did he, his hands trailing over her ribs, her stomach, till finally they were back between her legs.

But this time his lips had followed.

Kirsty almost jack-knifed off the bed when his tongue flicked over her exquisitely swollen clitoris.

"No," she gasped, but he ignored her and did it again, then again. His fingers slid back inside her as well, deeper this time, exploring, stroking. And amazingly she was back there, in that pre-orgasmic maelstrom, desperate for release once more.

When his tongue began to lick her, like a cat licking up cream, her whole insides contracted and her hands clutched at the bedding. She was going to come again. She couldn't stop it. She couldn't...

He'd been right, he thought as he felt her shudder and shake once more. She wasn't any different.

He left her lying there, naked and open, whilst he stripped, then drew on a condom. It infuriated him that his hands were shaking slightly. But, damn it all, did she have to watch him with that ridiculous look of awe in her eyes? Did she have to seem taken aback by his size? He wasn't any bigger than that damned vibrator she'd bought.

Well, okay, he was...a bit.

Still, it was *her* fault if he was huge. This was a first for him as well. It seemed virgins turned him on. Especially ones who came on cue.

When he joined her on the bed again, he rolled her over onto her side and spooned his body around her from behind.

"What...what are you doing?" she gasped.

"What you wanted me to do."

"You're not going to do it like this, are you?"

"Trust me." Most of the women he slept with these days really liked this position. They liked their

breasts and their clitoris played with as he pumped
slowly into them. On Ryan's part, he preferred any
position where he didn't have to look into the
woman's eyes. It was more impersonal that way.
Occasionally he tolerated a woman being on top, but
not often. Ryan liked being the one in control, di-
recting the action.

"Kiss me first," she pleaded with him.

"What?"

"Kiss me. On the mouth. Please."

Every instinct in Ryan warned him not to. But she
was already twisting in his arms, already reaching for
him.

"Oh, Ryan," she cried, just before her lips found
his.

Soft, they were. And sweet. And loving. Oh, so
loving.

Was that his undoing? Her being loving as opposed
to lustful?

"No," he vainly protested when her legs lifted to
wrap around his waist.

"Yes," she insisted against his mouth. "Yes."

"I'll hurt you like this. I'll go in too deep."

"No, you won't," she urged. And her hand
brushed against the distended tip of his penis.

"Don't," he warned, stunned to discover that he
was dangerously close to coming. He pushed her hand
away and took a firm hold of himself—both physically and mentally—then tried to ease into her.

Immediately the danger returned.

Ryan froze. What was going on here?

He decided it was because she was so tight. So
squeezingly, exquisitely tight.

When he thought he could safely continue, he did.

A soft cry escaped her lips and he stopped again, which was just as well. He was balancing on that precipice again.

"I'm hurting you," he said, shocked by the whole scenario.

"A little," she admitted in a small, pained voice.

He withdrew totally and she sobbed her distress. "No, no—don't stop. Please don't stop."

"But I'm hurting you." He couldn't think. His head was whirling, blood thumping in his temples, and elsewhere.

"I'll get over it."

She grabbed him herself and pushed him in, much further than he'd managed.

He gasped.

"There," she said, sounding satisfied. "That wasn't so bad. Now do it," she commanded. "Just do it."

Disarmed by her forcefulness, and relieved to be totally inside her without a catastrophe happening, he started just doing it. But slowly. Carefully.

She stared up at him with widening green eyes, her body quickly learning to lift in unison with his rhythm, her lips parting as she started to pant.

"Don't stop," she choked out. "Don't stop."

God! How could he?

"Kiss me," she demanded, and he did.

"Again," she insisted, every time he came up for air.

But he didn't mind. He couldn't get enough of her. He wanted it to go on and on. But then suddenly her fingers were digging into his back, and she started gripping him more tightly inside.

His mouth wrenched away from hers. "No, don't do that," he cried out, his face twisting into a grimace.

But it was already too late.

"Oh, God," he groaned.

His back arched away from her and he came with a violent shudder, his flesh pulsing powerfully. Kirsty stared up at him, taken aback by the primitive force of his climax and the wild ecstasy in his eyes. The thought that she had done that to him was thrilling!

But when his body finally stilled and he returned to normality she was left with the impression that he was none too pleased.

"You didn't come," he said, as though it was the most dreadful thing in the world.

"Does it matter?" She reached up to stroke his beautiful face, especially his mouth, which had given her such pleasure. "It doesn't to me," she murmured, feeling perfectly happy and content. Giving pleasure held as much satisfaction as receiving it, especially when you were in love. And she was. There was no point in pretending, certainly not to herself.

"Well, it matters to me," he growled, and within seconds he was out of her and off the bed, stalking into the bathroom, slamming the door shut behind him.

Soon she heard the toilet flush, and the shower go for a short time, but within no time at all he was back in bed with her, pushing any protests aside and playing with her quite mercilessly till she wanted him back inside her again. This time he did it to her the way he'd wanted to do it to her before, and she came, no trouble at all, only a second or two before him. As the complementary sensations rocked through her Kirsty appreciated why lovers thought coming together was the ultimate experience.

Or it would be, she thought blissfully, if she could look into Ryan's eyes at the same time.

"Happy now?" she murmured, even as her mind began shutting down with the most delicious weariness.

"Go to sleep," he ordered, and she did.

With an exhausted sigh, Ryan carefully withdrew, staring down at her for a few moments before shaking his head and covering her naked body with the quilt. Then he left the bed to go to the bathroom once more.

Just as well she's gone to sleep, he thought as he flushed the toilet then washed his hands. He was done. Quite done. More done than he'd ever been before.

Ryan glanced up at himself in the gilt-framed vanity mirror and tried to see if he looked different. Because he'd certainly acted differently out in that bed. Hell, he'd almost lost it several times before he actually had lost it. He'd certainly stopped being the machine Leanne had called him.

Why? Was it the circumstances? Or the girl?

Lord only knew. A virgin. Hell, who would have believed it? Nathan had been right after all.

Thinking of Nathan reminded Ryan of what he'd been originally hired to—something he'd totally forgotten in the heat of the moment. He hadn't even checked out the house properly when they'd come home, as he should have. Talk about being unprofessional!

Dragging on his clothes, he padded quietly downstairs and along into the family room. Jaws jumped up from where he'd been stretched out on a lounge and came straight up to him, tail wagging, brown eyes eager.

"Want to do the rounds with me, boy?" Ryan asked, scratching the dog behind his ears.

Jaws wagged his tail harder.

"Come on, then. A quick tour of the backyard, then the front. And if you want to lift a leg do it then, or you'll have to be put outside for the rest of the night, and you wouldn't want that, would you?"

Jaws woofed, as though he understood.

The air outside was brisk, but not freezing. A cloud bank had rolled in, covering the moon and the stars. The lights from the house, however, gave Ryan a good sight of the surrounds. Nathan had pretty good security, but not enough to stop a determined burglar or a vengeance-minded creep.

Ryan had waved off his man outside as he drove through the gates earlier tonight, thinking that to keep a watch over Belleview while he was inside with Kirsty was an unnecessary precaution and expense.

But maybe not…

Ryan walked over to the gates and looked up and down the street. No suspicious-looking cars parked anywhere, but he knew that could change in a flash. That car earlier tonight had jolted him for a while. He'd honestly thought they were being followed. Ryan had a sixth sense about such things.

Still, he seemed to have been wrong this time.

Thank heavens. The last thing he wanted to do was to have egg on his face after sending Nathan an ''Everything fine here. Gregory's not put a foot wrong' text message today.

Even so, a message had come straight back that he was to keep on the job, regardless of what things looked like. His orders were to stay vigilant twenty-four hours a day till he returned.

Ryan had to confess he hadn't been too vigilant for the last hour or so. Not that he'd been doing anything Kirsty's father hadn't expected him to do, the bastard.

Muttering under his breath, Ryan went back inside and put Jaws in the family room whilst he went to check every single window and door in the house.

All proved to be tight as a drum.

That done, he returned to the family room, where he checked the locks on all the glass doors. ''I'm going to leave a light on in here, and out on the terrace by the pool,'' he told Jaws. ''You bark like mad if you see or hear anything.''

Jaws opened his eyes only slightly from where he was already lying back down on the lounge. His walk outside seemed to have exhausted him. Or maybe it was the mountain of steak he'd eaten earlier.

''You are the biggest, ugliest, laziest con-artist of a dog I've ever met,'' he told the dog in a deceptively pleasant voice. ''But I like you all the same.''

Jaws yawned and closed his eyes again.

Ryan shook his head and went back upstairs to bed.

Kirsty stirred slightly when he climbed in beside her, rolling over and snuggling up to him as though she'd been doing it all her life. Her arms instinctively went round his chest, her lips brushing against his back with a muffled sigh. Soon she was sound asleep again, her naked body pressed tantalisingly against his.

Ryan lay there in an agony of instant need and desire. But he did nothing about either. How could he? Kirsty was obviously exhausted, and probably a little sore.

Which was another first for him—caring about someone else's feelings rather than his own.

Ryan almost laughed at the perversity of life. Okay, so he'd been wrong. It hadn't been the circumstances. It had been the girl.

CHAPTER THIRTEEN

"WAKEY-WAKEY," Kirsty whispered into Ryan's ear. If she'd had a hand free she would have tapped him on the shoulder.

He shot awake like a bullet out of a rifle, his abrupt sitting up almost upsetting the breakfast tray she was holding. "What? What's up?"

Kirsty, who was determined not to suffer from any silly morning-after embarrassment, laughed. "Do you always wake up like that?"

He glared at the breakfast tray, then up at her. "You said you weren't trying to trap me."

"I'm not. But I thought you deserved some serious refuelling if you were going to be any good to me tonight." She plonked the tray across his lap, happy to hide that part of him which would become decidedly X-rated if the quilt slipped any further.

Not that she needed another viewing to remember what he was like down there. Awesome was the word which came to mind. Kirsty's body was suffering from some after-effects of that awesomeness this morning. She would have to have a long soak in the tub today if *she* was going to be on deck tonight as well. And she intended to be, by hook or by crook!

"What time do you have to be at work?" she

asked, perching on the foot of the bed with her feet curled under her white towelling robe.

"Why, what time is it?" He snatched his watch up from the bedside table and groaned. "Oh, no, it's gone eight. I don't have time for this."

"*Make* time," she said, leaning over to press the table firmly into the mattress so that he couldn't get up.

"You're a bossy little miss, do you know that?"

"Yes," she said quite happily. "Now *eat*! I didn't slave down there in the kitchen for the last half-hour for nothing."

"But I only have muesli and fruit for breakfast," he told her, frowning down at what she'd prepared.

"Tough. Today you're having bacon, eggs, gourmet chicken sausages, fried tomato and toast, along with freshly brewed coffee.

"This would kill a brown dog."

"Actually, no, it didn't. Jaws had his plateful a while back and is still doing splendidly. He's stretched out on the lounge, watching cartoons."

"Does that dog do anything else besides eat, sleep and watch television?"

"Not often. Now, stop gasbagging and get that food into you."

She sat there, smiling, whilst he tucked into the fat-laden breakfast with increasing relish.

"Good, wasn't it?" she said after he'd polished off every morsel on the plate and was gulping back the coffee.

He drained the mug dry, then licked his lips. "All things which are bad for you taste good," he said, his eyes fastening onto her with meaning.

"I know. Care for another taste of me tonight?"

She held her breath till she saw that incredibly sexy mouth of his curve into a slow smile. "What do *you* think?"

Kirsty couldn't hide her delight. Nor did she try to. "Fantastic! But no detour to the Regency first. Straight back here."

"I like a girl who knows what she wants."

Kirsty laughed. "No, you don't. You don't at all. You want to run a mile, but you just can't resist the idea of educating your sweet little Kirsty in all things wicked and sexual."

"You're far from sweet sometimes. And not so little any more. But, yes, you're right. I'd like to do exactly that—provided you remember that that's all it is, Kirsty. Sex. Nothing more."

Kirsty wasn't ever going to lie to him or pretend with him again. "Maybe for you, Ryan, but not for me. I love you."

"You only *think* you do."

"If it makes you feel better to believe that, then be my guest. But I do love you. Sooner or later you'll have to come to terms with it. I already have, and, really, it's no big deal. So you'll give me the flick one day. I'll be very upset for a while…" Like for a hundred years or so. "But I'll survive."

He stared at her across the tray. "What kind of girl *are* you?"

"A crazy one. Now, you'd better get a move on if you're going to work."

"God, yes. Pity I didn't think to bring some fresh clothes with me. Now I'll have to go all the way back to Bondi first. What a pain."

"No need. Your suit and top are hanging up behind the bathroom door, nicely steamed clean and wrinkle-free. And your shorts and socks are at this very moment being dried in the dryer downstairs."

"And she says she's not trying to trap me," Ryan said ruefully as he put aside the tray. "Breakfast in bed. Clothes at the ready. Sex tonight without even having to pay for a single drink. Now that's a trapping trifecta if ever I heard one!"

Kirsty tried not to gawk when he threw the bedclothes back, swung his feet over the side of the bed and stood up. She'd seen him naked the night before, but her brain had been frying at the time and she hadn't had time to drink it in properly.

Wow, she thought as her eyes ate him up in the daylight.

Ryan had always been a well-built man, with a naturally good shape. Now he was super man, with the sort of body women liked to ogle in those all-male calendars. Fantastic tan; broad shoulders and chest; bulging biceps; six-pack stomach; long, strong, muscular legs.

And great buns, she added to the list when he turned and headed towards the bathroom.

"I won't lock the door," he called over his shoulder. "Just pop the rest of my things inside while I'm in the shower."

"Will do."

"And then you can come in and kiss my butt."

"Sorry. I draw the line at butt-kissing."

His laughter echoed in the bathroom.

Kirsty ran up the Opera House steps, annoyed with herself for not ringing and ordering the taxi for an earlier time. She should have realised the traffic would be heavier on a Friday night.

"Hey, wait up," Peter called after her as she hurried past him. "You're not that late. It's only twenty past seven."

Kirsty stopped and waited impatiently for Peter to catch up. "Josh likes us there a good hour before curtain call," she reminded him.

"Josh can go jump. Poofter bastard."

"Don't say things like that. He's a really nice man."

"Ooh. Teacher's pet. If I didn't know it would take a miracle, I'd think you were sleeping with him."

"I'm not going to listen to garbage like that." And she marched on ahead of him again. It was going to be hard pretending to be in love with *him* tonight. He was getting to be a right pain in the neck.

Still, that was what she got paid for. To pretend.

Thankfully, Kirsty didn't run into Josh on her way to her dressing room, but Mimi gave her a reproving look when she came in. Carla just smirked, her eyes going over to the spot on the long vanity table which was reserved for Kirsty, where a sheaf of white lilies was lying.

"Flowers for you," she said in a sing-song voice.

Kirsty walked over and stared down at the lilies. They couldn't be from Ryan. He wouldn't send her flowers at all, let alone lilies. No one sent white lilies, except to a funeral.

Kirsty's stomach fluttered nervously as she opened the plain white card.

You're dead, bitch, it read.

Her face paled with shock, till a reviving fury sent her whirling to face a still smirking Carla.

"You sent these, didn't you?"

"Me? Spend good money on flowers for you? You have to be kidding. I wouldn't spit on you if you were on fire."

"Stop this, you two," Mimi intervened sharply. "For what it's worth, Kirsty, when I arrived shortly after seven the lilies were already there. Carla was reading the note, but I don't think she would have to do that if she sent them. What did the note say, anyway? Obviously it wasn't nice."

"No, it wasn't." Kirsty ripped the rotten note into shreds and threw the pieces in the wastepaper bin under the vanity. The lilies followed. "If you think you can intimidate me with tactics like this, Carla, then you can think again. I'm going to be so good tonight you'll never get to play Helen. Not at night. Not *ever*!"

"Is that so?" Carla returned, that smirk still in place. "We'll see, Miss High and Mighty. We'll see."

"I can't stand this," Mimi muttered, and started getting her things together. "I'm going to share the other room with the other girls. You two can slug it out from now on all alone."

"Please don't go, Mimi," Kirsty pleaded, hating the thought of being alone with Carla every night.

"No, please don't go, Mimi," Carla said with feeling. "We common-as-muck girls have to stick together."

Mimi looked taken aback. "What do you mean, common-as-muck?"

"Oh, surely you've noticed. Kirsty here is a cut above the likes of us. You can't hide a private school education, you know. It's there, in the voice and the manner. And then there's the clothes, of course. I've been thinking about her today and I realised she doesn't have a sugar-daddy. Just a daddy with money. Lots of it, I'd say, by the look of her."

Mimi's eyes swept up and down Kirsty's clothes, a troubled frown bunching her high forehead. "Is she right, Kirsty? Do you come from a wealthy family?"

Kirsty felt the betraying colour zoom into her cheeks.

Mimi's frown deepened. "The day you got this part you told me you'd been supporting yourself with waitressing jobs whilst you went for auditions. Was that the truth, or all lies?"

"I haven't been lying. I've done every kind of mundane and menial job known to womankind over the last few years. Carla's just jealous. You know she's just jealous. She'll say anything to make me look bad."

"So your parents *aren't* wealthy?" Mimi persisted.

"I..." Kirsty almost lied, but there was something about Mimi which made it difficult to lie to her. "They...they do have money. Yes."

"*See?*" Carla sneered. "What did I tell you?"

"I haven't lived at home for years!" Kirsty declared defensively. "I haven't taken a cent from my father in all that time."

"What about Mumsy?" Carla piped up. "I'll bet she's been looking after her darling daughter on the sly."

"My parents are divorced. And my mother's living

overseas.'' Only a slight distortion of the truth. Her mother *was* actually in New York, for a season on Broadway playing the lead role in her ex-husband's most famous play *The Woman in Black*. She'd been called in when the American playing the role had been injured in a car accident a while back and the tough New York critics had savaged the understudy.

"Okay," Mimi said, "I'll stay. But this has to stop right now, you two. If there's one thing I can't stand, it's when the people I'm working with aren't professional. I also can't stand liars. You didn't exactly lie to us, Kirsty, but you haven't been telling the total truth about yourself. That hardly engenders a good feeling with your fellow cast members. I realise it's too much to expect everyone to be best buddies, but there should at least be some respect between us. With that in mind, I'm warning you, Carla, if there are any more flowers or notes or snide remarks, I'll complain to Josh myself and you'll be the one finding somewhere else to dress. Do I make myself clear?''

Kirsty nodded. Even Carla looked chastened.

"I didn't send those dumb flowers," she muttered.

"Maybe not," Mimi agreed, though Kirsty held her tongue. Carla had sent them all right. "But you've still been a total bitch to Kirsty from day one of rehearsal.''

"I can't help it. I don't like her."

"Too bad. Learn to hold your tongue. Learn to *act*. Now, I suggest we all shut up and get ready. The curtain goes up in twelve minutes.''

"Oh, gosh!" Kirsty gasped, and started stripping.

She was ready, but still flustered when the five-minute call came. When Josh came over to her in the wings she wondered if he knew how late she'd been, or what had just happened between herself and Carla. The theatre's gossip grapevine was incredibly fast, if inaccurate at times.

"Did you get those awful lilies?" he whispered.

"What? Oh, yes. Yes, I did."

"Who in God's name would send anyone lilies?"

"I don't know. There wasn't any name on the card." No way was she going to tell him what the note had said. "How did you know about them?"

"Some guy collared me at the main door when I arrived and said they were for you."

"Some guy? What kind of guy?"

"Short. Skinny. Wore a baseball cap. Not my type, so I didn't look too hard. I doubt he was the buyer of the flowers. Just the delivery man."

"Oh."

"Don't let it worry you. It won't be the last lot of anonymous flowers you'll get sent in your life— though let's hope your next secret admirer has the gumption to send roses. Lilies are for funerals, aren't they? Okay, the curtain's going up. Now, see if you can swing into the role a bit more quickly than you did last night, sweetie. You were great after a while, but that first scene didn't quite do it for me."

The curtain went up and Kirsty scooped in some deep breaths. She had a few minutes before her own entry on stage. Not long to get herself into character.

Damn, but it was difficult to forget about those rotten lilies! What a bitch that Carla was! Obviously she must have dropped into a local florist on the way here and ordered the flowers to be delivered immediately. Kirsty doubted that the note had been sent. No florist would agree to attach such a nasty message. What Mimi had seen was Carla checking what *she'd* just written, not reading the darned thing.

But what kind of mind would do such a thing in the first place?

A jealous, vicious, ambitious mind, that was what!

Forget Carla, Kirsty ordered herself as the time ticked down to her going on stage. Forget the lilies *and* that ghastly note. Because if you don't then you'll be doing exactly what Carla wants. Letting her affect your performance. She doesn't really want you dead. She just wants you to die out there on the stage, in front of everyone.

Over my dead body, Kirsty vowed, and took another deeply gathering breath.

Time to be brilliant again. Time to pretend Alastair was Ryan once more, and that she was madly, crazily in love with him. Piece of cake! She only had to think about last night.

But just before Kirsty's cue to step forward from the wings to knock on the set door Carla materialised beside her.

"Break a leg, rich bitch," she whispered. *"Literally."*

CHAPTER FOURTEEN

RYAN knew something was wrong straight away. Kirsty just wasn't her usual vibrant self. But he didn't tackle her about her mood till they were over the bridge and well on the way to St Ives.

"What's wrong, sweetheart?" he asked quietly whilst they sat at a set of traffic lights in Chatswood.

Kirsty sighed. "It's my understudy. She hates me."

"How do you know?"

"Trust me. I know. She won't be happy till I fall flat on my face."

"What happened?"

"Oh, nothing you can do anything about. Needless to say we had words, and it somehow came out that I was from a wealthy family, which didn't go down too well with Mimi. And I *like* Mimi. It all really upset me."

"And?"

"I thought I had it all together, but Carla told me to break a leg—literally—just before I went on stage and it rattled me. I made a right hash of the opening scene again," she confessed with another unhappy sigh. "If I don't start off more convincingly tomorrow night I honestly think Josh might give Carla a go."

"Did he say he would?"

"No. But I saw the look on his face afterwards."

"You were good the night I saw you."

"Well, I wasn't tonight. Especially the bit where Alastair is supposed to seduce me behind the bar."

"I see. Well, that's a pretty difficult scene, isn't it?" ·

Ryan didn't like to admit he'd never actually seen that part of the play. He'd been outside taking her father's call the first night, and hadn't arrived till after intermission on the second. Tonight he hadn't gone to the play at all, because he'd driven down to Campbelltown after lunch and watched Nick Gregory himself for several hours. He'd wanted to get a personal feel for the man and his supposedly changed character. He'd wanted to reassure himself that the man was no longer a risk.

As it turned out, the reports he'd had about him seemed spot-on. Gregory had worked solidly all afternoon, only stopping for a short afternoon tea break and a trip to the gents. In all the time Ryan had watched him he hadn't made, nor taken, a single phone call—hardly the action of a man plotting immediate revenge. He'd knocked off at five, then driven straight home to his uncle's house. Around six-thirty he'd taken his aunt's small white car down to a local shopping centre where he'd picked up a pizza and a couple of videos before driving home again. He hadn't even gone to the pub with his uncle for a Friday night booze-up, like most blue-collar workers did at the end of the week.

By the time Ryan had handed over the stake-out to the next operator, around eight p.m., he'd felt pretty confident Kirsty was in no danger from Gregory. But, as per his client's orders, he'd told his man to remain vigilant and not take anything for granted.

"I know what you're thinking," Kirsty said with a wry smile on her face.

"What am I thinking?" Ryan couldn't stop a smile of his own. Because she had no damned idea what he was thinking. How could she? She knew nothing about Gregory's release, or about the new and unexpected feelings for her he'd been fighting all day.

"You're thinking I can't act out a sexual position I've never experienced."

"Is that a hint?"

"What?"

"Your dad has a very nice new bar in the front living-room, I noticed."

"Ryan! I wasn't… I didn't…" She blushed beautifully, her green eyes wide and glittering. "It…it was just an observation, not a hint."

"Fine," he said, rather liking seeing her rattled. But her indignant blush didn't fool him. She wanted him to do it to her up against her dad's bar. She wanted him to do it to her in all sorts of ways and all sorts of places.

Which was fine by Ryan.

He'd already decided that the safest way to conduct his affair with Kirsty was to keep focusing on the sex. There was no point in his entertaining any silly romantic hopes himself, because girls like Kirsty might imagine themselves in love with men like him but they didn't end up with them. All she wanted from him, basically, was the experience of being in love. The illusion of romance.

And, of course, the sex.

"Nevertheless, perhaps we should remedy your inexperience of just such a scenario," he said, slanting her a wicked look. "Give that scene some credibility for tomorrow night's performance."

She stared over at him with shock in her eyes. But she didn't say no, he noticed.

"Do you have a short swishy skirt at home, much the same as the one you wear in the play? And a sexy halter-neck top? And high strappy shoes?"

"No, of course not. It's winter. And I don't live at Belleview, remember? I've only brought the bare essentials with me for my stay."

"Pity. We'll just have to improvise, then. You can wear the leather jacket I've got on, plus those sexy boots of yours. And nothing else."

"Ryan. I couldn't. Honestly."

He laughed. "Oh, yes, you could."

And, yes, she did.

But once again she surprised him, turning something which could have been a dark and decadent encounter into a crazy fun thing. She alternated between laughing and moaning; between telling him she didn't believe she was doing this and surrendering herself to him with a total trust which was mind-blowing.

Once again *he* struggled to contain his own desires, only able to control himself by the use of distraction, stopping every now and then to gulp a mouthful of the straight Scotch he'd poured himself when she'd first walked into the very formal and elegant living room dressed in nothing but his black leather jacket and her black boots.

And she looked incredible. The black leather contrasted wickedly with her soft blonde hair and still innocent face, the mixture of virgin and vamp both entrancing and arousing him to a level which sent warning bells clanging through his brain.

She'd stood there shyly for a split second before suddenly laughing, then strutting across the room like a professional dominatrix. She'd marched right up to him and whisked the drink out of his hand, plonking it on top of the bar before shoving his then free hand up under the leather jacket onto her bare buttocks.

"Ve haf vays of making you suffer," she'd teased.

It really was a wonder he'd done as well as he had.

"That was amazing," she murmured with a sated sigh, her upper body still lying prone across the bar, her hands no longer clutching the far edge but flopped near her head. "Don't move. I could stay like this for ever."

Ryan, who was only just recovering from his own torrid release, couldn't have moved if he'd tried to. Frankly, he needed the fusion with her body to keep himself upright. She groaned when he reached over for the whisky glass and its last remaining mouthful.

Slowly, the blood began to seep back into other areas of Ryan's body, his legs found terra firma and his brain cells eventually reactivated.

"I might have to come see that play again tomorrow night," he said wryly. "See what you do with the opening scene now that you know what the real thing feels like."

She giggled. "My God, if I acted like I did just then, they might call in the police. I'll have to deliver a watered-down version, don't you think?"

"Well, perhaps a quieter one."

Kirsty was giggling when Jaws's loud barking suddenly reverberated through the house.

Kirsty stopped laughing, her head and shoulders lifting off the bar. Ryan was already frowning at what was not Jaws's usual feed-me, let-me-in bark. And why would it be? They'd already fed him and let him in to watch television as soon as they'd got home.

"Maybe he thinks we're noisy burglars in here," Kirsty suggested, even as Ryan was zipping up his trousers.

"Maybe," he muttered, trying not to feel alarmed. "I'll go see what's bothering him."

Jaws was standing at the glass door leading out onto the terrace, staring out towards the pool, growling ominously.

"What is it, boy?" Ryan asked, hurrying over to the dog, whose hackles were right up. "Did you see someone out there? Hear something?"

Jaws pressed his nose hard up against the sliding glass door and growled some more.

Ryan couldn't see anyone in the reasonably large area the lights reached, but it was a big block, with lots of garden beyond the pool and loads of places to hide. He wished he had his gun on him, but it was strapped under the front seat of his car.

"Ryan?" Kirsty stood in the doorway, her eyes worried as she raked her hair back from her face. Though still in her leather gear, she didn't look at all like the whip-wielding dominatrix of half an hour ago, but more like the frightened girl he'd once rescued. The thought that anything might happen to her whilst in his charge made Ryan feel physically ill.

"What is it?" she asked. "Is there someone out there?"

"I don't know. Look, why don't you pop upstairs and have a shower? And lock the bathroom door."

"Lock the door? But—"

"Don't argue with me," he snapped. "Just do it."

She opened her mouth briefly, then shut it and left.

Ryan decided not to go out into the backyard first. To just walk out there into the light without knowing who could be watching and waiting for him in the shadows would be a foolish move. And foolish he was not.

He went to get his gun first. But as soon as he opened the front door Ryan heard a car engine start up in the street outside and tyres screech as it accelerated away. He leapt down the front steps and ran across the front lawn with more determination than an Olympic sprinter in the hundred metres final, his speed crashing him into the iron gates. Gripping the shuddering bars, he peered through them.

Too late. All he saw of the car was a lingering trace of blue smoke. Whoever it was had gone.

Ryan swore, then swore again.

He trudged back to the house, muttering angrily under his breath. He supposed it could have been some burglar, checking the house out first before breaking in later. It was amazing how many homes were conveniently robbed when the occupants were away on holiday. Ryan had some theories on that, which went from owner-organised insurance fraud to professional criminals getting lists of passengers from airlines and shipping companies.

He could not discount, however, that it might have been Gregory.

Ryan returned to the family room, where he'd left his mobile phone on the breakfast bar. He snatched it up and began to press buttons. He had people to ring, things to check on and arrangements to be made.

From now on Belleview was going to be staked out all day and all night, not just till he arrived. He would have to inform Nathan of these developments, of course. But that could wait till tomorrow. He didn't think Nathan would appreciate him contacting him at such an hour. He'd send a text message in the morning. But if he didn't hear from him by late afternoon he'd have to ring Nathan himself, and to hell with the consequences.

CHAPTER FIFTEEN

NATHAN leant on the railing of the front upper deck, his arm around Gemma's waist, just watching the water roll by. The sun was shining and the afternoon sea breeze wasn't as bracing as it had been on other days.

It was very relaxing. Actually, this cruise had been much more relaxing so far than he'd anticipated. Not being able to sleep with Gemma hadn't been so much of a trial after all.

They had actually talked—about so many topics. And they'd done things together. Gambled in the casino last night. Been to the on-board movies twice already—something they hadn't done together in ages. They'd exercised on his-and-hers stairwalkers in the very well-equipped gym every morning, and swum in the pool every afternoon. They'd even strolled hand in hand in the moonlight on the deck last night.

Nathan had resisted kissing her, however. Despite Gemma perhaps wanting him to.

He'd been accused of being a sadist in his life, but never a masochist.

Gemma had never appreciated the power of his love for her. Or the depths of his desires. Once let loose, they were difficult to control.

He'd been controlling them for four days now, and

controlling them superbly. But it was just as well she'd given him the green light over lunch today.

He'd contemplated sweeping her back to their suite for an afternoon of unbridled lust. But only for a split second. It had literally been years since Gemma had welcomed his body in hers with the kind of uninhibited passion she'd once shown.

Their sex life had left a lot to be desired for far too long.

But tonight, Nathan vowed, he would seduce his wife back into being the willing little love slave he'd once created for himself. He'd use every weapon at his disposal. The romantic atmosphere. Champagne. Jealousy.

Gemma had tried to hide it, but she'd been showing definite signs of jealousy over the attention he received from women every evening, either over dinner or in the various bars and clubs they frequented afterwards. As was usually the case on cruises, the women far outnumbered the men. The cabins were chock-full of widows and divorcees and desperately seeking singles, all looking for a man.

Any man.

He could have had his pick, even if he *hadn't* been rich and famous and good-looking. As it was, he could have laid the entire female passenger list over eighteen, if he'd a mind to. One little madam in particular—she couldn't have been more than twenty-one—zeroed in on him every chance she got.

She couldn't compare with Gemma in true beauty, but she was a sexy piece and she knew it. Nathan suspected she hadn't been a virgin for some years. She had that look in her eyes which spelt experience, and lots of it. She was the sort of girl who always carried condoms in her purse and had to top up her supply every other day.

Her name was Jackie. She had a slender but bosomy figure and very long red curly hair—a colour which always made Gemma's blood boil. Nathan's ex-wife had flaming red hair.

He wouldn't have to flirt with the girl to get the reaction he wanted. Just somehow contrive to sit at Jackie's table at dinner, and Mother Nature would do the rest.

Nathan smiled to himself.

"You know something, Nathan?" Gemma said with a sharp look and an ever sharper tone. "I've always hated it when you smile like that."

"Like what."

"Like you know something I don't."

He turned Gemma into his arms, stroking her hair back behind her ears when it blew across her face.

She had a lovely face, and lovely skin which tanned easily and always carried a honey-brown hue, even in the winter. Her rich brown hair was thick and wavy and shiny, and just long enough to play with when down. Her eyes were big and brown and heart-stoppingly expressive, her mouth full and lush and just made for love.

"Darling," he crooned softly, stroking a thumbpad softly over her beautiful lips. "There's no secret to why I'm smiling. I'm thinking about tonight."

"Oh…" Her mouth stayed open and he stroked along her lower lip, watching with great satisfaction when her eyes started to dilate.

"I don't think we'll go on to the casino after dinner," he went on silkily. "I'll order a bottle of champagne from room service and we'll retire early."

"If…if that's what you want."

"It's what I want."

He suspected she did, too. In fact, unless he was much mistaken, she'd be quite happy if he suggested going back to their suite right now.

But Nathan wasn't taking any chances. He wanted her hot for him. So hot that she'd combust into flames with a single touch.

Waiting was sometimes the best foreplay of all.

Which was why he stopped stroking her lip.

Her eyes betrayed disappointment when he did.

"Why don't you go off and have the works at that excellent beauty salon this afternoon?" he suggested smoothly. "I've been missing doing my weights, so I'm going to hit the gym for a while."

"You think I need the works?" she shot back indignantly.

He refrained from telling her what he thought she needed, and smiled instead. "Of course not. I just thought it might relax you. Oh, and if you have a pedicure make sure they paint your toenails red. I've always had this thing for red toenails."

"Really?" she said waspishly. "I thought it was red hair you had a thing for."

"If you seriously think that, then why not have your hair dyed red as well?"

"I had auburn highlights put in it the other day. Or hadn't you noticed?"

"Oh, I noticed. I notice everything about you, my darling. But, speaking of things I have a thing for…"

He bent forward and whispered something into her ear.

She gasped. "You don't seriously think I'm going to ask them to do that, do you? I'd die of embarrassment."

"Then let me do it," he suggested.

"Nathan, don't be so disgusting!"

"Do it yourself, then. How can that possibly be disgusting?"

She stared at him, shock in her eyes but excitement in her pink cheeks. His Gemma was basically sensual. And quite naughty, once you got her going. But she had always had difficulty coming to terms with what she wanted in the sexual department. In the early years of their relationship he'd always had to seduce and coerce. For a while, after Alex had been born, she'd become beautifully bolder, but then that unfortunate business had happened after Richard's arrival and all Nathan's good work looked as if it had been wasted.

He was glad to see that she hadn't really changed. She'd just been hiding the creature he'd created.

"No one will know but me," he said softly.

"*I'll* know. Even when I'm dressed I'll feel... naked. And horribly aware."

"Yes. Of course. That's precisely the point."

"You really are a wicked man," she snapped, and flounced off.

Nathan smiled as he watched her go. Maybe she'd do it. And maybe she wouldn't. But she'd think about it, and that was just as good.

By tonight she would be ripe and ready for plucking.

And then there'd be no looking back. Gone the nights of frustration. Gone the feeling that she might not love him any more. He'd hated that more than the lack of sex. Sex he could get anywhere, if he really wanted it. But no one could love him like Gemma could.

If she ever stopped loving him, or left him...

Nathan brushed aside such negative thinking. His Gemma would never leave him. Never. Soon she'd be pregnant again, and everything would be right in his world.

Nathan was whistling as he made his way down to get his gym clothes.

Kirsty waved Ryan off, then watched his car till it disappeared. Scooping in a deep breath, she turned and started to walk slowly towards the main steps of the Opera House.

It was just on two-thirty, the sun was shining and the water shimmering. The place was buzzing with people.

Sitting or walking by Sydney Harbour on a warm winter's day was the stuff tourist dreams were made of. Sydneysiders appreciated it too, especially at the weekends. All the outdoor cafés along the foreshores would be very busy, Kirsty imagined.

What a pity she had to spend the rest of Saturday afternoon sitting inside, being "on hand" for the matinee performance in case she was needed.

For the first time since rehearsals began Kirsty actually didn't want to go to work today. Not just because of the weather, or her problems with Carla, or her own dodgy performance the previous night, but because she hated being away from Ryan.

She'd had such a wonderful time with him since waking this morning, even the more mundane chores of life being incredibly enjoyable when she did them with him. Making the bed. Feeding the dog. Cooking breakfast. Stacking the dishwasher afterwards. Popping down to the supermarket for a few groceries.

Of course, Ryan had interspersed the housework with some seriously erotic activities. In the short space of a few hours they must have made love at least four times in various places in the house.

No, five, she amended, remembering what they'd done in the shower. Though did that count? They hadn't actually had sex as such.

Kirsty decided it did.

A delicious shiver rippled down her spine as she made her way slowly up the never-ending rise of steps. She'd really *loved* doing that to him. Amazing. She'd always thought she'd hate it.

Still, there wasn't anything she didn't like doing with Ryan. He made her feel so…safe.

Kirsty stopped with a jolt. The word *safe* had popped into her mind—instead of excited or turned on.

What had *safe* got to do with her feelings for him?

Maybe a lot, she realised as she resumed her slow walk up the rest of the steps. It was the first feeling she'd had when he'd rescued her five years ago. It was what she'd felt last night when he'd finally come upstairs and told her not to worry, it had just been a stray cat in the backyard. It was perhaps why she could surrender her body to him so completely and with such mindless rapture.

Because she knew Ryan would never hurt her.

Feeling safe with a man was not to be underestimated.

But was it love?

Her mother had always insisted it wasn't love she'd felt for Ryan but a form of gratitude and hero-worship. Ryan himself had told her she didn't really love him, that it was just liking and a strong sexual attraction between them. And Ryan was no fool.

Kirsty had to concede that the sex between them *was* incredible. But it definitely wasn't the only thing. They complemented each other in more ways than just physical ones. They met needs in each other. The need to love, and to be loved in return. Life for both of them had been very deficient so far in that regard. Ryan's maybe more so than hers. At least she had always had a loving family around her, regardless of their trials and tribulations and differences of opinion.

As much as she might resent her father's controlling ways, she knew that underneath he really loved her.

One day Ryan would see that *she* really loved *him*.

And then…then he might open himself to really loving her in return.

Kirsty was hugging that optimistic thought to herself and just reaching the top step when, out of the corner of her eye, she saw someone running towards her from the side. She barely had time to turn her head when a rough shoulder contacted hers and she was sent flying backwards.

Her head twisted round mid-scream and she caught

a glimpse of a figure in a navy tracksuit running off down the very steps she was about to crash down.

He didn't stop, and somehow she managed not to fall on her back. But she still fell hard, her side hitting the cement ridges of the steps with considerable force, taking all the breath out of the body.

She ricocheted down several steps before stopping in a hunched, hurt huddle at the feet of a very large lady.

"My God, honey," the woman said in an American accent, reaching down to help a seriously winded Kirsty to her feet. "Are you all right?"

"I…I think so," she said as she brushed down her clothes and looped her bag back over her shoulder.

But she wasn't. She'd twisted her ankle in the fall and it was awfully painful to put any weight on it. On top of that, her left hip and elbow were throbbing like mad. She'd be black and blue tomorrow. Her only consolation was that she hadn't scraped off any actual skin, possibly due to wearing jeans, boots and a jacket. Her face had thankfully escaped damage as well.

"You could have been killed," the tourist lady said in shocked tones. "That crazy guy, running down these steps like that. And he didn't even stop. People these days. So rude! Now, are you sure you're all right? That ankle's bothering you, isn't it? You should have it seen to straight away. You don't have to walk too far, do you?"

"No, I work in there," she said, and pointed to the Opera House.

"Lucky you. It's some building, isn't it? And the setting's amazing. Here, let me help you, honey. Lean on me. So what do you do in the Opera House? Tourist guide?''

''No, I'm an actor.''

''An actor! I should have guessed. You are one very pretty young lady. Oh, wait till I tell Bert. He'll be so jealous. Still, I told him not to go to a stuffy old museum when he could walk around somewhere as lovely as this. So what are you acting in, honey?''

''I have one of the main roles in a play on here at the moment.''

''Which play is that? We'll come see it, if we have the time.''

''*Sisters in Love*. There's a matinee on at three. But I won't be in that. I go on tonight, at eight.''

''Are you sure you'll be able to?''

Kirsty gritted her teeth. ''You know the saying. The show must go on.''

''Brave girl. What is it that they say in the theatre? Break a leg? A silly saying, really. You could have done just that a minute ago and that would hardly have been good luck.''

Kirsty stopped hobbling and looked up at the lady, her mind whirling at what she'd just said. ''Did…did you happen to get a look at the fellow who knocked into me?''

''Not a good look. Let me think. He wasn't big. Kinda short, actually, and real skinny. And he was wearing a navy tracksuit and joggers. Oh, and a baseball cap. But I didn't see his face. Why? You don't think he did it on purpose, do you?''

''No. No, of course not,'' Kirsty lied. ''Thank you so much for helping me,'' she said at the door.

''My pleasure. You look after yourself, now.''

Kirsty made her way slowly and thoughtfully along the main corridor towards the dressing room. It was too much of a coincidence—that baseball cap, plus the slight build.

Kirsty's heart quickened along with her temper. So Carla had upped the ante, had she? First the lilies, and now this.

It had to be Carla behind both incidents. There just wasn't anyone else. She must have paid—or per-suaded—some creepy boyfriend of hers to deliver the flowers last night, and then, when that hadn't worked well enough, to push her down the steps today. Carla had made the threat last night.

Break a leg, rich bitch. Literally.

Which was what had almost just happened.

Kirsty was fuming by the time she limped into the dressing room. Naturally Carla was already there, pre-tending to be getting ready for the matinee perfor-mance whilst probably waiting for the good news that her nemesis would not be going on tonight. She cer-tainly looked surprised when Kirsty hobbled in. Maybe she'd been hoping she'd have to be carted off to hospital. Which could quite easily have been the case.

Mimi, Kirsty noticed with a degree of disappoint-ment, was absent. She'd have liked her to be there as a witness.

"What on earth happened to you?" Carla asked.

Kirsty slumped into a chair, wincing as she propped her already puffing ankle up on another chair. "As if you don't know," she threw at her.

"What does that mean?"

"It means you'd better watch yourself or you'll

find yourself arrested. I intend to press charges,'' she bluffed. ''Once the police find the man responsible for this, and he's facing a jail term, he'll tell them who put him up to it. There was a witness,'' she added for good measure. ''One who can identify him.''

''I don't know what you're talking about.''

''Of course not,'' Kirsty countered tartly. ''Just like you didn't send those lilies last night.''

''I didn't!''

''Oh, for pity's sake. Mimi's not here now. There's no one else to hear your lies, so you might as well tell the truth. Okay, so you didn't *personally* send me those flowers. You had one of your deadbeat boy-friends do it for you—the same one who just pushed me down the Opera House steps.''

Kirsty had to admit that Carla looked genuinely taken aback. But then she *was* an actor. Of sorts.

''You're insane!'' Carla snapped, returning to brushing out her long blonde hair and putting it up into a ponytail. ''I might want the part of Helen, but I don't need to go to those lengths to get it. After last night it won't be long before Josh gives me my chance. By the look of you, that might just be tonight. A bit difficult for Helen to swan sexily around the stage with a sprained ankle.''

Kirsty wanted to jump up and scratch the bitch's eyes out, but she was hard pushed to even move. Tears pricked at her eyes once she realised Carla was probably right. How could she possibly go on to-night?

But how could she *not*? Kirsty agonised.

All these years of battling to get a good part in a

play and what happened? She was in danger of losing it. She might even get a reputation for being unreliable into the bargain. It wouldn't take much ingenuity on Carla's part for a rumour to get around that she'd fallen down the steps because she was drunk, or stoned.

Mimi coming in at that moment was a godsend. Kirsty had never been so glad to see someone in all her life.

Mimi frowned at Kirsty's teary face, then down at her rapidly swelling ankle.

"What happened to you?" she asked as she dumped her bag on the floor beside her locker.

Carla glared over at Kirsty and Kirsty shrugged.

"I collided with some maniacal jogger on the steps outside."

"Is your ankle broken?"

"No, just sprained."

"I'll get some ice," she said, and was gone in a flash.

"Florence Nightingale to the rescue," Carla sneered.

"Don't you start on Mimi. She'd do the same for you. She's a really nice person."

"Unlike me, you mean," Carla sniped back.

Kirsty pulled a face. "Wow. She does know how to tell the truth after all."

Carla's blue eyes narrowed. "I *have* been telling you the truth, you stupid cow. You're the liar around here. I didn't send you those bloody lilies. And I didn't have you pushed down the bloody Opera House steps. If I'd thought of it, I'd have done it myself weeks ago."

"Oh, hush up," Kirsty said wearily. "If we're fighting when Mimi gets back, she'll leave."

"Who gives a stuff? She's almost as bad as you, the way she sucks up to Josh."

"Shut *up*!" Kirsty screamed.

Carla finally shut up, leaving Kirsty to sink into a deep and dark depression. Not even thinking about being with Ryan later tonight could snap her out of it. She was going to fail, just as her father said she would.

She'd fail with Ryan, too. Eventually.

By the time Mimi came back with an ice pack and an elastic bandage she was almost beyond help. Emotionally anyway.

Mimi gently arranged the ice pack around her ankle, wrapped a towel around it, then propped her foot carefully back on the chair with an added cushion underneath.

"How about a cup of coffee?" she asked kindly, and Kirsty almost burst into tears. But she managed to hold it together by the skin of her teeth.

"That'd be great," she said, her voice still catching. "Thanks, Mimi. For everything."

"Coffee for you too, Carla?" Mimi offered more brusquely.

Management had recently installed a self-serve coffee machine just down the hall.

"Can't," Carla replied curtly. "I have to get my make-up on. Curtain call's in a few minutes."

Mimi, like Kirsty, didn't have to get made up or dressed. She too was just "on hand' in case something happened to her understudy.

Mimi went for the coffee and Kirsty counted down

the minutes till Carla would leave to go on stage. Mimi might have been thinking the same thing because she certainly took her time getting the coffee. She didn't make a reappearance till Carla got the five-minute call.

"Wish me luck," Carla said as she sashayed out, wearing an identical outfit to the one Kirsty wore as Helen in act one—although hers was a size larger, courtesy of her bigger boobs and behind.

"She doesn't need luck," Mimi muttered, carrying the mugs of coffee over to the vanity table, putting Kirsty's within easy reach. "What she needs is some talent. Either that or a non-gay director."

Kirsty was surprised by the catty comment. "You don't think she has any talent?"

"Not compared to you. And she knows it." Mimi pulled out her chair from the dressing table and swung it round to face Kirsty. She sat across it backwards, her forearms resting along the wooden back.

Kirsty thought how sexy she looked in her black jeans, black polo-necked jumper and black ankle boots. She wasn't what you'd call strictly beautiful, but striking-looking, with incredibly pale skin, deeply set grey eyes and a wide full mouth.

"So what really happened out on the steps?" Mimi asked. "I got the vibes you were holding something back."

Kirsty hesitated to tell Mimi. She had no real evidence against Carla and might be beginning to sound paranoid.

"Just like I told you. I collided with this jogger on the steps and fell."

"Did he stop?"

"No."

"You didn't get a look at him, then?"

"No… Why?"

"It crossed my mind that Carla might have put someone up to it. I wouldn't put it past her."

Kirsty heaved a huge sigh of relief. "I'm so glad you said that, because I was thinking the same thing but I didn't like to say so. There *was* a witness, you know. She—"

"A witness!" Mimi broke in, excited. "Who?"

"An American tourist. She said it was some guy wearing a baseball cap. You know, Josh told me the chap who delivered the lilies last night wore a baseball cap."

"Really? That does sound suspicious. But it's hardly conclusive. I mean…there's nothing much you can really do."

"No."

"Of course the one thing you *can* do is not let Carla win."

"Meaning?"

"You go on tonight regardless."

"I can't go on wearing that big bandage and limping all over the stage."

"No, you certainly can't. So we won't strap your ankle up till after the performance tonight. Meanwhile you keep the ice on it, and an hour before you go on you pop a couple of strong painkillers."

"But I don't have any strong painkillers. I never take anything stronger than paracetamol."

"I've got some. My doctor prescribed them for me. I have a damaged disc in my back which bothers me sometimes."

"What are they?"

"Strong," Mimi said with a dry smile. "Trust me, for several hours you won't feel that ankle one little bit."

"I...I don't like taking anything prescribed for someone else."

Mimi's eyes hardened, giving Kirsty a glimpse of the tough character which lay beneath Mimi's surface amenability. "Then let Carla go on tonight," she said with an indifferent shrug. "It's your choice."

Kirsty thought about the look on Carla's face if she heard she'd be playing Helen on a Saturday night.

Kirsty knew she simply couldn't bear it. She'd rather die.

"I'll take the tablets," she said.

CHAPTER SIXTEEN

NATHAN let himself back into their suite around four, happy to see that Gemma was still out. But when he went to open the bathroom door it was locked.

"Who is it?" Gemma squeaked in a panicky voice on hearing the rattling knob.

"It's just me," Nathan returned. "Let me in."

"I'm in the bath."

"So? I've seen you in the bath before." Though not for quite a long time. "I need to have a shower. I'm all hot and sweaty from the gym."

"Well, you *can't* come in," she called back, defiance now in her voice. "You'll just have to wait till I'm finished."

Nathan's eyebrows lifted. Finished what, exactly. Dared he hope she was doing what he'd suggested?

The thought thrilled him. Only a woman in love would do that for her man.

Or a woman in lust, came another less thrilling reason.

Gemma *was* getting to that age where sex could be a powerful force in a woman. Maybe he'd unleashed that force in her on this cruise with all his clever little strategies. Maybe she didn't really love him after all. She just wanted release from her escalating frustrations.

After all, if he'd thought their sex life hadn't been much to rave about for years, then she must be feeling the same. Since Gemma was not the sort of woman to be unfaithful, then he, as her husband, was the only man she could use to vent her frustrations on.

The thought of being used did not sit well on Nathan.

"How long will you be?" he asked sharply, his earlier happy mood deteriorating.

"A while," she returned, much more coolly. "Go sit on the balcony for a while. Have a drink or something."

A drink was a damned good idea, Nathan thought grumpily, and poured himself a Scotch from the mini-bar. He was adding ice from the freezer tray when he remembered he hadn't checked his message bank all day.

Putting the glass down, he hurried to retrieve his phone from the bedside chest and pressed the appropriate buttons. Ryan's very brief text message jumped out at him and Nathan swore.

"How long do you think you'll be?" he called out again to Gemma through the bathroom door again. "Give me a rough idea."

"For heaven's sake, Nathan, why didn't you have a shower at the gym? They have plenty there. I'll be quite some time yet. Ten, fifteen minutes, maybe."

"Fine. Just wanted to know. I'll go have that drink you suggested."

"Have two," she snapped.

Nathan left the drink untouched, however, and dashed out onto the balcony, dialling Ryan's home number first. It was Saturday, after all.

He answered on the fourth ring.

"Ryan Harris."

"Nathan. You said to call. Has something happened?"

"Not exactly. But I think there was an intruder in the grounds of Belleview last night."

"You *think*? What does that mean?"

"Jaws was growling and—"

Nathan cut him off with a laugh. "That dog growls at his own shadow."

"Not this time. There was a car parked out in the street which took off as soon as I went outside."

Nathan didn't like the sound of that, and said so.

"I agree," Ryan said. "I want to put a watch on Belleview twenty-four hours a day. Just for the time you're away. But I needed to ask you first. You're already spending a small fortune and it'll be expensive."

"Hang the expense. Do it."

"I also want to get Kirsty away from Belleview for a couple of days."

Nathan frowned. "But...where? I mean...what will you tell her?"

"That I'd like her to come stay at my place for the rest of the weekend."

"And she'll agree to that?"

"Yes. Provided I bring Jaws with us."

"And you think he'll go as well? Don't forget I told you he doesn't travel well."

"I'll use a closed-in van instead of a car. And he'll be able to sit with us all the time. Jaws and I have become quite good friends."

"And Kirsty?"

"We're *more* than good friends."

No news could have made Nathan happier.

"Splendid," he said, smiling.

"You might like to know there was no affair with any married man. She meant me."

"Ahh. Now everything makes sense. That's good,' then. *Isn't* it?" he added when Ryan remained silent.

"It's flattering, I guess. But I still don't feel happy about deceiving her over the reasons behind our meeting up again. Still, it's too late now. If I tell her the truth she'll think I'm a creep."

"She would never think you a creep, Ryan. But you're right. Telling women the truth can be hazardous if it's something they won't want to hear. And, let's face it, Kirsty is not going to want to hear about Nick Gregory being out of jail, or that I hired you to protect her. Best let her believe what she's always believed about you."

"Which is what?"

"That you're her own personal and private hero. Which you obviously still are. No other man has gotten to first base with her before, as I'm sure you are now aware."

"I'm no hero and you know it," Ryan said sharply. "I'm just a man."

"A man my daughter loves."

"*Thinks* she loves."

Nathan heard the cynicism in Ryan's voice and understood it. It was exactly how he'd felt about Gemma's feelings for him to begin with. That was the one drawback with virgins. You never could be quite sure if it was the real you they loved, or just the fact you were their first lover.

"I know how you must feel," he said with a sigh. "She's young and inexperienced. And— Oh-oh."

"What?"

"Christ."

"What's going on?"

"Gemma's just come out of the bathroom."

"And she's seen you talking to me?"

"Spot-on," Nathan bit out, his mind whirring.

"Just do what you always do, then," Ryan said drily. "Lie." And he hung up.

Nathan stared down at the dead phone for a few seconds in amazement. That son of a bitch—having the hide to speak to him like that. And then to hang up.

Kirsty would have her hands full with the likes of him.

But Kirsty was the least of Nathan's worries at that moment.

Gemma was already crossing the room, staring at him through the glass doors, her expression half-curious, half-disbelieving.

Nathan slipped his mobile into his tracksuit pants pocket and had his story at the ready by the time she slid back the glass door and stepped out onto the balcony.

The sea breeze immediately whipped apart the ivory silk dressing gown she was wearing, and not even a desperate lunge by his wife's hands could prevent him from seeing that she was totally nude underneath. And he meant...*totally* nude.

Nathan swallowed.

"Who were you calling?" she asked, one hand

clutching the sides of the robe together whilst the other tried to hold her hair in place.

Clearly she'd had it done at the salon earlier, up into that sexy tousled style which probably took ages to do but always looked as if they'd just shoved a few pins in. Her nails were red, Nathan noted as well. Fingers and toes. Nathan immediately knew he could not wait for tonight.

It had to be much sooner than that.

"It wasn't the boys, was it?" she went on with a frown before he could launch into his excuse. "You made *me* agree not to contact anyone onshore while we're away. You said we both needed a total break from everyone and everything."

"Very true. And, no, it wasn't the boys. Or family at all. Just a business colleague of mine telling me of an unexpected development and wanting a decision."

"So are you saying *he* called *you*? I didn't hear any ring."

"No, he sent me a text message on my mobile to call him ASAP, so I did. I left my mobile number with various people in case of any emergency."

"Really. So who's *he*? Your accountant? Solicitor? Bank manager? Broker? Who? Give him a name, Nathan," she finished, suspicion written all over her.

"It was Zachary, if you must know. He promised to look after things for me while I was away, but something came up and he wanted to check with me first before he took the appropriate action."

"What, exactly?"

"Gemma, for pity's sake, you won't understand it. It's business."

Her eyes flashed fury at him. "I want to know what

was so important that Zachary couldn't attend to it for a few miserable days. Or wasn't he smart enough, in your humble opinion, to understand your business either?''

Nathan could not believe how difficult he was finding it to lie to her. But it had to be done. Especially now, at this moment, with his flesh on the rise and his desires about to run riot.

''Some shares we own in one of those new Internet companies have dropped alarmingly,'' he invented. ''He wanted to know whether to sell or not.''

She blinked, her shoulders sagging from where she'd been holding them in tense rebellion. ''Oh. Is that all? And what did you tell him?''

''Sell, of course.''

''And have we lost a lot of money?''

''Not enough to worry your pretty little head about,'' he said, prying her hands away from her robe and hair and letting the breeze have its wicked way with her.

''Nathan!'' she gasped, glancing frantically around in case there were any people on the neighbouring balconies.

He solved any possible problem by pulling her into his arms, thereby hiding any exposure of full-frontal nudity.

''Put your arms up around my neck,'' he said, and she did.

His own hands curved over her silk-encased buttocks and he kissed her, hard, his fingertips digging into the peach-shaped globes whilst he rubbed his erection against the soft swell of her stomach.

''I can't wait till tonight,'' he murmured harshly

against her mouth when he came up for air. "Inside," he ordered thickly, and bundled her back into the bedroom.

"No," she moaned when he pushed her back across the bed and started to unsash her robe. She actually grabbed his wrists and tried to stop him.

"Don't be silly," he said, gently but firmly putting her hands aside, then peeling the robe back so that he could see what she looked like.

Because he knew she *wanted* his eyes on her. *And* his hands. *And* his mouth.

His gut crunched down hard when he looked at her freshly shaven pubis.

"Glorious," he murmured, stroking her legs apart, then stroking *her* till she began to make soft little moaning noises. When she turned her face away, and stuffed a fist in her mouth to muffle her moans, he bent his mouth to her smooth, sweet-smelling flesh, running his tongue over the satiny tops of her thighs before dipping into the moist valley between them.

Now she began to make serious sounds, gasping her shocked delight each time he licked her clitoris, then groaning when he sucked on it. When her thighs started quivering and her back arching off the bed, he stopped and stood up. Her eyes whipped open to gaze up at him with an agony of frustration in their depths.

But she never said a word, holding his gaze almost angrily whilst he stripped. Their expression showed a measure of satisfaction when she saw the state he was in, as though she was glad he was as desperate as she was.

Any other time he would have gone back down on her, given her a climax before entering her himself.

But that was not what he wanted at this moment. He wanted—no, needed—to be inside her, deep. And he needed to see her eyes.

He stepped up to the bed, between her legs, and slipped his hands up under her bottom, lifting her body till he could angle himself directly into her. Her mouth parted on a startled cry when he penetrated her fully, with a single powerful push, but her flesh closed around him like a vice.

He groaned, worried suddenly if he could last. For she was just so hot, and wet, and tight.

But last he would, even if it killed him.

His fingertips dug into her buttocks as he began to move, withdrawing almost to the tip each time before ramming himself home. Her eyes widened, then squeezed shut, her face grimacing as she tried not to come. But she had no chance, after what he'd already done to her. No chance at all.

"Oh, God," she moaned as she shattered apart, propelling him into a counter-climax more intense than any climax he could ever remember. The force of her spasms sucked the seed from his body in great gulps, bringing a moment's regret that it was the wrong time of the month for her. Because surely a pregnancy would have resulted from such a primal mating.

Nathan sagged at the knees afterwards, his body slipping out of hers as he sank to the floor, his forehead coming to rest on the bed between her legs. He could not move for ages, and when he finally lifted his head it was to find her lying there, arms and legs still outstretched, staring blankly up at the ceiling.

"Are you all right, Gemma?" he asked as he got

to his feet. A stupid question, perhaps, but it was what came out.

"I'm fine," she said in a flat voice.

"You don't sound fine. You sound...upset."

She sent him an odd look before drawing her legs together and wrapping the sides of the robe around her naked body. "Now, why would I be upset, Nathan? I just had the most fantastic orgasm. What more could a wife possibly want?"

He sighed and ran his hands through his hair. "I wish I knew, Gemma. I've done my best to make this second honeymoon a success. Honestly."

She sighed too. "I know you have. I'm sorry, Nathan. I'm acting like a shrew." She scooped herself off the bed and sashed the robe properly around her. "I'm going to the toilet, then you can go in and have that shower you wanted."

"Why not have one with me?" he suggested, thinking of showers they'd shared in the dim and distant past. Not so dim or distant, however, that he could not remember them.

She would not meet his eyes. "Not this time, Nathan. I'm in need of a glass of water and a couple of aspirin. I have a terrible headache."

"When did you get that?" She wasn't going to use the old headache excuse, was she? He'd been planning on a whole evening of undiluted and very satisfying sex. He'd already decided not to go to dinner but to order a meal from Room Service, plus champagne and whatever else they fancied.

"When do you think?" she threw at him wearily.

He frowned. "You don't usually get a headache when you come."

"Well, I did this time," she said tautly. "I'll be fine in a little while, so don't worry. I won't do anything to spoil your fun later."

"But I want it to be fun for you, too, darling."

"For pity's sake, Nathan. Give me a little time and you can do whatever you like, okay?"

"Really?" All sorts of interesting scenarios popped into his mind.

"I promise."

"You know, Gemma, you shouldn't make promises you might not keep."

"I always keep my promises, Nathan." And she swept past him into the bathroom, locking the door behind her.

Nathan stared at the shut door and saw it suddenly as a symbol of their relationship. Gemma's body might have reopened to him, but her heart hadn't.

He didn't like that. He wanted her to love him, not just want him, or tolerate him.

Yet it was impossible to *force* her to love him. All he could do was keep making love to her and hope, after she got pregnant, that things would come right.

He thought once again of telling her about his vasectomy reversal, but just couldn't bring himself to take the risk. She might react very badly to his doing something again without consulting her. Far better he hold his tongue and let nature take its course. Clearly she wasn't about to leave him. Time was on his side.

The bathroom door opened and Gemma emerged, her glance exasperated. "Must you stand around naked all the time?"

"Well, I *am* about to have a shower. And I *am* planning on some more lovemaking later."

"Yes, I already know that. But I'll need at least half an hour for the painkiller I just took to work. So, after your shower, would you mind slipping on a robe till then?"

The thought that his being naked bothered her so much pleased Nathan no end. All those weights he'd been doing were paying dividends. Or was it the fact his erection hadn't entirely subsided? "If you insist," he said with deceptive mildness.

"I insist," she said.

He smiled. "In that case, a robe it is."

"Thank you," she said, and he strode into the bathroom.

CHAPTER SEVENTEEN

GEMMA paced around the bedroom, seething with resentment as she listened to Nathan humming happily in the shower.

Once again he'd got what he wanted, hadn't he?

He was the devil incarnate, she decided as she recalled the feverishly frantic state he'd reduced her to earlier, where she'd wanted nothing but his hands on her. And his mouth. And his body. Over and around and inside her. Everywhere. Anywhere.

By the time she'd come her head had literally exploded! Her headache was no figment of her imagination. It had been cripplingly, cruelly real.

Unfortunately the headache was already receding and her traitorous mind—and even more traitorous body—had begun anticipating the pleasures in store for her when Nathan emerged from his shower. She was even tempted to join him in there, as he'd suggested.

This realisation brought even more resentment, as did the memory of the way she'd weakly obeyed his other erotic suggestion. Yet shaving herself totally had excited her unbearably, as he'd known it would. When her husband had wanted to see for himself what she'd done, she'd been overwhelmed by an amazing

mixture of emotions—from the fiercest embarrassment to the most feverish excitement.

He'd been right, of course, to brush aside her feeble
struggles to stop him looking at her and touching her.
Because by then, underneath her rather hypocritical
inhibitions, she'd wanted whatever he'd wanted.

Which was exactly what she'd feared when she
came on this cruise with him. That their relationship
would revert to what it had been at the beginning of
their marriage, with Nathan the erotic slavemaster and
she his mindless love slave.

She'd broken away from his spell over the last few
years, but now she was in danger of going back—
back into the prison of Nathan's merciless making, a
dark, erotic dungeon where nothing was taboo and
everything seemed oh, so right.

The memories of the amazing nights she'd once
spent with him came back. Not to haunt but to tempt
her.

*Go to him. Take off that robe and walk in there,
naked. Now. Do it. Do it.*

"No," she moaned aloud at the last second. "Do
something else. *Anything* else."

Whirling away from the bathroom door, she spied
the clothes which Nathan had discarded earlier on the
floor. She supposed picking up after him was just another form of slavery, but it was better than wimp-
ishly going into that rotten shower with him.

Gemma walked over and snatched up Nathan's
tracksuit pants. When his cellphone slipped out of the
pocket and fell out onto the carpet she scooped it up
and was about to place it onto the bedside chest when

a thought suddenly struck. It was Saturday today. The Stock Exchange was closed on a Saturday.

He lied to me, she realised with a nasty jolt, and stared down into the phone. Nathan *lied* to me. It probably wasn't even Zachary he was talking to.

But if it wasn't Zachary, then who?

Gemma pressed the callback button and it connected straight through to the last number Nathan had called. A man eventually answered, but the line was crackling and fading in and out, and she couldn't quite catch his name. She realised then why Nathan had gone out onto the balcony to make the call. For better reception. Disconnecting, she hurried out and rang the number again. And this time she heard the man come through quite clearly and rather impatiently.

"Ryan Harris. Who *is* this?"

Gemma's eyes rounded. Ryan Harris! Not Zachary or the boys, or even Byron. Nathan had called Ryan Harris!

She disconnected straight away, her heart racing. But with anger, or fear? Gemma knew exactly who Ryan Harris was. How could she forget the handsome young private investigator who'd rescued Kirsty then been so kind to her afterwards?

But why on earth was Nathan calling a private investigator? What was going on back home that she didn't know about?

The moment Nathan saw Gemma standing there, with his mobile in her hands and that look on her face, his stomach flipped right over.

God, what a difference a few seconds made. There he'd been, so happy with the way things were going.

And now this…

He sighed. "So what is it that you've found out?" he asked resignedly. "Or suspect?"

"It's Saturday," she said, her voice trembling. With rage? "The Stock Market isn't open on a Saturday."

"The Sydney one isn't," he countered. "But New York is."

"Don't you dare tell me more lies," she snapped, her cheeks going bright pink. "I pressed the callback button and I know who you were talking to. It was Ryan Harris. I haven't forgotten who Ryan Harris is, what his job is. I want to know why you've hired a private investigator. And I want to know the truth. If you lie to me again, Nathan, and I find out later, then I will divorce you. That I promise."

He didn't really think she would, but he just couldn't risk it. "Ryan isn't working as a private investigator any more," he told her. "He's head of security at IAS these days. That's a fancy word for a bodyguard."

Gemma sucked in sharply at this news. "And who is it in our family needing a bodyguard?"

"Kirsty."

"Kirsty! But…but…but…*why*?"

He told her why, although he didn't tell her about the possible intruder at Belleview last night. He made it sound as if he'd only been taking sensible precautions for Kirsty's safety whilst they were away, and that Ryan had been reporting to him through text messages on his mobile. He pretended the call today had just been a check-in call, that everything was A-okay.

Gemma sank down onto the side of the bed, her face pale. "Are…are you sure the boys aren't in any danger?" she asked with alarm in her lovely eyes.

"They're safe as houses."

"But how can you say that? They might have been in some danger, especially in the beginning. Just because this Nick Gregory seems to be behaving himself now? You didn't know that before he got out of jail. I remember him from the trial. He was always shouting threats, not just at Kirsty but at you too, Nathan. Our sons could well be a target if he's out for revenge."

"I didn't see it that way."

She stared up at him, then jumped to her feet. "*You* didn't see it that way. My God, that's just so typical of you, Nathan. You never do see—or care about— anyone else's point of view. Everything's always about what *you* want. You wanted me on this cruise, and you knew if you told me the situation with Gregory I wouldn't have come."

"That's not fair. I only—"

"Did what you thought was best," she mocked. "Yes, I know."

Nathan prayed for patience. "You would only have worried."

"So what? I have a right to worry. They're my sons."

"They're mine, too," he snapped. "Do you think I would put them in danger? They are perfectly safe where they are with Jade, well away from Belleview."

"And what about poor Kirsty, *staying* at Belleview? How safe is she?"

"Very safe, since I hired Ryan as her personal bodyguard."

"And how did you manage that little trick without telling Kirsty the truth? Because I'll bet my bottom dollar you didn't tell her the truth, did you?"

"No," Nathan said tautly, feeling the noose tightening around his neck.

"So, Merlin the Magician, would you like to inform me what lies you *did* tell your daughter?"

"I didn't tell her any. That was Ryan's job."

She looked perplexed. "Ryan's job? I don't get it. I…"

He saw the penny drop, and the shock which quickly followed. Nathan knew then that he was in real danger of losing everything. He had to talk, and talk fast.

"Oh, Nathan, you didn't," Gemma was already saying, disbelief in her voice. "You couldn't. Not knowing what Kirsty once felt about Ryan. That's cruel. He's a married man."

"Not any more, he isn't."

"He isn't?"

"No. He divorced that tart of a wife of his a couple of years ago. You should see him now, Gemma. He's nothing like he used to be. He drives a Porsche and dresses in suits. Owns an apartment overlooking the beach at Bondi. And he genuinely likes Kirsty. They're already lovers."

"*What?* But…but…"

"Yes, I know. She was still a virgin. Well, she isn't any more. And high time, too. Beautiful, passionate young girls like Kirsty shouldn't be virgins. They're made for love. And for marriage. If my plans work out, she'll give up that silly acting nonsense too— marry Ryan and have a family. There's no happiness for her on the stage. Trust me on that. She's just not talented enough, for starters. Believe me, the last thing in the world I ever wanted was for my daughter to become an actor, like her mother. I—''

Nathan broke off, sensing all of a sudden that his explanations weren't working in his favour. Gemma was beginning to look at him not as if he was a magician, but a monster.

"You just don't understand, do you?" she said, shaking her head at him. "It's not about what *you* want, Nathan, but about what Kirsty wants. And she *wants* to be an actor."

Nathan did what he'd used to do when they were first married and he'd felt Gemma slipping away from him. He tried to take her into his arms.

"No, don't touch me," she snapped, shrugging him off. "I can't bear for you to touch me."

"But you promised," he reminded her, anger and frustration heating his blood.

"Well, that was before I knew about this. So I'm breaking my promise."

Nathan clenched his teeth down hard in his jaw. She couldn't knock him back. Not tonight. Not now. He loved her and he needed her. Didn't she understand that?

"I don't think that's a very good idea, Gemma," he bit out.

"Why? What are you going to do about it? Rape me, like you did once before?"

*   *   *

The moment the ugly words were out of her mouth Gemma regretted them.

Nathan rocked backwards, almost as though she had physically hit him. His face went an ashen grey and the lights in his eyes went out. He stared at her for what felt like ages.

"It's over, isn't it?" he said at last, his voice cold and dead. "Our marriage. It's over."

Gemma wanted to cry. Because he was right. It had been over the day he'd had that vasectomy. Yet his actually saying so sent shockwaves through her body.

"I…I think a separation might be a good idea," she said shakily. "I do need a little space."

He laughed. "Space. Can't stand that weak word. Why not just say it as it is? You don't love me any more and you want a divorce."

His aggression fired up some much-needed spirit. "All right. I want a divorce."

"So be it. I'll get dressed, then give you some of that much-needed space you want. I'm sure they'll be able to find me another cabin for the rest of the cruise. You can stay in here and sulk like the child you still are."

"There's no need to insult me."

"There's every need. Why do you think I keep things from you? Because you can't handle the truth."

"I can so!"

"Can you? Then here's some home truths for you. You knew what I was when you married me, Gemma. You knew my faults and my flaws. I'm not perfect. But I have always, *always* loved you. You told me once that you would always love *me*, and I foolishly believed you. Now I find out that you never really loved me at all! The fears I held for our relationship right at the beginning have been finally proven. All you wanted from me back then was sex.''

"That's not true!'' she denied.

"You're quite right. That's not true. After a while you wanted something else. My sperm. No wonder our relationship foundered when I cut that off. But don't think I couldn't still seduce you, little girl, if I wanted to. I could have you flat on your back and begging in no time. Or up on your hands and knees. You always did like it that way, didn't you? Once you got over your pretend shyness.''

His steely eyes locked onto hers and she shivered.

"But you know what? That kind of seduction no longer has any appeal for me. For one thing you might accuse me of rape afterwards. I have a hankering for a partner who actually *wants* me to make love to her. Who welcomes my advances and even makes some of her own. In short, my darling wife, I don't want you.''

Gemma stood there, shaking like a leaf, whilst her husband dragged his black dinner suit out of the built-in closet and dressed. Swiftly. Elegantly. His black bow tie done up, he strode into the bathroom and combed his hair, before spraying on some of his very expensive cologne.

She watched him with a drying mouth, unable to believe this was happening. He was leaving her. Not only leaving her, but leaving her to go and make love to another woman.

"Don't do this, Nathan,'' she cried after him as he stalked towards the door.

He wrenched at the door, then stopped to glare over his shoulder at her. "Don't do what?"

"Sleep with that awful Jackie girl just to hurt me."

He laughed. "Is that what you think I'm going to do?"

"I *know* that's what you're going to do."

He shot her one of those awful smiles which she hated. "And will my doing that hurt you?" he asked coolly.

"Yes." It was a cry, and a plea.

"Good," he snarled, and slammed the door after him.

CHAPTER EIGHTEEN

RYAN'S phone rang again half an hour later. Was it Nathan's wife again? Would she actually speak to him this time? Or change her mind again?

Those two calls had definitely come from Nathan's mobile phone. But it hadn't been Nathan on the other end. It had been a woman. He had heard her breathing. If there was one thing Ryan was familiar with, it was women breathing on the other end of a phone.

Ryan decided that if Mrs Whitmore was checking up on her husband's calls then best he didn't answer it.

But the damned phone just kept on ringing.

Oh, what the hell! It wasn't *his* fault if Nathan was lying to his wife.

Scowling, he strode into his living room and snatched up the receiver. "Ryan Harris," he said sharply.

"Ryan. It's Kirsty. What is it? You sound angry."

Relief and pleasure washed through him like a cleansing wave. "Not with you, sweetheart. It's just that I've had a couple of weirdo calls this afternoon. Ones where no one says anything when you answer."

"Probably a wrong number," Kirsty suggested, "and they were too embarrassed to say so."

"Yes. You could be right. So what's up? Do you want me to come to the play tonight after all?"

"No! No, please don't. I might get nervous if I know you're in the audience."

He laughed. "But I did so want to see that first scene, with you and Pretty Boy up behind the bar."

"Oh, God, don't remind me. Please don't come, Ryan," she begged.

"And don't *you*," he teased.

"Ryan, don't be wicked! As if I would. Or could, without you."

"You said you were going to pretend he was me."

"Yes, but that's not the same as *being* you. And it's all just simulated, you know. He doesn't even really touch me with his...er...um...thingummy."

"Dick, darling. The word you're looking for is dick. And he'd better not."

"Ooh. You're jealous. That's sweet."

He *was* jealous, too. Yet he hated jealousy. It was such a destructive emotion if it got out of hand. But a little jealousy was comforting. And telling. Kirsty had been jealous of Leanne the other night. And he'd liked it a lot. Unlike his responses to his ex's maniacal over-possessiveness. She'd driven him crazy with her jealous tantrums and off-the-wall accusations.

Still, Kirsty was nothing like Tina—for which he was eternally grateful.

"So we'll meet around the same time, same place?" he said.

"Yes. Yes, I suppose so."

"You *suppose* so? Kirsty, what aren't you telling me?"

"Well, the thing is, Ryan, I...I tripped on the

Opera House steps this afternoon and fell over. I...I've sprained my ankle.''

''You poor thing. Why didn't you say so straight away? That's why you rang, isn't it? To tell me you're a clumsy clot. I'll bet you were running.''

''Well...''

''Those steps are not made for running up *or* down. Will you be able to go on tonight?''

''Wild horses won't stop me!''

He smiled at the determination in her voice. ''That's my girl. Okay, so this is the situation. You're still going on, I'm not to come see you in the play, and you'll be hobbling out to our usual spot afterwards for me to carry you down to the car.''

''Would you do that?''

''Wild horses won't stop me,'' he said softly, and she sighed.

''My hero.''

Ryan wished she hadn't said that. He was far from being her hero.

''I've been thinking, Kirsty, if we bring Jaws with us, would you like to spend a few days over at my place at Bondi?''

''Oh, wow, I'd love that. But I'm not sure you'll be able to coerce Jaws into your car. He has a problem with travelling. Has to be dragged in, even with Gemma behind the wheel.''

Ryan gnawed at his bottom lip. He'd almost forgotten that he wasn't supposed to know about the dog's road paranoia. He'd almost put his foot in it then.

''I see,'' he said, pretending this was new news. ''Look, we have several closed vans at work which we use for spying operations, all with lounge-like seats in the back and blacked-out windows. I'll bring one with me tonight, instead of my car. And I'll pop in my spare portable TV. That way Jaws will hardly know he's on the move. He'll think it's a home away from home—especially if you sit with him and tickle him behind the ears all the way.''

''You know, I think that just might work.''

''Of course it will work. And, once there, the wicked Black Prince is going to carry the beautiful blonde princess into his boudoir and consign her faithful pet to his place on the leather lounge in front of the television whilst he ravishes said princess for days on end.''

She laughed. ''That sounds lovely, Ryan, but Josh wants us in here first thing Tuesday morning for some directorial nitpicking. We've all been a bit hit and miss so far with our performances and I think he's going to read us the riot act.''

''That still gives us tonight, all Sunday and daytime Monday. I'll take Monday off work.''

''Can you do that?''

''Of course I can. I'm the boss. Besides, I can see to most things via my mobile. They can call me in if there's a real emergency. I don't live far away from the city, do I?''

''No. I...er...I have to go now, Ryan, The matinee's finishing and I have to get a new ice pack for my ankle. This one's melting.''

''Sounds pretty bad, Kirsty. Are you sure you should go on?''

''I'm positive! Oh, and don't worry if I'm a little bit late getting out to you tonight. Mimi is going to strap my ankle up afterwards, and of course I will be hobbling, not hurrying.''

''Can I come inside and carry you from wherever you do the strapping up?''

''Lord, no, I'll never hear the end of it. No, I'll be fine. Just don't think I'm not coming and go home without me.''

''As if I would. Bye, sweetheart—and, please… take it easy on that ankle.''

''I will. B…bye.''

She hung up, leaving Ryan frowning down into the receiver. She'd sounded quite shaky at the end there. Teary, even.

Still, sprained ankles could be very painful. He'd done a few in himself during his martial arts training years.

Ryan hung up and walked back towards the kitchen. Poor Kirsty, having to perform with a bunged-up ankle. But he would expect nothing less. She had guts, his girl.

His girl…

Ryan's heart did a flip-flop. Yes, he accepted with a sigh, she *was* his girl. In every way.

Frankly, he could not wait to bring her home with him tonight, bung ankle and all. He really fancied the idea of looking after her, of cosseting and pampering her. He'd bring her drinks in bed, rub her legs, massage her feet, suck her toes. He'd do everything he knew women liked—not for his usual reason, just to screw them silly, but because he wanted to make Kirsty feel as special as she was to him.

He supposed he could tell her he loved her.

But he decided that could wait. Tonight—and for

the next two days—he'd *show* her he loved her, in every way he could think of.

Ryan grinned as he started counting up how many lovemaking positions catered for ladies with injured ankles.

One hell of a lot!

CHAPTER NINETEEN

GEMMA lay, dry-eyed, on the bed, still in shock. Yet it was ages since Nathan had stormed out. Everything he'd said to her kept revolving around her head. His calling her childish. His telling her that she'd never really loved him. His final thrust that he'd didn't care if he hurt her.

"Over," she croaked out loud. "My marriage is over. Nathan doesn't love me any more."

At this very moment he was probably having dinner with that girl, that red-haired slut. Afterwards he'd take her dancing, or to the casino. Nathan never rushed things. He would make love to her with his eyes all evening, and with his hands. He was a toucher when in the mood, was Nathan. He'd drape an arm sexily around her shoulders. Or tightly around her waist, keeping her close by his side, letting the heat of his body seep in through her clothes.

What little there would be of them.

Then, later, when the evening was drawing to an end, he'd let her take him back to her cabin. He might even let her undress him. She was just the type who'd do that. Bold as brass. And bad through and through, the kind who gave blow jobs instead of goodnight pecks.

Gemma could see that slut now, sinking to her

knees in front of *her* husband, opening those lush, glossed lips of hers whilst glancing up at Nathan with eyes which spoke of more decadences to come. And Nathan would reach down to wind his fingers into those long rich red curls and he'd hold his new lover's head, as he'd once held *her* head, then lose himself as only Nathan could lose himself in the dark pleasures of the night.

With a sob, Gemma rolled over and curled up into a foetal ball, the knuckles from her fists jammed tight into her mouth. She didn't cry. She moaned, long, tortured moans which sounded like an animal in pain.

She was that animal, and, yes, she was in pain. The pain which came when a wife realised only after she had lost her husband that she really did love him, with all his faults and flaws.

Nathan was right. She'd known what kind of man he was when she married him. Older. More experienced. Super-intelligent, super-rich and a super-stud.

If she was brutally truthful with herself, she'd been excited by the very faults and flaws she'd been warned about. Right from the start she'd been turned on by his rather ruthless dominance in the bedroom. If their relationship had been largely physical for a long time, then she only had herself to blame. She'd liked playing slave to his master.

Nathan was right. She was the one who hadn't grown up in their marriage. She hadn't moved on. Not really. For a few miserable months during her first pregnancy she'd stood up for herself. On the surface. But she'd soon slipped back into her old role after Alexander's birth. They both had.

And whilst their sex life had been stunning at the

time, it had restricted any growth between them as a couple in other areas. Gemma could see now that this had mostly been her fault—finding any excuse not to accompany him on the invitations they'd both received, as a couple. All because she'd felt inferior, or insecure. At the time she'd pretended it was enough, being Alexander's devoted mother during the day and Nathan's devoted wife in bed at night.

But the narrowness of both roles had gradually had a detrimental effect, with the sacrifice of her own person and personality. She'd become addicted to making the men in her life happy, and forgotten to make herself happy. Gradually, all decisions became left up to Nathan, except mundane things like what brand of baby napkins to use, or what meal to prepare that night.

Resentment over her life must have been there all along, simmering underneath. And when Nathan had had that vasectomy without telling her all hell had broken loose. For Gemma, her whole happiness and self-esteem had become bound up in being both a wife and a mother. If she couldn't be one any more, she'd resented being the other. Nathan had deprived her of more children so she had deprived him of the one thing she knew mattered one hell of a lot to him.

The pleasure they shared in the bedroom.

Yet he'd wanted *her* today, not that slut. Wanted to make love to *her*. Wanted *her* to make love to *him*. Willingly, for a change, not reluctantly. She was the one he'd wanted on her hands and knees before him. His wife. The woman he loved.

And he *did* love her. Of course he loved her. No man would have put up with what he'd put up with

these past few years if he hadn't. Not a man like
Nathan, anyway.

He'd have walked out long ago.

But he hadn't. He'd stayed and he'd tried. She
could see now how hard he'd tried. All he'd wanted
from her tonight was willingness. And what had she
done? Thrown his desire for her back in his face.

And now he'd gone looking for what he needed
with another woman.

Gemma groaned and rolled back and forth on the
bed.

"Oh, God," she wailed. "God."

But then, suddenly, she stopped the futile wailing
and the thrashing back and forth. Her eyes shot to the
small digital clock on the dressing table. Nine past
nine.

Maybe it wasn't too late to do something, to fight
for the man she loved. Nothing was to be achieved
by staying where she was, wallowing in self-pity. *Get
out there, girl. Do something. Don't just let that slut
have him. Have some guts! You come from Lightning
Ridge. You're tough. And resilient. And brave.*

She bounced off the bed and raced into the bathroom.

"And bloody beautiful!" she told the determined
face in the mirror.

Nathan placed his chips on red, number six, then
brushed his lips over the back of the hand of the redhead glued to his side.

"That's for luck," he said in slightly slurred tones.

She grabbed his face and kissed him properly, her
tongue snaking in like the serpent from Eden.

He pulled back as soon as he could manage, his head spinning like the wheel. "Down, girl," he said with a husky laugh.

"Not here, honey," she whispered in his ear, that insidious tongue of hers darting in so deep she could have been doing brain surgery. "But we could slip out on deck, if you like."

He had a sudden image of her giving him a blow job whilst he chucked up over the side of the ship. His stomach swirled with nausea and he almost vomited on the spot. He shrugged her off his ear and reached for the rest of his drink. The hair of the dog sometimes worked with him.

"Let's go somewhere, honey," she persisted. "I have a really nice room."

"Not just yet, sweetheart," he muttered back. "It's way too early."

And he was way too drunk. Hell, he probably couldn't even get it up. Not that he seriously wanted to. He didn't want sex at all. Not with Jackie. Not with anyone.

Except his Gemma.

She's ruined me, he decided, his stomach lurching again, though not with nausea this time. With despair.

He had to get out of here.

His gaze was searching the smoke-filled room for the nearest exit when he saw her walking towards him through the haze, her hips swinging from side to side, a strange little smile on that luscious mouth of hers.

She was dressed in blue. Tight slinky blue from top to toe. Long sleeves. High neck. No bra. He could tell because there was a diamond-shaped keyhole between her breasts and there was nothing but bare flesh beyond. On top of that, when she walked, her full breasts jiggled like jelly beneath the bodice of the dress.

And then there were her nipples.

Gemma's nipples had grown larger with breast-feeding. Larger and longer and slightly less sensitive. They could take a delicious degree of rough treatment now without her telling him to stop. At the moment they were poking provocatively into the crushed velvet material, screaming their excitement at him.

She sauntered right up to him, that saucy little smile still in place.

"So this is where you've got to," she purred. "Naughty man. I should have known. And is the lovely Jackie bringing you luck so far tonight?" She directed this towards the redhead, who had stiffened by Nathan's side.

"I thought you said you weren't coming," Nathan growled, not sure if he was angry or amused. He was certainly amazed. He would never have imagined she'd have it in her to do something as bold as this. Not his sweet, shy little Gemma.

There was nothing sweet or shy about the way she looked, or the way she was acting. Every male head in the place had swung round at her entrance. And why not? She was stunning, with her hair up, full make-up on and long diamond drops dangling from her ears.

The perfume she was drenched in was pretty powerful too.

"I changed my mind," she said nonchalantly, moving her slender shoulders enough to set the earrings swaying and sparkling under the lights of the overhead chandelier.

"So I see. Nice dress."

"Yes," she said, preening visibly at the compliment. "One of my own choices."

"You should choose more."

"I aim to, in future."

His eyebrows lifted whilst his heart pounded. She was talking about the future. *Their* future.

"Nathan," Jackie said in a whiny voice, clutching at his arm. "I thought it was going to be just you and me tonight."

"Sorry to disappoint you, honey," he returned, "but my first priority has to be my wife. Now that she's got over that dreadful headache of hers it's *au revoir* to this. And to us." And he handed her the rest of his whisky.

"Actually, it's *adieu*, Nathan," Gemma said, surprising him that she knew the difference. "Better luck next time, toots," she directed at Jackie as she slid her arm around Nathan's other elbow and gave him a firm tug. "You'd have done fine ten years ago. Nathan was right into cradle snatching in those days. Although, to be frank, even back then he liked his lays a little less laid. Come along, darling…" She smiled a truly wicked smile. "I have something interesting to show you which you didn't look at properly this afternoon."

Gemma left Jackie spluttering with unrequited rage whilst she dragged a stunned Nathan out of the casino and into the balmy night air. Since reaching the calmer and warmer waters of the Whitsundays, the evening air out in deck was very pleasant.

"I have to warn you," Nathan said as his wife dragged him in the direction of their suite, "I'm plastered."

"I've been with you when you've been plastered before," she returned with superb panache. "I rather like it."

"How's that?"

"You always take for ever to get it up, then even longer to come. Just what the lady ordered."

He stopped and stared at her. "Am I with the right person here? You are Gemma Whitmore, aren't you? Wife of Nathan Whitmore and mother of Alexander and Richard Whitmore?"

"The one and only. I also happen to love said Nathan Whitmore with all my heart."

He could not help it. He almost cried. Instead, in his struggle to keep control of his emotions, his face became hard.

"You don't believe me," she said, instant panic in her voice.

"I…" His voice choked off, for fear of it breaking.

"I do, Nathan. I swear to you. I know I've been wrong, acting the way I have. I have been silly and childish."

"No." He shook his head. "No, you haven't been childish at all. And I was the one who was wrong. I should have talked to you before I had that vasectomy. I don't know why I didn't. I guess it's a normal male reaction to try to protect the woman he loves. That's why I haven't told you other things as well. I was just trying to protect you. But I can see now that by trying to protect you too much I've done you a grave disservice. There's a fine line between protectiveness and possessiveness. I'll try not to step over it again.''

''Oh, Nathan, you do really love me, don't you?''

''Love you? I'd *die* for you.''

Tears of happiness glistened in her eyes. ''There's no need to go that far. I'd much rather you live for me. And make love to me. I want you to make love to me, Nathan. Now.''

''Nothing would give me greater pleasure, but there's something else I have to tell you first. I tried to tell you the first day of this cruise, but we had that little spat and I was too worried then to tell you.''

''What?'' she said, her eyes instantly wide. With fear, he thought, and could have kicked himself. But it was too late now. He had to tell her.

''It's nothing bad. At least, I hope not. Just please don't go off the handle because I didn't tell you before now. I wanted it to be a surprise. A pleasant surprise.''

''Nathan, tell me before I burst!''

''I had my vasectomy reversed whilst I was over in New York. I found the best microsurgeon in the world and he assured me I'm so potent now I could impregnate a room full of fertile females at forty paces.''

Nathan's own fears immediately disintegrated at the joy which shone forth from her eyes. ''I think I want you to make love to me now more than ever.''

''Take me by the hand, then, my darling, and lead me to the promised land.''

Gemma had him flat on his back and utterly exhausted several hours later.

"Enough," he moaned after she'd ridden him to a virtual standstill and was even now lying beside him, propped up on one elbow, her free hand playing with him again with merciless intent.

"I never thought I'd hear you say that," she smiled, and bent to lick the tip of his flaccid penis till it twitched with life once more.

"I don't know where you learnt such things," he groaned.

"I had an excellent teacher."

"He should be castrated for corrupting so sweet a creature. Good God, don't *do* that!"

"Don't do what?" she said, sounding oh, so innocent whilst what she was doing was *far* from innocent.

"What you're doing," he choked out.

"You really want me to stop?"

"No. Yes. Ahh... For pity's sake, Gemma, I'm going to come again."

"Really? Oh, goodie." She was on him like a flash, gobbling him up into her woman's body, rising and falling on him in a voluptuous rhythm which his tortured flesh found both pain and pleasure. In retaliation he reached for her breasts, and pinched her nipples till she cried out, and came.

He came too, and it was the most gloriously decadent, beautifully loving orgasm he'd ever experienced. She collapsed across him afterwards and his hands wound into her hair, holding her gasping face to his chest.

"I love you," he whispered.

"And I love you," she panted back. "Till the day I die."

"Well, I hope I'm already dead when that happens," he returned thickly. "Because I simply couldn't live without you, my love."

Her head suddenly jerked up, her hair tumbling down around her flushed face. "That sounds promising. Presumably, if you love me that much, you'd just about forgive me anything, is that right?"

His heart jolted. "Er...that depends on what *anything* is." If she'd been doing even a fraction of what she'd just done with him with another man then she was in big trouble.

"I lied to you."

"About what?" he asked worriedly.

"About my period. It finished two weeks ago."

CHAPTER TWENTY

RYAN emerged from his kitchen with two glasses of freshly squeezed orange juice in his hands, and was heading across his living-room to the north-facing balcony when he stopped and just stared.

The sun had not long risen but it had already moved round to the north and the balcony was drenched in sunlight, the soft winter rays bouncing off Kirsty's blonde hair as she sat at the table, head bent over the morning newspaper. She was wearing an old grey sloppy joe of his, which reached down to her knees and looked sexier than the most provocative negligee. Jaws, the lazy lug, was asleep at her feet— exhausted, no doubt, from keeping up with Ryan on his early-morning jog.

It was Tuesday, and Kirsty had been living with him for less than three days. But Ryan knew, as he looked at her, that he wanted her to live with him for the rest of his life.

Still, it was a bit too soon to say that. Too soon to tell her of the extraordinary depth of his love for her. Perhaps because he wasn't used to it himself yet. He'd never known such a love existed—or, if it did, that he would ever feel it. Just looking at her brought him the most intense pleasure. He especially liked looking at her when she was asleep, naked, beside him, and his eyes drank in the perfection of her lovely face and body.

But it wasn't just her physical beauty which captivated him. It was the beauty of her bright, bubbly soul. She was optimistic where he might have been cynical. She was light and joy where he would have been brooding and dark.

Nothing bothered her for too long. And she was so brave. Fancy going on on Saturday night after such a bad fall. He'd been horrified when he finally saw the state of her after getting her back to Belleview that night. Her ankle had quickly blown up like a balloon, and all down one side she'd been very badly bruised.

Yet she hadn't complained. She'd laughingly told him that after Mimi's painkillers she hadn't felt a thing, *and* she'd been bloody brilliant as Helen into the bargain. She'd saucily added that if he wanted to make love to her he had about two hours before the effect of the tablets wore off.

He hadn't made love to her. Not that night, anyway. He'd brought her back here and looked after her instead, and in doing so had discovered how much he loved her. Sex was all very well, but nothing compared with that special satisfaction he'd felt as he'd gently tended to her ankle and rubbed cream into her bruises. He hadn't minded getting up to get her some more painkillers in the middle of the night, or rubbing her back till she drifted off again. And when she'd murmured how much she loved him, this time he hadn't told her she was a fool.

Of course he still wasn't convinced Kirsty loved him in the way he now loved her. She was very young, and he *was* her first lover. Ryan wasn't going to kid himself that her feelings for him were going to last for ever, but, damn it all, he was going to grab what happiness he could while it did last.

Her head suddenly lifted from the newspaper to throw him a bright smile. "What's the delay? Don't just stand there like a dork, waiter. Bring me my juice, pronto. Or I won't give you a tip."

"I was just admiring the view," he said as he placed the juice down next to her. "So? Where's my tip?"

"Don't be so damned accommodating or I might decide to move in here with you permanently," she quipped.

"Huh?"

"That's my tip."

"Oh." He laughed, then decided to take advantage of the moment. "Er...would you like to? Move in permanently, that is?"

"Ryan!" she exclaimed with teasing lights in her clear green eyes. "Have you forgotten your rules?"

"Totally."

She looked smug. "I knew you would after you discovered that virginity does not necessarily equate with vulnerability. Or inhibitions."

"How right you are," he said drily. "I'm never going to look at any of my furniture—or floors—in quite the same way. Anything worth reading in the paper?"

"Is there ever?" She handed it to him, drained her orange juice and stood up, no longer wincing when she put weight on her ankle. "I'm off to have a shower and get decent. Then you'll have to drive me and Jaws back to Belleview."

"But you didn't give me an answer."

"I didn't think you'd need one." She bent to cradle his face with soft hands and give him an upside-down kiss on his mouth. "Yes, of course, you silly man. As soon as Dad and Gemma get home on Thursday." And she was off.

Ryan wished she hadn't mentioned her father. It depressed him every time he thought of the way they'd been brought together. The only good thing about Nathan's return to Sydney would be that he'd finally be able to have done with the job he'd been hired to do.

Nick Gregory was obviously not a risk. Ryan continued to tell Nathan just that in his text message report every day. And not a soul had gone near Belleview since that last incident. Ryan hoped and prayed Nathan never, ever told Kirsty about Gregory even being out of jail. There was nothing to be achieved by doing so and she might put two and two together and get five.

Kirsty finding out her father had paid him to date her was his worst nightmare.

Still, Nathan wasn't likely to tell her, was he? It wouldn't make him look too good either.

Ryan picked up the newspaper and lightly scanned the headlines. Kirsty was so right. There was never anything worth reading. Just bad news. Life was difficult enough without reading about other people's misfortunes. Even the football was boring these days. It was all about money and nothing to do with club loyalty. No wonder crowd numbers were down.

He put the paper back down and picked up his orange juice, sipping it and leaning back to soak in the view which made living here so fantastic. The sea, sparking like diamonds under the morning sun. The expanse of clear blue sky. The golden stretch of beach. The feeling of space and light, yet being so close to the city.

Ryan glanced back at the front-page headline about some poor innocent high school kid being shot in a drive-by killing. Who needed to read about that? He closed the paper and pushed it well away from him.

The gossip column on the back page was right there in view, but it went unread and unnoticed. Including the paragraph about Kirsty.

If only he'd seen it, Ryan was to think later. Maybe it might have changed things. Yet that was unlikely. The events of the coming day had been set into motion years ago. Nothing would have stopped it except death.

Nothing *did* stop it except death.

CHAPTER TWENTY-ONE

"I've been waiting for you," Josh said curtly as he collared Kirsty in the main corridor shortly after two.

"I'm not that late," she defended. "Only a few minutes. Why? What's up?" She immediately thought he was going to tell her she'd been demoted to understudy. Though why she couldn't guess. She'd been darned good last night.

"Have you seen this?" He jabbed at the back page of the newspaper he was holding.

"Seen what?"

"This paragraph about you."

"About *me*?" She grabbed the paper and zeroed straight in on her name.

"Oh, no," she groaned as she read the whole unfortunate and unflattering item.

A little birdie told me yesterday that previous bit-part player Kirsty O'Connell is none other than Kirsty Whitmore, daughter of playwright Nathan Whitmore and the present toast of Broadway, Lenore Langtry. Kirsty made the headlines a few years ago after an unsuccessful kidnapping attempt. I hear it's not just her name which has been changed but her hair, which has gone from bright red to peroxide blonde. Her role as the younger

sister, Helen, in Sisters in Love *is supposed to be
a sizzling one, but I gather that on opening night
Kirsty didn't sizzle at all. She was as flat as the
flattest champagne. Pays to have a famous father,
doesn't it?*

"*Are* you Nathan Whitmore and Lenore Langtry's
daughter?" Josh demanded to know.

Kirsty didn't appreciate his aggressive attitude and
her hackles came up. She wasn't *ashamed* of her par-
entage. She'd hidden it because she hadn't wanted to
take *advantage* of it.

"Yes, I am," she returned defiantly. "Kirsty
O'Connell's my stage name. What of it?"

"What of it? For pity's sake, girl, you're not stupid. You must know how this makes me look."

"Clever?" she suggested.

"Don't take that tone with me. Dear God, Kirsty,
think about it. Carla was already bitching that I fa-
voured you over everyone else, especially her. Now
she thinks she knows why. She was positively livid
when she came in. I can understand how she feels."

"Why didn't you just tell her the truth? That you
didn't know who I was when you cast me."

"I did. But it didn't wash."

"So what are you going to do about it? Cave in
and give her my part?"

"I have my career as a director to think of."

Kirsty heard his unsaid words and felt physically
sick. "If you replace me with Carla people will think
you're running scared," she argued desperately. "A
director has to be strong."

"A director has to be sensible. Carla's now the

girlfriend of one of the producers, and he's already been on the phone to me about you. Your father is not the force in the theatre world he once was, Kirsty. He has nothing to do with productions these days. People just buy the rights to his plays and that's that. My contract states I can hire and fire as I see fit. I'm not firing you, but from today you're the understudy."

"No!" she cried.

"Yes," he bit out.

"I...I'll quit."

"If you do, no other director will ever hire you again. You're a talented girl, Kirsty. But you made a mistake, lying to people about who you are. No one likes to feel they've been made a fool of. Don't stuff up your career further by putting on a turn and letting people down. Play the understudy with good grace and I guarantee that you'll survive this. *And* you'll go on to much better parts than Carla will ever get."

That was no consolation to Kirsty at that moment and her chin began to quiver.

Josh gave her shoulder a sympathetic squeeze. "I'm sorry, sweetie. Really, I am. But that's life."

Kirsty burst into tears. She was still crying when she reached the dressing room. But she pulled herself together before going in. No way was she going to let Carla see how upset she was.

"Did Josh give you the good news?" Carla jibed straight away.

Kirsty gave her a killer look and walked past her with her head held high.

She saw Carla in the mirror, smirking at her back.

"I guess I'd better get out there on stage for to

day's run-through since I'm in the first scene now,'' she said gleefully. ''Coming, Mimi?''

''I'll just be a minute.''

Kirsty didn't want to look at Mimi. If she was ashamed of not telling the truth, it was not telling Mimi. She literally had to force herself to face the girl she now counted as a friend.

''I'm sorry, Mimi,'' she said remorsefully. ''I should have told you.''

''I'm sorry, too,'' Mimi returned with genuine sadness in her face.

The tears started up again then, as they did when people were sympathetic. Kirsty snatched up some tissues and blew her nose. ''Josh says to grin and bear it. He said I'll come through this. He said I'm more talented than Carla.''

''That's good advice, because he's right. You are. But why *did* you keep your identity a secret?'' Mimi asked, clearly puzzled. ''I mean…if Nathan Whitmore was *my* father…'' She shook her head in obvious bewilderment.

''I wouldn't wish that on my worst enemy,'' Kirsty muttered, and Mimi looked startled.

''But…but he's a genius!''

''He's a bastard. Look, I really don't want to talk about my father.''

Mimi frowned, then shrugged. ''Fine. Shall we go out there, then, and show certain people we have more character than they do? And more talent?''

Kirsty straightened, buoyed up by Mimi's kindness and encouragement. ''Absolutely!''

Kirsty did her best to keep her chin up during rehearsals. But it was appallingly difficult, especially with Carla acting like some pathetic prima donna all the time. When Kirsty started thinking about pushing *her* down the Opera House steps, she knew she was close to cracking.

It was a relief when Carla swanned out of the place as soon as Josh called it quits at a quarter to five. Kirsty had made plans for Ryan to meet her on the steps at five-thirty. They were supposed to be going out somewhere for a bite to eat before returning to Belleview—and Jaws—for the night.

She sat in the dressing room, waiting for the time to tick away, glad to have the distraction of Mimi's very pleasant company as the other girl changed from her rehearsal uniform of tights and top into a smashing red dress and matching coat.

"You have a special date?" Kirsty asked, wondering if *she* should have brought something nice to change into instead of always wearing jeans and jumpers. But all her good outfits were back at her bedsit and she'd just been too busy to go back there.

"No. I'm going to one of those arranged dinner parties for singles."

"What? *You?*"

Mimi smiled a wry little smile. "Yes. Me."

"But I thought you'd have men dripping over you all the time."

"Unfortunately not the right kind. The only single straight men I meet are actors—and goodness knows who'd want to end up with one of them? When I lowered myself recently to go to Peter's place for so-called drinks, I realised I'd reached the bottom of the barrel. I didn't want to go to a normal dating service, because I hear the creeps you meet that way are even worse than actors. But I've heard some good things about this style of introduction. At least you're in a group, and in public at a restaurant, so you can escape without having to fight off some sleazebag trying to get into your pants before you've even had your first drink. You must have met the type.''

''Oh, yes. Many times. But I have a really nice boyfriend now. I'm going to marry him. He just doesn't know it yet. I have to go meet him right now, actually.'' She stood up and looped her bag over her shoulder.

''Kirsty…''

''Yes?''

''Nothing. See you tomorrow afternoon.''

Kirsty grimaced. ''Oh, yes, my debut as understudy. Gosh, what a comedown.''

''Don't think like that. You'll make it to the top eventually. I'm sure of it.''

''Thanks, Mimi. That's nice of you to say so. But then, you're a really nice person.''

''Oh, I'm not so nice,'' Mimi muttered under her breath as Kirsty walked out of the door.

Kirsty's heart lifted when she saw Ryan waiting for her. What did it really matter about being relegated to understudy? Mimi was right. She'd make it. And in a way it was relief that the cat was out of the bag about who she was. She wouldn't try to keep it a secret ever again.

''What are you looking so pleased about?'' Ryan said when she ran up and hugged him.

''Just seeing you.''

''Flatterer.''

''No, I mean it. Being with you matters more to

me than anything. So how was your day?'' she asked, linking arms with him and steering him towards the steps. ''I hope it was better than mine.''

The instant concern in his eyes soothed her. ''Something was wrong with your day?''

''Some journalist found out my real identity and printed it in a gossip column in this morning's paper. Josh was seriously put out. On top of that, Carla's now shacking up with one of the play's producers and he put added pressure on Josh to give Carla my part and demote me to understudy. So he did.''

Ryan looked outraged. ''But that's not right!''

''No. But, as Josh said, that's life.''

''Geez, I detest that saying,'' he muttered, scowling.

''Can't say it's my favourite either.''

''It was actually in the paper that you are Kirsty Whitmore?''

''Yep. That same paper we both didn't read properly this morning. But I'm not upset about it any more, Ryan. Honest. In a way, it's a relief.''

''Mmm. I guess it had to come out one day.''

''My feelings exactly. So where are you taking me for dinner?'' she asked as she stopped by Ryan's car. They'd walked quickly as they talked.

''Wherever you'd like to go,'' Ryan replied, and opened the passenger door for her.

''Try hell,'' came a gravelly voice from somewhere.

Kirsty was glancing around in surprise when a figure in a navy tracksuit and baseball cap stepped out from behind a nearby cement column.

Kirsty stared, first into the coal-black eyes of Ryan's ex-wife, and then at the gun in her hands.

CHAPTER TWENTY-TWO

RYAN absorbed the situation in one horrifying flash. It would remain snapped in his memory for ever.

"Tina, *no*!" he cried out, before it was too late.

She turned slightly towards him and the gun came too, away from where it had been pointed, right at Kirsty's chest.

It wasn't much, but it was something.

"No, Ryan?" she said in the coldest, deadliest voice. "You don't want me to kill her like she deserves to be killed? And why would that be, I wonder? Because you love her and can't bear to live without her?"

Ryan tried not to panic, calling on what he'd learned during that negotiating course.

If all else fails when negotiating with a terrorist, or a suicide threat, or an insane ex-wife about to murder the girl you adore, just tell them what they want to hear. Buy yourself some time.

"No, of course not," he returned placatingly. "You know the only woman I ever loved was you. I don't want you to kill her because you'd end up in jail doing a life sentence. How could we possibly get back together again if that happens?"

Ryan saw Kirsty's head jerk towards him, shock and confusion in her eyes.

Tina laughed. "You think I believe that bullshit?"

"It's not bullshit. You always had it wrong about her. You broke up our marriage because you were jealous, but that jealousy just wasn't warranted."

"*I* broke up our marriage?"

"Well, of course. You don't think I really wanted a divorce, do you? How could any woman compare with you? Remember what it was like between us. I couldn't keep away from you. I wanted you all the time. You think I could ever want *her* like that?"

"You're sleeping with her. I know you are."

Ryan shrugged, ignoring Kirsty's wide eyes on him. "So I'm sleeping with her. So what? I've slept with lots of women since our divorce. That doesn't mean they mean anything to me."

"Yes, but this is the first one you've taken back to where you live. All the others you met in hotels during the day. The Regency mostly, as I recall."

He couldn't totally contain his shock.

"That surprised you, didn't it?" she said with an ugly laugh. "You thought I'd stopped following you, but I hadn't. I just stopped doing all those other silly things which pissed you off enough to call the police. I've been following you all this time, Ryan, making sure you *never* gave another woman what you wouldn't give me."

"A baby, you mean?"

"Hell, no. I never wanted any stupid bloody baby. I just wanted you. You, in my bed every night. You, loving me."

"I never stopped loving you, Tina."

"Stop lying to me!" she screamed. "I know the truth, damn it. You love this rich bitch. You can't keep away from her. You've been with her every night for the last week. You're besotted with her. I can tell.''

When Ryan saw the gun swing back towards Kirsty he laughed, hoping that would distract Tina again. And it worked.

''What I'm besotted with, Tina, is the fifty grand her daddy is paying me to do just that. Stay with her day and night till he gets back from his holidays. He called me the day before he left on a cruise. Last Tuesday, it was. He'd found out that Nick Gregory— one of the men who kidnapped Kirsty—was getting out of jail the next day.''

Ryan heard Kirsty gasp, but he didn't look her way. His focus remained totally on Tina.

''Daddy was worried for his precious daughter's safety. He knew I wasn't keen on the job. That's why he offered me so much money.''

Tina's black eyes showed the beginnings of doubt. Lord knew what Kirsty was thinking.

''You didn't *have* to sleep with her,'' Tina said, her black eyes pained.

''It was the only way I could stay close enough to do the job properly. Her father didn't want her to know about Gregory being out. As it turned out he could have told her. Gregory's not at all interested in revenge, or making trouble,'' he added, more for Kirsty's benefit than Tina's.

''But we weren't to know that beforehand,'' he continued with an indifferent-looking shrug. ''I was just killing two birds with one stone—doing my job and, yes, getting some easy sex at the same time. You can't blame me for that, honey. You were the one who gave me a real yen for female flesh. But if you think I'm in love with this spoiled little show pony then you don't know me very well.''

He flashed Kirsty a scornful look to make his words more convincing. She looked pole-axed, of course. But still beautiful.

Tina, on the other hand, looked simply awful. Thin and gaunt, with sunken cheeks and dark circles under her eyes. Hard to make anyone believe he'd prefer her to Kirsty. But he had to try.

''Hell, just look at her,'' he jeered. ''Totally up herself. I like a down-to-earth woman who knows how to please a guy. I never did go for the silver-spoon-in-the-mouth kind who thinks she's God's gift to men and wants her dates to do all the work in bed.''

Ryan knew he'd probably just cruelled his chances with Kirsty for ever. But it was better than her lying dead in the city morgue. That was a very accurate hand gun Tina was holding. And she was far too close to miss. Too far away, however, for him to risk trying to disarm her with a flying tackle. He'd never reach her before she fired.

''I dare say you might only be screwing her for the money,'' Tina said grudgingly, ''but *she* loves *you*. I can't allow that either.''

''Love him!'' Kirsty burst out. ''I don't love that mercenary bastard. Not any more. Hell, you can have him.''

Tina laughed. ''Good try, rich bitch. But *you* I don't believe. You love my Ryan. You always did. I saw it in your eyes that night I came to that fancy dinner party. And I saw it the other night when you were dancing with him. You didn't see me, of course.

Either of you. I didn't stay long. Just long enough to find out what was going on. I followed you for a while after you left, but not for too long. Ryan has a right nose for my following him. But I knew as soon as he went over the bridge where he was going.

"And I was right, wasn't I?" she threw at him. "You took her back to that fancy house and made love to her all night like you used to make love to me. I sat outside in my car and pictured what was going on inside and I almost went crazy. I told myself you'd stop seeing her after a couple of times, like you stopped seeing all the others. But you didn't, Ryan," she groaned in anguish. "You didn't."

Ryan could see she was losing it. Desperation forced him to say anything, just so she didn't shoot.

"But I will, Tina. I promise. It was just the money making me stay. But as of tonight it's over. I'll go with you now, if that's what you want. The only reason I haven't contacted you since the divorce is because I thought you didn't want me any more. Sure, you made me angry with all that stalking business, but afterwards I realised how much I missed you. Why do you think I've never had a real girlfriend, just pick-ups? Because I'm still in love with you."

For a split second he saw another flicker of doubt creep into her eyes. But then, suddenly, they went hard and cold again. "I don't believe you, Ryan. You're lying to me. You do love her and you're trying to save her. But it's too late to save her. I did warn you, rich bitch."

When the gun swung back towards Kirsty Ryan tensed, ready to spring. But then he saw that the safety catch was still on. Maybe if he talked to Tina a bit more, got a bit closer...

"What do you mean? You warned her?" he asked, sliding one foot forwards slightly.

"You mean she didn't she get my note and my lilies? Maybe that raging poofter kept them for himself. Pity. Pity she didn't break her neck when I pushed her down those steps, too. But no such luck. I realised after she got up again that I needed something much more reliable. I needed a gun. But getting myself a gun was easier said then done. Still, I eventually got one. And now I'm going to do what those stupid kidnappers should have done five years ago. Wipe her off the face of the earth."

With two very steady hands outstretched, she pointed the gun right at Kirsty's heart and flicked the safety catch off. Horror galvanised Ryan when he saw her trigger finger begin to squeeze.

"Nooooo!" he screamed, and launched himself sidewards in mid-air, his arms outstretched as wide as possible to cover as much of Kirsty as he could.

The bullet meant for the girl he loved slammed into his chest. He grunted, then fell, hard, onto his side on the cement floor.

Kirsty screamed, and so did someone else. Ryan caught a glimpse of a woman in red rushing towards them, shouting. He blinked up at Tina, who dropped the gun and just stood there, staring down at him, anguish in her face.

"Oh, no," she cried. *"No!"*

He groaned and rolled onto his back, his arms flopping wide as the pain in his chest mushroomed and a black curtain started to come down in his head. His last thought was that he would never now be able to tell Kirsty that he hadn't taken her father's money, that he had been lying to save her, that he really, truly loved her.

Kirsty dropped to her knees by Ryan's side just as Mimi materialised and swooped down upon the gun. "You crazy bitch!" Mimi screamed at an ashen-faced Tina. "You've killed him."

"No... No. I would *never* kill *him*."

"I saw you. You shot him."

"No..." Tina began backing away, shaking her head. "No. I would never hurt him. I love him." She stared down at his unconscious body and shuddered. "Oh, dear God, dear God..." Suddenly, she turned and ran.

"Mimi, help me," Kirsty pleaded, shock and panic sending her blank. "I don't know what to do."

Mimi wrenched off her beautiful red jacket and rolled it into a ball. "Here. Press this against the wound. I'll ring for an ambulance." She'd already pulled out her mobile and was punching in the emergency number.

Kirsty did as ordered, tears streaming down her face. "Don't die, Ryan. Please don't die. I don't care if Dad did hire you to protect me. I don't care about anything you said just now. I don't care if you don't love me."

"Of course he loves you," Mimi said, hunkering down on the other side of Ryan's prostrate figure. "He was prepared to die for you, wasn't he? The ambulance is on its way."

Kirsty sobbed, and prayed for the ambulance to hurry. When she heard the screech of tyres, for a split second she thought it was them. But even paramedics couldn't get there that quickly. A small blue car screamed past then, and rocketed up the ramp towards the exit. The driver wore a baseball cap.

"She's insane!" Kirsty said.

"Who is she?" Mimi asked.

"His ex-wife."

"Ahh." Mimi nodded in understanding, then put her fingertips to Ryan's throat. "He's going to make it, you know. Strong pulse."

"You're just saying that."

"No. No, I don't just say things. I have this awful habit of being brutally honest."

"Then I hope you're right, because I don't know what I'd do if Ryan died."

"You'd survive," Mimi said. "Just not happily."

Two hours later Kirsty was pacing the hospital waiting room, trying not to go insane herself. The ambulance had been reasonably quick, and Ryan had been rushed into surgery as soon they arrived. But she'd had no word since. The nurses kept saying she'd be informed of his condition as soon as he was out of Theatre and in the recovery room.

"You don't have to stay, Mimi," she told the girl, who'd been like a rock all this time.

Mimi smiled from where she was sitting, on one of the plastic chairs which lined the wall. "Now, Kirsty, where would I go? I'm no longer in the mood for a dinner party. I rang and cancelled that as soon as we arrived. Besides, I want to be here when they tell you that your Ryan is going to make it. It's important to me."

Kirsty heard something in Mimi's voice which puzzled her. "Why is it important to you?"

"Because I feel guilty enough about you today as it is. I want to see you happy again."

"I'm not sure I know what you're getting at?"

"I was the one who rang that journalist at the paper. I was the one who told him who you really are."

Kirsty could not have been more surprised if Mimi had told her she was a serial killer. "*You*. But why? And how? I mean…how did you even know who I was in the first place? I don't understand. If you knew who I was, why didn't you say something sooner?"

Mimi sighed. "I didn't know. Not till I was looking through some old newspaper files on Monday at the State Library and came upon the reports of your kidnapping. There were photographs of you, and even though you do look different with short fair hair your features are the same."

"So it was just a coincidence you found out?"

"Not quite a coincidence. I was looking up everything published on Nathan Whitmore and his family."

"But *why*? Just because he wrote *Sisters in Love*?"

"No. And, please…try not to be too shocked. It was because he's my father too."

Kirsty gaped. Then stumbled over to sit down. Then gaped some more.

"Yes, I know," Mimi said drily. "I'm a few years older than you, which makes your father quite young when he fathered me. He was sixteen, to be exact."

"Sixteen!"

"If you think that's bad, wait till I tell you how old my mother was."

Kirsty could well imagine how old her poor mother

was. Probably well under-age, if she knew her father. He liked them young.

So she was shocked to the core when Mimi told her the age of her mother, and the circumstances of her conception.

"My God!" was all she could say.

"I only found out your father *was* my father when my mother died recently. A friend of hers thought it was her duty to enlighten me. I didn't believe her at first, but she insisted it was true, and of course the resemblance is quite remarkable—especially when you look at photos of your father and myself side by side. Look, I'll show you a couple."

She retrieved two photographs from her handbag and handed them over to Kirsty.

"That's a copy of an early one of your father I got from the library archives. And this is one of me a few years ago when I was touring Australia with a Shakespearean company. I had short hair back then."

Kirsty held the two photos side by side, her gaze switching continually from one to the other. Mimi was right. The likeness *was* amazing.

"The old lady who told me thought I had a right to know," Mimi went on. "And a right to tell your father I was his daughter. Possibly for what I could get out of him. But in the end I just didn't see it that way. I thought he must have suffered enough at my mother's hands and would not welcome me as his daughter. I, like you, have a strong sense of pride."

"Poor Dad," Kirsty said, getting an inkling, for once, of what might have fashioned the man he'd become. His relationship with Mimi's mother was hardly a normal first sexual experience. Who knew what effect it had had on him?

"You called him a bastard earlier today," Mimi said with a worried frown. "Why? Is he really as bad as all that?"

Kirsty shook her head. "No. Not really. He just has this compulsion to control everyone and everything around him."

"You mean he cares too much?"

"Yes. Yes, I guess that's one way of looking at it."

"I heard a bit of what your boyfriend said to that woman, about your father paying him to protect you. Do you think that's true? Or was he just trying to stop her from shooting you?"

"Well, I do think he was trying to stop her from shooting me with some of the things he said. Ryan told me he'd never loved that witch and I believe him. But I suspect the bit about one of my kidnappers being out of jail was true enough, as well as Dad hiring Ryan to protect me. That's exactly the sort of thing my—*our* father—would do."

"I see. Well, I wouldn't mind a bit of that kind of caring, I can tell you. My mother was a hopeless mother. And a drunk to boot. I've had to look after myself since I was a tiny tot and, quite frankly, I'm so tired of it. I want someone I can lean on occasionally, and love. I feel like I've been alone all my life."

Kirsty looked at her half-sister and felt her heart fill with a very real affection for this beautiful and brave girl. "Well, you have *me* from now on, Mimi," she said with a catch in her voice. "I've always wanted a sister. You can lean on me. And love me. And I'll love you right back.''

Mimi's eyes flooded. "You don't mean that. You can't! Not after what I did."

"Don't be silly." Kirsty went over to sit on the chair beside Mimi and hold her hands. "You did me a favour. It was becoming a strain, actually, trying to hide my true identity."

Mimi groaned. "You don't know how much I regretted doing what I did. When Josh gave Carla your part I could have cut my throat. It's just that when I first found out who you really were I was momentarily overwhelmed by this incredible burst of jealousy. I'd made that horrible call before I had time for second thoughts."

"That's all right," Kirsty said, and gave her a big hug. "I understand perfectly, and I forgive you."

Mimi pulled back and stared at her. "You are the nicest but strangest girl. And you know something even stranger? I was drawn to you right from the start. I used to think… She's like me, this girl. I didn't know how much at the time."

"I liked you too, even if you were rather stand-offish."

"That's just a self-protective shield I've developed. I don't have a doting father to hire handsome bodyguards to look after me, and sleep with me as a bonus."

"Kirsty Harris?" someone called out from the corridor. "I'm looking for a Kirsty Harris?"

"Here—here!" Kirsty jumped up and dashed out into the hallway. Mimi followed.

A middle-aged and very tired-looking doctor stil

in theatre garb frowned over at both of them. "Which one of you is Mrs Harris?"

"That's me," Kirsty said.

"Mmm." He stared down at her ringless hand, which Kirsty quickly whipped behind her back. "Your husband's out of surgery. He lost quite a lot of blood, and his right lung was punctured, but the bullet missed his heart. He'll make a full recovery."

Kirsty didn't know whether to burst into tears or whoop for joy. When her face just crumpled, she opted for a restrained weep.

"There, there," the doctor said, patting her shoulder. "No need to cry. He's strong as a bull, your husband. He'll be fine. His blood pressure's good and he's breathing comfortably. You should be able to see him when he comes round. Can you wait? Are there any little Harrises you have to get home to?"

"No. Not yet."

He looked her up and down. "Only a matter of time, I don't doubt." And he was gone.

Mimi came up and gave her a hug. "I told you so."

Kirsty sniffled and her half-sister produced a tissue.

"Mrs Harris, eh?" Mimi said drily. "When did you come up with that?"

"Well, you know nurses," Kirsty said with a sheepish smile. "They only tell close relatives the real condition of a patient."

Mimi glanced down at Kirsty's stomach. "And could there be any little Harrises on the way? Have we been getting carried away just a bit with the handsome bodyguard's attentions?"

"Good grief, no. Do I look seriously stupid? I have

no intention of having children for yonks. I'm only just twenty-three.''

''I thought you said you were going to marry the man?''

''I am. Well, I *was*, before this happened. I mean… maybe he won't want to marry me. Maybe he doesn't really love me. I mean…maybe he *was* just with me for the money.''

''In the words of his ex, that's bullshit, Kirsty. What does your heart tell you?''

''He loves me.''

''I agree.''

''Either that,'' Kirsty added, ''or he takes his work very seriously.''

Mimi laughed. ''No one takes their work *that* seriously.''

''Ryan is an unusual sort of man. I think being a hero is a compulsion with him.''

''Only with you, I'll warrant.''

''You think so?'' Kirsty asked hopefully.

''Love has a way of bringing out the best in people.''

''Oh, that's sweet.''

''Yes, it was, wasn't it? Your sweetness must be catchy.''

''You think I'm *sweet*? I'm not sweet at all!''

Mimi cocked her head on one side and smiled. ''No. Perhaps not. Perhaps you're more like our father than you think.''

Kirsty grinned. ''Perhaps. Oh, and speaking of our dad—are you or are you not going to tell him that he *is* your dad?''

''No,'' Mimi said thoughtfully. ''No, I don't think

I am. And I don't want you to either. It'll have to be enough, having you for my sister.''

"Oh, Lord, you're actually trying to protect him, aren't you? You don't want him to feel bad—or guilty—about you." Kirsty rolled her eyes. "Dad is the last person you have to protect from guilt. He doesn't know the meaning of the word."

"Everyone knows the meaning of guilt, Kirsty. I was brought up on it."

"He'd *adore* you."

"He'd *hate* me. I'd remind him of a time he'd rather forget."

"Oh. Yes, you could be right there. Okay, we won't tell him."

Mimi sighed. "Thank God you agree. Promise?"

Kirsty winced. "Do I have to? I hate making promises."

"Promise!"

"Oh, all right, I promise," she said grudgingly. "Truly, you're family!"

Mimi's heart almost exploded with happiness. Family. Kirsty had just called her family.

"Mrs Harris?"

Kirsty's head whipped round to find a nurse smiling at her. "If you'd like to come see your husband, he's awake now and asking for you."

"You go," Mimi insisted.

"Will you wait for me?"

"Of course." She'd waited to feel a real sense of family all her life. She wasn't about to run out on that lovely feeling now.

CHAPTER TWENTY-THREE

''NOT too long, now,'' the nurse warned at the door. ''He needs his rest.''

Kirsty nodded and made her way quietly into the room. Shock at the sight of all the machines and tubes Ryan was hooked up to faltered her progress for a while, but she eventually moved over to the side of the bed and peered down into Ryan's grey-coloured face.

He looked as if he was asleep, lying there with his eyes shut. But they suddenly flicked open, and he looked straight up at her.

She smiled. ''My hero again,'' she murmured.

His eyes carried a pain which wasn't just physical. ''Not quite.'' He glanced away from her over towards the far wall. ''I don't want you being nice to me out of gratitude. I know what you must think of me.''

Kirsty sighed. Men! And they called women drama queens!

''What I think, Ryan Harris,'' she said, ''is that you should have told me about Nick Gregory yourself. And about Dad hiring you. You should have trusted my love for you. But I forgive you all the same. I know you must love me very much to do what you did tonight.''

His eyes came back to hers, disbelief in their pale blue depths. "Are you saying you still love me?"

"Don't you mean I still *think* I love you? Or have we finally moved beyond that?"

"Well I... I..."

Kirsty sighed again. "You're still not sure, are you? You think I'm too young and inexperienced to know the difference between love and sex. Well, I do know the difference, Ryan Harris. Love takes a bullet in the chest. Sex doesn't. And love forgives a man for taking fifty grand to sleep with her. Sex doesn't. Though I have to confess I'm very annoyed with my father for offering such an obscene amount of money. He must believe no man would ever want to sleep with me for myself and myself alone."

"I didn't take the fifty grand," Ryan said, and Kirsty blinked.

"You didn't?"

"No. I told your dad I'd be happy to date you for nothing."

"You did?"

"But he *was* paying me to protect you while he was away. And, yes, he knew darn well that my becoming your lover would be the best way I could manage that without telling you the truth."

"Mmm. Something smells here, Ryan."

"He knew you were a virgin," Ryan supplied. "I don't think he liked that any more than he likes your being an actress."

"Actor," Kirsty corrected. "You know what? I think that's it. I think Dad had a secret agenda when he hired you. *He* was the one killing two birds with the one stone. And hopefully killing off my career at the same time. He thought I'd fall madly in love with you again, get married and have half a dozen kiddies before I turned thirty. Well, he's got a lot to learn about me yet, has dear old Dad. No way am I going to give up my chosen profession. If anything, I'm even more determined to succeed on the stage after what happened today.''

"Er...what about the rest of it?''

"The rest of it?''

"The falling madly in love with me again bit?''

"Oh, well, you know I did that. That was a foregone conclusion.''

"Do you think he bargained on my falling madly in love with you in return?''

Kirsty's heart jolted to a stop, before thudding into wonderful life again. "But of course,'' she murmured, bending down to rain soft kisses all over Ryan's mouth. "His plans...didn't have a chance...unless that happened. Why else would a man like you propose...except if you fell madly in love?''

She finally stopped kissing him.

"And would you marry me if I proposed?'' Ryan asked.

"But of course. Eventually,'' she tagged on.

"And the six kids before you're thirty?''

"I'm sorry, my darling, but children don't figure in my life plan till I'm at least thirty. And even then there won't be six. Two at the most.''

"Sensible number.''

The door opened and the nurse popped her head in, her expression firm. "Time's up, Mrs Harris.''

"Could you give me just one more minute, Sister, please?" she begged.

"Well…not a second more." And she left, but the door stayed open.

"Mrs Harris?" Ryan said, smiling softly.

Kirsty wrinkled her nose at him. "Sounds good, doesn't it?"

"How long is eventually?" he asked. "And before you answer, trust me when I say I approve of and fully support your acting ambitions. Being an outgoing, creative and talented person is who you are, Kirsty. And I love who you are. But I don't want to wait years for us to be married. I want you to live with me soon, as my wife."

"I want that too, my darling, but proper weddings take time to plan, and I aim to have a proper wedding. Make dear old Dad pay through the nose. How about November? Belleview looks beautiful in the spring…"

He reached up to stroke her cheek. "Not as beautiful as you will as a bride."

"Tell me again that you love me, Ryan."

"I love you. I'll always love you."

Tears filled her eyes. "And I've always loved you."

The nurse bustled back in, this time with a policeman in tow.

"I don't know about this," she grumbled. "Did you get the doctor's permission to talk to this patient?" she asked the policeman.

"I certainly did, ma'am. I explained to him that it was best Mr Harris knew of these new developments. Stop him worrying about the person who shot him."

"Well…just don't be too long."

When the nurse glowered over at Kirsty, Kirsty steadfastly ignored her and she flounced out.

"You've arrested her, I hope," Ryan said straight away.

"There's no need. Your ex-wife's been killed in a fatal accident on the Bulli pass, Mr Harris. Only one car involved. It plunged over the side of the road and down a ravine. Witnesses aren't sure if it was an accident or suicide. They said she was speeding and might have lost control. Either way, she's gone. Permanently."

Kirsty sighed a huge sigh of relief, as did Ryan.

"Thank God," he said. "She never would have stopped, you know."

"Yes. We gathered that. We've been to her flat and the walls of her bedroom are covered with photographs of you—all taken covertly, by the look of them. She was clearly obsessed. Not in her right mind."

"Tell me about it. She stalked me for two years after I first left her. Drove me crazy, ringing up at all hours of the day and night, tailing me everywhere, slashing my tyres, writing filthy graffiti over the walls of places I lived. It was only after she was arrested and warned by a judge that he'd send her to jail if she continued that she stopped the obvious harassment. I thought it was finally over. But it wasn't at all…"

Kirsty listened to what had happened to Ryan at Tina's hands and finally understood why he'd adopted such a seemingly callous attitude towards women.

"I should have guessed she was just lying low," Ryan muttered.

"Stop thinking about her," the policeman advised. "It *is* over now. Death is rather final."

"True. Thanks for stopping by, Officer," Ryan said. "You've taken an enormous load off my mind."

"Just doing my job," he said, and strode out.

"Are you going back to Belleview tonight?" Ryan asked a thoughtful Kirsty.

"Have to. Jaws will be starving by now. Why? Surely you're not *still* worried about my staying there alone."

"I am a bit."

"But you said Gregory wasn't a risk. Was that a lie too?"

"No. Not at all. I'd bet my Bondi apartment on his being rehabilitated. It's just that big empty mansions like Belleview are always a target when their owners are away in holidays."

"Tell you what. I'll ask Mimi to come home with me. She's still waiting for me outside."

"Really? That was kind of her."

"She's a kind person."

"You like her, don't you?"

"You could say that."

Ryan gave her an odd look.

"What?" she asked, feeling guilty without knowing what she was feeling guilty about.

"There's something you're not telling me."

"Who, me?"

"Yes, you. The one who didn't tell me about the lilies. Or about being *pushed* down the Opera House steps. I might have guessed it was Tina if I'd had those little snippets of information. So what is it you're keeping from me this time?''

''I can't tell you.''

''Why not?''

''I promised.''

''Kirsty…''

''Oh, all right. I suppose I did only promise not to tell my father. But then you have to promise not to tell anyone else.''

''Good God. All right. Just tell me before that nurse comes back and tosses you out. Be quick.''

''Well it's like this…''

CHAPTER TWENTY-FOUR

November, five months later...

MIMI was putting the final pins into Kirsty's head-piece when someone knocked on the bedroom door.

"Who is it?" she asked. "If it's Ryan, then you can't come in. It's unlucky for the groom to see the bride before the wedding."

"It's not Ryan," Nathan answered. "It's only me. The father of the bride."

Only me.

Mimi smiled to herself. There was nothing *only* about the father of the bride—a fact confirmed when he came in.

Guests at the wedding today could have been excused for thinking Nathan was the groom, rather than the father of the bride, he was so handsome and young-looking. Yet he was *her* father as well.

Mimi still couldn't get used to that extraordinary reality. Nathan Whitmore still overawed her, even now, after she'd been a frequent visitor to Belleview with Kirsty during the past few months.

He wasn't a bastard at all, in Mimi's opinion. She thought he was rather wonderful. And incredibly attractive. If she hadn't been his daughter she might have been seriously infatuated. As it was, she still

thought he was a dish. No wonder his wife was besotted.

"Ready yet, love?" he asked Kirsty, who was
looking like a dream in the most feminine wedding
gown Mimi had ever seen. Made of cream silk, it had
a tightly boned bodice and a low sweetheart neckline
outlined with pearls. The skirt was full and flouncy,
making Kirsty's waist look extra tiny. There wasn't a
train, but her veil was long, stretching out from a
coronet of pearls which held her hair up and firmly
in place. Pearls dropped from her lobes and encircled
her throat, the choker necklace being the "something
old', given to Kirsty by her stepmother to wear that
day.

Nathan smiled as he walked over and took Kirsty's
hands in his, drawing them out wide as he admired
his very beautiful daughter. "You look indescribably
lovely," he said. "Ryan's a lucky man."

"Mimi looks lovely too," Kirsty said.

Mischievously, Mimi thought. She was a devil
whenever they were in their father's company. Mimi
was almost beginning to consider telling Nathan she
was his daughter to stop Kirsty's infernal mischief-
making.

When Nathan's eyes swung her way Mimi felt
slightly self-conscious, as she always did under his
coolly enigmatic gaze.

"Indeed she does. Red suits her."

Mimi's bridesmaid gown was made of silk as well,
in a similar style to Kirsty's wedding dress, but minus
the pearls and minus the full skirt. It followed her
hourglass figure like a glove, right to the floor, and

had an attached piece which draped around her hips and ended in an imitation bustle at the back.

"Why do you think I chose red for her?" Kirsty told her father before smiling over at Mimi. "I'll never forget that lovely red jacket you had which you whipped off and gave me the night of the shooting. Which reminds me. Did Ryan's blood ever come out?"

"I don't know. I never got the jacket back. I think it must have been thrown away."

"Oh, what a shame. That was such a smashing outfit. I'll have to buy you another one. Dad, tell her we'll buy her another one."

Nathan gave Mimi a long, thoughtful look. "I don't think Mimi would want us to buy her another one, Kirsty."

"But why ever not?"

"Because she likes to be independent. Isn't that right, Mimi?"

Her chin automatically lifted. "Yes, Mr Whitmore. You're perfectly correct."

"When are you going to call me Nathan?" he suggested smoothly, and Mimi felt herself growing warm in the face.

"Or Dad, if you like," he added quietly, and both girls gasped.

A whole host of emotions bombarded Mimi, who quickly looked at Kirsty.

She shook her head vigorously. "I swear to you, Mimi, I didn't tell him."

"Well, you must have told *someone*," Mimi complained in anguish.

"Just Ryan. Oh, and Gemma—eventually. I can never keep anything from Gemma."

"Yes, it was Gemma who told me," Nathan admitted. "About a month ago. I have to confess I didn't take it all that well at first, Mimi, so possibly your instinct was correct in not telling me. I needed some time to adjust to the idea. I do have this problem with my past, especially my wayward teenage years, but I've been watching you this past month and I have to confess I see little of your mother in you.

"Gemma tells me that's because you've taken after me, which I'm not sure is a compliment or a liability. I have a tendency to look at things in a negative light. But Gemma also says you are a clear demonstration that good things can come from a not so good situation. And you know what? I have to agree with her. You are a fine person, with a fine character and an even finer acting talent. If I was forced to choose which one of my two daughters is the better actor I would be hard pushed. You are both incredibly talented."

"Did you hear that?" Kirsty burst out, grinning from ear to ear whilst Mimi was struggling not to cry. "My God, I wish I'd had a tape recorder in here. My father, telling me I'm incredibly talented."

"I can admit I'm wrong on the rare occasion that I am," he said drily. "So, are we ready to go, daughters? Nothing more to do?"

"No. We're ready," they chorused, both of them now beaming with happiness.

"One thing before we do. Since today is Kirsty's day, Mimi, I won't be announcing the fact to all and sundry here that I now have an additional daughter

But, trust me, I won't be keeping it a secret either, at least not with close members of the Gemma says that there's been too many secrets family over the years and it has to stop.''

"Hear, hear!'' Kirsty agreed, whilst Mimi just glowed. He hadn't rejected her. He was welcoming her into his and Kirsty's family.

And what a family they were!

Mimi had met them all at the pre-wedding party Byron Whitmore had thrown for Kirsty and Ryan last weekend at his magnificent harbourside home. Kirsty had filled her in over the last few months with endless gossip about various members of her family. But seeing them in the flesh had been an eye-opening experience. Talk about the bold and the beautiful!

Mimi didn't doubt they were capable of the many scandalous goings-on which Kirsty had salaciously related.

"Flowers!'' Kirsty suddenly exclaimed. "We don't have our bouquets.''

"Ah, yes,'' Nathan said with a nod of his handsome head. "I forgot. Gemma has them on the hallside table outside. She's waiting to come in with them. She didn't want to intrude whilst I…er…made my disclosure. I'll just go get her. Actually, Gemma has a disclosure of her own to make as well.''

Mimi shot Kirsty a questioning glance as Nathan strode out into the hall to collect Gemma.

"Well, she can't be pregnant,'' Kirsty whispered. "Dad had one those operations after Richard was born.'' And she made snipping gestures with her hand. "The doctor said it was too dangerous for Gemma to have any more babies.''

"What, then?"

"Nothing bad, I'm sure. No way would Gemma tell me anything bad on my wedding day."

True, Mimi thought. Gemma was such a nice lady. And a very beautiful one.

Gemma came in wearing a royal blue outfit which wasn't at all matronly or stepmother-of-the-bride. Still, at only twenty-eight, why *should* she be looking matronly?

She came straight over and gave Mimi a warm hug. "I'm so glad Nathan told you he knew. Now I don't have to be careful over what I say. You know, you look just like your father. The resemblance is quite incredible."

"Gemma, darling," Nathan interrupted, "isn't there a little something you want to tell the girls before we go downstairs? I mean, you've told just about everyone else down there already."

The joy which spread across Gemma's lovely face was a joy in itself.

"I'm going to have a baby," she said, her hands automatically coming to rest on her stomach, which did have a slight rounding, now that Mimi looked "Just on four months."

Kirsty looked gobsmacked. "But… But…"

"I had my vasectomy reversed," Nathan explained.

Now Kirsty looked worried. "But, Gemma, thought…"

"I'm going to have a Caesarean," her stepmother reassured her. "So no trouble at the delivery end of things."

"Do you know yet whether it's a boy or a girl?"

Mimi asked Gemma, feeling very happy for her. She was clearly a born mother and thrilled to pieces with her news.

"I found out yesterday. It's a little girl. A daughter. I'm going to call her Opal. After the opal which brought Nathan and myself together."

"Oh, that's sweet," Mimi said. She'd heard all about that opal from Kirsty. It had been called the Hearts Of Fire and was worth a fortune. It had also been the catalyst behind a lot of the conflicts which had torn the Whitmore family apart for several decades. Yet it had been Gemma's finding that same opal which had finally brought them all back happily together.

What a fabulous story that would make, if ever anyone wanted to tell it. Chock-full of enough secrets and sins for several books. A series, even.

"So, you've got *three* daughters now, Dad," Kirsty said teasingly. "What do you think of that?"

"I'm very pleased. And it won't be stopping there. Gemma's already informed me that she wants another child after this one, and I'm happy to oblige. As long as she realises I'm not as young as I used to be. It took two whole months of exhaustive trying to get her pregnant this time. Lord knows how long it might take in another year or so."

Mimi was taken aback at the wickedly X-rated look which flashed between Nathan and Gemma. Being a fly on *their* bedroom wall would be an education, she suspected.

"Right, now, back to the matter at hand, girls," Nathan commanded, handing the white roses to the bride and the red roses to Kirsty, who promptly swapped bouquets.

"Truly, Dad!" Kirsty said with a roll of her eyes. "You might be a creative genius writing-wise, but you have no head for colour or design. The red goes with the white, and the white with the red."

"Okay, okay, don't start lecturing me. I'm only a mere man. And so is Ryan. Trust me when I say if we don't get downstairs soon the poor boy is going to faint dead away. He was already looking a little green around the gills when I left him propped up against the bar, having some hair of the dog. Perhaps I shouldn't have organised his stag party for the night before the wedding. Or hired quite so many strippers. But what's done is done. The groom won't be much good to you tonight, though, I'll warrant, daughter dear."

"Dad, you didn't!" Kirsty exclaimed, horrified, whilst Gemma and Mimi laughed.

"He's pulling your leg, Kirsty," Mimi said. "Can't you tell?"

"No," Nathan said in dry amusement. "She never can. I see I'm going to have to be more subtle with *you*, missie."

"Mimi," she corrected him, and he laughed.

"Oh, yes. *Much* more subtle. Right, Gemma, off you toddle and get the bridal music going." He straightened his bow-tie, slicked his golden head of hair into place with his hands, then slid a masterful arm through Kirsty's. "Ready, daughters of mine?"

"Ready!"

"Good. Because it's showtime!"

How right he was, Mimi thought as she walked

sedately down the sweeping staircase, dozens of pairs of eyes trained upon her. Several guests were still sipping champagne in the front living-room, not yet gone along to where the family room had been cleared of its normal furniture and set up as a mini-chapel. Kirsty had refused to even consider an out-door wedding, because of the possibility of spring rain, but as it turned out the day was clear and sunny.

One particular pair of eyes drew Mimi's attention, and she recognised their owner as Kirsty's step-brother. Emery. He was the elder son of Kirsty's mother's second husband. Mimi had been introduced to him last weekend. He was a lawyer and worked for the Department of Public Prosecutions. Thirtyish, very tall, single—and quite attractive if you fancied the darkly brooding type, which she didn't. He'd to-tally ignored her the other night, after they'd been introduced, yet now he was staring at her over the rim of his champagne glass as if she was water and he'd been lost in the desert for six months.

Mimi was grateful when she'd passed him by, but even then she could feel his dark eyes boring holes into her back, especially where her dress dipped in a deep V almost down to her waist, showing quite an expanse of bare flesh. The effect on her body under-neath her clothes was quite startling, making her grateful for the tightly boned corset confining her sud-denly wayward flesh.

Emery's sexually charged scrutiny and her sexually charged response demonstrated that, whilst her brain was not attracted to his type, her body definitely was. How annoying!

It took an effort of will to put her mind back on

the job at hand. Being her sister's bridesmaid was very important to Mimi and she didn't want to stuff it up. When she reached the doorway into the family room, and the strip of red carpet which bisected it, she walked slowly up the makeshift aisle, smiling sweetly at the sea of faces left and right, careful to keep one eye on her feet. She didn't want to trip over. The stiletto-heeled shoes Kirsty had picked out for her were a bit on the deadly side.

Several of the female guests stood out, however, with their striking looks and stylish clothes. Kirsty's outrageous aunt Jade was impossible not to notice, in a candy-pink outfit with a matching picture hat. And the blonde with the gorgeous hunk on her arm was none other than Kirsty's great-aunt Ava—*my* great-aunt Ava as well, Mimi realised—though not looking at all great-auntish, in very sexy black.

And speaking of black…

Mimi's eyes zeroed in on the woman with the jet-black hair and jet-black eyes, her gorgeous figure draped in a designer dress of purple satin.

When Kirsty had introduced Melanie to Mimi the other night as having once been her pops' house-keeper, all sorts of scandalous scenarios had jumped into Mimi's far too imaginative mind. But had been wise enough to keep them all to herself—especially considering the woman's husband had been standing right next to the lady in question.

Mimi glanced from Melanie up at where Byron Whitmore was standing, next to Ryan, proud as punch at having been asked to be Ryan's best man. Although in his late fifties, Pops was still an impressive figure of a man, his grey hair not making him look older,

just more distinguished. Impossible to think of his
living in the same house as a woman like Melanie
and something not going on between them—and neither of them had been married back then.

Had an affair been one of the secrets Nathan had
been talking about?

Who knew?

Maybe she'd find out one day.

As Mimi approached the spot at the end of the red
carpet where the ceremony was to be performed, she
noticed that Gemma's dog had somehow snuck in
from the backyard and was skulking behind Byron's
big frame.

She almost laughed, thinking of the look to come
on her father's face when he saw his canine nemesis
lurking nearby. There was certainly no love lost between those two.

Ryan, however, had Nathan's full approval—even
if he hadn't succeeded in coercing Kirsty away from
the stage.

Mimi smiled at the superbly turned out groom, who
showed not a single sign of a hangover, only a slight
impatience. His eyes were glued to a spot over her
shoulder. Mimi took her position on the left and
turned just as Nathan and Kirsty moved into sight at
the far doorway.

All the guests gasped as one. Ryan especially.

And why not? Kirsty had never looked more beautiful.

Mimi was watching the bride's slow walk up the
aisle on her father's arm when she noticed Emery slip
into the back of the room. Every nerve-ending she
owned went on red alert and, try as she might, she

couldn't tear her eyes away from him. She was glad when the ceremony got under way and she had reason to face the front again.

Yet witnessing Kirsty marry the man she loved, and seeing how happy they both were, didn't prove the most ideal distraction. By the time the ceremony was over Mimi was feeling just a little sad. And, yes, lonely. What she wouldn't give to find a man who would love her even half as much as Ryan loved Kirsty. Or a quarter of the way her father loved his Gemma.

The smile plastered on Mimi's face felt very forced after the ceremony, as she walked back down the aisle on the best man's arm.

It was then that she saw him again, watching her. No, *staring* at her.

Angry all of a sudden, she threw him a defiant and very saucy smile. He seemed startled. Shocked, even.

Which he was. Emery had not thought for a moment that a woman as gorgeous and vibrant as Mimi would give him a second glance. Yet he'd been mesmerised by her from the first moment they'd been introduced. His only defence against his instant infatuation had been to try ignoring her.

But how could you keep ignoring a star which shone so brightly?

And here she was…smiling at him in an incredibly encouraging and provocative fashion.

A blown-away Emery decided chances like this didn't come along every day of the week.

So he started smiling back…

EPILOGUE

"NEVER has a wedding given me so much satisfaction and pleasure," Nathan said as he climbed into bed that night.

Gemma emerged from their *en suite* bathroom, wearing Nathan's favourite nightie. It was mauve and made of satin, a long clingy slip thing, which showed every curve of his wife's luscious figure. Nathan especially liked the thin straps which were oh, so easy to slide off his wife's slender shoulders.

When she turned away from him and walked over to her dressing table her back view was as tantalising as her front, especially with her hair down. She'd been growing it, and it now fell past her shoulder-blades.

Nathan's gaze was very admiring. Like a good wine, Gemma was getting better with age. Being pregnant suited her, he realised. Her skin was glowing. And so was she.

"Why's that, Nathan?" she asked, flashing him a quick smile before picking up a tube of perfumed body lotion, squeezing a pool of it into both her hands and slowly massaging it into her arms.

"All I've ever wanted for Kirsty is for her to be truly happy," he pronounced. "I used to be sceptical at weddings, if you recall. And cynical over how long marriages would last. But not today. Today I felt confident that Ryan and Kirsty are right for each other.''

''I agree. They have a lot of love to give to each other, those two. And, speaking of Kirsty, didn't she look absolutely beautiful today? No, radiant. That's the word. And so happy. Ryan, too. All they need now to complete their happiness is a baby. It's a pity, really, that Kirsty doesn't want children till she's at least thirty.''

Nathan sat bolt-upright in bed. ''What? I didn't know that. When did she say that?''

''She's always said that, Nathan. She wants to concentrate on her acting career for a while.''

''*Stupid, stubborn girl!*''

Gemma smiled. ''I wonder who she takes after? But not to worry, darling. Kirsty'll change her mind. You wait and see. She just needs a little time to enjoy her present success on the stage. Her getting the lead in that new drama was a real coup. We'll have to go and see her in it when it opens.''

Nathan pulled a face. ''I hope it's a flop.''

''No, you don't.''

''Yes, I do. I hope any play I didn't write is a flop.''

Gemma laughed. ''You're incorrigible. Here, catch this,'' she said, and tossed him the tube of lotion. ''You can rub some of it into my tummy for me, so I don't get stretch marks.''

''Gemma Whitmore. You don't fool me. You're trying to seduce me.''

''Could be,'' she said, and sashayed over to the side of the bed. ''You're very sexy-looking in a tux, you know,'' she purred, slipping the straps of her nightie and letting it slide down to the floor.

Gemma didn't get any lotion rubbed into her stomach till a good fifteen minutes later.

''That's nice,'' she said dreamily as Nathan's hand worked in circles around her slightly stretched navel. ''Don't stop.''

''They are my favourite two words in the English language,'' he drawled, and squeezed some more lotion onto her skin.

''Ouch. That's cold.''

''Not for long.''

''I'm very happy about having a girl, Nathan,'' she murmured. ''Did I ever tell you that?''

''Only about a thousand times.''

She laughed softly. ''I wonder who she'll look like?''

''That's a lottery, isn't it?''

''Yes. I guess so. Jade looked well today, didn't she? She's very happy with Kyle.''

''Yes. I have to admit she is. But then he's just the right sort of husband for Jade. She needs someone strong and self-assured—a man not afraid for his wife to have a career.''

''That's what Celeste said today about Byron.''

''Well, it wouldn't have done Byron any good to object to your mother still running Campbell Jewels after they were married, would it? But I'm not so sure he likes her being so consumed by her career. He told me today he'd like to spend more time with her. He's thinking about opening a store in New York. Or Paris, even.''

"How will that achieve his spending more time with her?"

"He's going to ask her to help him search out the right location. She won't be able to resist such an offer."

"The devious old devil! I didn't know he had it in him."

"Trust me, Gemma, about your real father. Byron has got plenty in him. He might be rising sixty, but his testosterone is still working overtime. Of course, married to your mother, it would be."

"Are you blaming the women of the family for the Whitmore men's sexual excesses?"

"I'm blaming the whole female sex. They know just what to do to get us poor males going, and they start damned young. Did you get a load of Melanie's little girl today?"

"Tanya? Oh, yes. I saw what she was up to, the little minx. But you have to agree she's an incredibly beautiful child."

"Child! She was born old, that one. Eight years going on eighteen. Royce'll have his hands full with her later, you mark my words. Both Alex and Richard didn't know what hit them. They were her little slaves all day—running around getting her anything and everything she wanted just so she'd flash those gorgeous big black eyes of hers at them."

"We females do have to learn young to use what talents we have," Gemma said, picking up Nathan's hand and moving it a little lower. "After all, it *is* a man's world."

Nathan's hand stopped. "Man's world, my eye! This is most definitely a woman's world!"

She stifled a moan. "Are you trying to pick a fight with me so that you can stop rubbing my tummy?"

"Not at all. Just stating the truth."

"In that case, please resume what you were doing."

He did. Oh, bliss!

"Speaking of talented females," Gemma said, "Ava looked well, didn't she? Almost unrecognisable from the dumpy, timid little thing she used to be. She tells me she's off to New York soon, for an exhibition of her latest watercolours. And Vince is going with her. His mother's going to mind Vincente Junior whilst they're gone. Ava's very excited. She's never been to New York before."

"What is it about New York?" Nathan grumped. "Lenore can't wait to get back there. She's flying out tomorrow. And Zachary's going with her again to play nanny to their little girl. I'll have to get myself another solicitor soon, because he's just never here in Sydney any more. Frankly, I don't know what Lenore thought she was doing, having a baby at her age."

"Now, Nathan, don't be mean-spirited. Lenore wanted a baby as soon as she married Zachary, but the poor girl had a couple of miscarriages first."

"Really? I didn't know that. Still, that's just what I mean. Things go wrong after a woman gets to a certain age."

"A woman always wants to have a baby by the man she loves if she possibly can," Gemma pointed out. "Celeste said if she hadn't had me she'd have been devastated at not being able to have Byron's baby. And what about Ava? She was thirty-five by the time she had little Vince Junior. You didn't say she was too old at the time.''

''That was different.''

''I don't see how.''

''Ava's a Whitmore. The Whitmores are a superior species.''

''Thank you,'' Gemma said, smiling. ''I'll take that as a compliment. After all, genetically I'm the Whitmore in this marriage, not you, my sweet. Which means you won't object to my having babies till I'm at least thirty-five. That's seven years away, and possibly three more babies after Opal. I always did want six children.''

''But I'll be fifty by then!''

''Yes, and I'll bet you won't look a day older. Do you know what Celeste said about you today?''

''Dare I ask?'' Nathan said drily. ''Let's face it, I've never been your mother's favourite person.''

Gemma laughed. ''You could be right there. She said she wouldn't be surprised if you had a portrait in the attic which is going all wrinkled and depraved-looking.''

Nathan pulled a face. ''Very funny. Did you tell her we don't have an attic?''

''Yes. I defended you to the death. Told her you weren't depraved and never had been.''

Nathan groaned. ''Wait till she hears about Mimi.''

''She knows all about Mimi. I told her ages ago.''

''And?''

''She was very understanding and sympathetic towards both of you. And she was very proud of you for accepting the girl as your daughter. She likes

Mimi. Everyone does. Especially Emery, if you noticed.''

"What? What are you talking about?''

"Nathan Whitmore, do you go round with your head in the sand all the time?''

"Well, I was pretty busy today, playing father-of-the-bride. What happened between Emery and Mimi?''

"They fancy each other.''

"I find that hard to believe. He doesn't seem her type. Too serious and sullen.''

"He wasn't too sullen when they left together at the end of the night. He looked besotted and so did she.''

"Don't take too much notice of Mimi leaving with some guy. If she's anything like me she likes her sex. It doesn't mean she's in love, you know.''

"You underestimate your genes, darling. You are a one-woman man, and that kind of depth of feeling gets passed on. Kirsty is an example, and I think Mimi has the same trait.''

"Balderdash!''

"Time will tell, won't it?'' Gemma smiled a very private little smile. "Er…just a little lower, would you, darling?''

Nathan was wrong. Mimi became Mrs Emery Marsden eighteen months later.

Nathan walked her down the aisle not at Belleview, but in St Mary's Cathedral, in the city. Gemma looked on happily, with her adored Opal by her side. The little girl was just walking, and was the image of her grandmother, Celeste.

Afterwards, the reception was held at the Regency.

All the old crowd were in attendance, even Melanie and Royce, who used any excuse to travel out from England to sunny Australia for a holiday. Their by then ten-year-old daughter, Tanya, once again wielded her escalating charms on the boys at the reception—even on little Vincente, who at five was already breaking a few hearts of his own at kindergarten.

Kirsty and Ryan were there, of course, with Kirsty as chief bridesmaid opposite the groom's best man—his brother, Clark, who was a pilot in the RAAF. And, yes, Gemma had been right. Kirsty had changed her mind about babies after seeing little Opal born, and had taken time off from her acting career to have a baby of her own. A little girl, too, as it turned out. Named Hope, and just eight weeks old.

Hope meant the world to Ryan. In spite of—or perhaps because of—the bad example his own father had given him, Ryan was the most devoted father. A hands-on father. A blessed father.

He'd even started going to church on Sundays, because he wanted his little Hope to have everything he had never had as a child. A world surrounded by love, and goodness—and, yes, hope. For life without hope for the future was a bleak existence.

Ryan knew. He'd lived that kind of life. Hating every single day, loving no one, hoping for nothing. It had been sheer hell.

Life was very different for him now.

He'd found love.

And life was good.

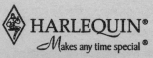

If you enjoyed what you just read,
then we've got an offer you can't resist!

Take 2
bestselling novels FREE!
Plus get a FREE surprise gift!

Clip this page and mail it to The Best of the Best™

IN U.S.A.
3010 Walden Ave.
P.O. Box 1867
Buffalo, N.Y. 14240-1867

IN CANADA
P.O. Box 609
Fort Erie, Ontario
L2A 5X3

YES! Please send me 2 free Best of the Best™ novels and my free surprise gift. After receiving them, if I don't wish to receive anymore, I can return the shipping statement marked cancel. If I don't cancel, I will receive 4 brand-new novels every month, before they're available in stores! In the U.S.A., bill me at the bargain price of $4.24 plus 25¢ shipping and handling per book and applicable sales tax, if any*. In Canada, bill me at the bargain price of $4.74 plus 25¢ shipping and handling per book and applicable taxes**. That's the complete price and a savings of over 15% off the cover prices—what a great deal! I understand that accepting the 2 free books and gift places me under no obligation ever to buy any books. I can always return a shipment and cancel at any time. Even if I never buy another book from The Best of the Best™, the 2 free books and gift are mine to keep forever.

185 MEN DFN
385 MEN DFN

Name	(PLEASE PRINT)	
Address	Apt.#	
City	State/Prov.	Zip/Postal Code

* Terms and prices subject to change without notice. Sales tax applicable in N.Y.
** Canadian residents will be charged applicable provincial taxes and GST.
All orders subject to approval. Offer limited to one per household and not valid to current Best of the Best™ subscribers.
® are registered trademarks of Harlequin Enterprises Limited.

BOB01   ©1998 Harlequin Enterprises Limited

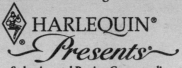